The Fox and the Hound

The Fox and the Hound

A Novel

Daniel P. Mannix

OPEN ROAD

INTEGRATED MEDIA
NEW YORK

ISBN: 979-8-3372-0092-7

This edition published in 2025 by Open Road Integrated Media, Inc.
180 Maiden Lane
New York, NY 10038
www.openroadmedia.com

The Fox and the Hound

1

The Hound

The big half-bred bloodhound lay in his barrel kennel and dreamed he was deer hunting. Of all the quarry he had ever trailed, deer was the hound's favorite, although it was usually strictly forbidden. He had been whipped, beaten with a club, and even hit in the flanks by bird shot for this crime; yet once, after an interminable journey to a faraway place, he had been allowed to track a deer. Now he smelled again that warm, rich odor as he toiled after the quarry. Again he heard the rapid *toot-toot-toot* of his master's horn blowing the "Gone away," and the notes made him yelp with excitement. He was not running now, but flying over the ground, and the scent was growing stronger. The quarry must be almost in sight. The hound kicked convulsively in his barrel and whined with eagerness.

He was vaguely aware of a distant noise so remote he was barely conscious of it. Yet the noise grew louder and more irritating. It was a shrill *Yip-yurr!* repeated over and over. The hound tried to banish it from his thoughts and concentrate on the glory of the chase, but the yapping forced itself on him. Gradually the splendor of the hunt began to fade, driven away by that infuriating, sharp yipping. With the noise came a penetrating odor that obliterated the glory of the thrilling deer scent. With a cry that was half bark, half growl, the hound came awake. He lay for an instant unsure of what was going on. Then he smelled the pungent scent of fox, and fox very close. At the same moment, the taunting yipping came again.

With a roar of fury, the hound burst from his barrel into the false light of early dawn. There, only a few yards away, a fox was sitting grinning at him. So crazed with rage he could not think, the hound flung himself at the intruder. The fox did not move. As his jaws were about to close over the stinking red interloper, the hound was flung on his side and lay groveling on the hard-packed earth. He had come to the end of his chain and been jerked backward.

By now every hound in the pack, as well as the fierce mongrel catch dogs, had been awakened and were raging at the ends of their chains. The fox cocked his triangular head to grin at them, knowing he was safe. Then he turned to the hound and barked again in the same teasing way. The taunt set the hound completely out of his head with madness. He flung himself the full length of the chain, rolled on the ground, tore at the metal links, and screamed with frustration while the fox still sat scoffing at him. The fox clearly knew to a foot the length of the chain—no difficult feat, for the fan-shaped strip of padded earth around each kennel showed the boundaries beyond which the captive dog could not go—and was enjoying himself immensely. He had stopped barking, as he could not have been heard above the tumult, and sat gloating over the chaos he was causing.

The headlights of a car swept the hill slope, illuminating briefly the coat of the fox so that it glowed as if with an internal light. Instantly the fox dropped his gloating, confident air. The grin vanished; he crouched down and turned to look at the lane leading to the isolated cabin below him. The lights of a second car glided over him, making the fox crouch even lower. Then as the clamor of the dogs increased in volume and frustration, the fox skulked away, beginning to run as soon as he was clear of the light, and vanished into the scrub-oak thickets.

The hound was the first to stop his frustrated screaming. In spite of the noise of the pack, he recognized the distinctive sound of his Master's car. A few moments later, he was able to identify the second vehicle. It belonged to men who came occasionally to his Master's home, and their presence always meant that his services would be in demand. He could identify half a dozen cars by their sound, although he could not recognize them by sight. When this particular car came, he was always called on to track a man. The hound didn't like tracking men especially—the scent was always poor, and there was no killing at the end of the trail. Although not bloodthirsty like the catch dogs, he did enjoy those last exciting moments of the chase, the anticipated crack of the rifle, and smelling the dead quarry. Still, anything that got him off the tiresome chain was a relief. So he stood hopefully, his tail wagging with doubtful eagerness, as there was still a chance his services might not be required.

He saw the cars stop and men get out. He thought one was his Master; but at that distance he could not be sure, for he was shortsighted. The men went into the cabin and then came out again, starting up the hill. The pack began to bark now, partly in warning and partly in expectation. As the men came closer, the hound could see that the figure in front was his Master. He recognized him by his manner of walking rather than by his appearance. He began to wiggle with excitement.

The Master came up to him and the hound saw that he was putting on a heavy leather belt and carried the long leash that meant man-tracking. He was to go and the rest would be left behind. Frantic with pride and delight, he groveled on the ground, turning his had sideways to expose the jugular vein as a sign of utter abjection to ingratiate himself further with his Master, whom he recognized as a stronger animal. The Master patted him and spoke his name, "Copper," together with other words the hound could not understand but which, from the tone, were gentle. Encouraged, the hound sprang up and, putting his forepaws on the Master's chest, tried to lick his face as he would the face of another dog who had showed friendliness. He was good-naturedly repulsed. The snap of his kennel chain was released and the tracking leash fastened to his collar.

Copper at once started for the cars. He did not throw his full weight on the leash until he heard the click of the snap on the other end of the lead being fitted into the eye socket on the belt. Then he pulled on the leash with all his strength, hurrying the Master toward the cars. There was a young Trigg hound named Chief, an excellent tracker and brave fighter who was the Master's favorite. Copper hated Chief with a hatred surpassing the hatred of a jealous woman. He was mortally afraid the Master might take the Trigg too and wanted to get him away from the other dogs as quickly as possible.

When they reached the cars, Copper hesitated. Sometimes the Master took him in one car and sometimes in the other. The Master spoke to the two men whom Copper recognized primarily by the smell of their leather leggings. He had gone out with them several times before. The Master unclipped the lead, opened the door of his car, and ordered the hound to get in. Copper sprang in promptly, jumping up to his special seat on a rack behind the driver, and lay down, thumping the boards enthusiastically with his tail. There was an apprehensive quality to the thumping, as he still was not absolutely sure that the Master might not go back after that accursed Chief. But the Master climbed in and started the car. As soon as it moved, Copper relaxed and stopped his tail wagging. No doubt now, he was safe.

When they reached the paved highway, the second car passed them. A flashing light appeared on its top and it gave off a moaning wail. Both cars speeded up. Copper would have loved to have been able to lean out the window of the car, drinking in the wind, especially as the car accelerated. The rush of air through his open mouth into his lungs gave him an intoxicating sensation. As this was forbidden, he had to be content with the current of air that came in through the open window. Lying quietly, he sucked it in through his broad wet nostrils. The motion of the car soothed him, and he dozed.

He was awakened by the car turning off the smooth highway and jolting over a dirt track. It was broad daylight. Copper yawned and stretched as well as he could in his cramped quarters. The other car was still ahead of them, throwing up dust that made the hound sneeze. He put one paw over his nose as a shield.

The cars stopped and there was a sound of voices. Copper stood up, tired and cramped by the journey and eager to be let out. The Master opened the door and allowed him to jump down and relieve himself against some bushes. There were a number of men here, all talking, and Copper ran around investigating the new smells and pausing to eat a little saw grass, for the ride had made him slightly nauseated.

Copper heard his Master's angry voice and glanced up, apprehensive that he had done something wrong, but the Master was speaking to one of the men who had come from a cabin with something in his hand. The Master snatched the object and came toward Copper. He held it out and the hound realized it was a scent guide, an object that would give him the scent of the man he was to track.

The object was cloth, and Copper smelled it carefully. There were several human scents, including that of the man who had just handled it and of course the Master's scent. This last didn't bother the hound; he naturally recognized and eliminated that particular odor, but he had no way of telling which of the other scents was the important one.

The Master put the tracking leash on his collar and Copper prepared for work. When he heard the familiar click as the leash was snapped to the belt, he started off. All the men began to follow them, but to Copper's relief the Master shouted and all but one dropped back. He was one of the leather-smelling men, and followed a few feet behind.

The Master took Copper on a long swing around the cabin. The hound worked slowly, sorting out the different scents that came to him. Animal scents, such as rabbit and squirrel, he ignored. Occasionally he crossed patches of wild mustard or mint that gave off an odor that tended to mask other scents. In such cases he skirted the patches to be able to work on uncontaminated ground. Twice he crossed clearings where the hot sun had burned off most of the scent. He worked these carefully to make sure of not missing a faint trail.

At last he hit a clear man track. Copper stopped instantly, sniffing long and loudly. Then he went back to the Master for the scent guide. The Master held it out and Copper sniffed the guide. Yes, one of the odors, and by far the strongest, was the same as that of the track. Without any more hesitation Copper went back to the trail and started out.

It was damp and cool under the trees and the scent held well. Copper forged ahead, at times dragging the Master after him, for the man could not pass under low-hanging boughs as easily as the hound. A few times the hound lost the scent, but by pressing on he was able to pick it up within a few yards. Occasionally, though, the quarry had turned off at an angle at places where the scent had sunk into dry ground or been blown away by a wind. Here Copper was at a loss. The Master had to take him back to the last sure place and start him over. By working slowly and systematically from one wisp of scent to the next, the hound was able to unravel the line. In one especially bad spot he had to dig to find the scent where it had soaked into the ground an inch or so below the surface. In another, the scent had been blown completely away, but Copper found a suggestion of it lodged under the edge of a fallen tree.

They came out on a dirt road. The quarry had sat down to rest—the scent was quite strong—and smoked. But here the trail ended. Copper circled the spot to make sure. Then he lifted one leg and urinated as a sign that the quarry had vanished. As a young hound he had followed trails with so much enthusiasm that he had never had time to relieve himself until the scent ended. Then he had wet. The Master had come to recognize what he meant, so now the act of wetting was a code sign between them.

The Master called to the leather-smelling man who came up. They talked while Copper lay down and rested. It had been a long pull, and he was tired and thirsty.

Finally the Master came over to him. He poured water from a canteen onto the rim of his hat, and Copper drank eagerly. Then the Master washed out his nose and massaged his feet. Finally he shook the leash and said, "Go on, boy. Go find 'em."

Copper looked up reproachfully. He had already indicated that the trail stopped here. Yet the Master was insistent. With an almost audible sigh, the hound rose and checked again. Yes, the scent definitely stopped here. Copper tried to think what to do.

Although there was no scent of the quarry, there was the scent of an automobile. Copper could easily smell the odor of the rubber tires, gasoline, and oil as well as the individualistic metal odor of a machine. As he had to track something, and there was nothing else to track, he began tracking the car.

Following the car was fairly simple, although the hot mud hurt his pads. Copper soon found that enough of the scent had blown off the road and clung to the grass along the edge for him to follow it there. The grass was still partly damp and its many blades offered a perfect trap for the scent particles. Even better, the sun was making the scent rise so it floated a few inches above the ground and the hound did not have to drop his head.

After a time he came on the man scent again by the side of the road. It was quite clear, although not fresh. It led into the woods, and Copper started after it eagerly, jerking on the leash. The Master pulled him up and he and the leather-smelling man bent down to look at something. Copper hurried over. They had found a white object that smelled heavily of tobacco but had so little of the man scent that Copper turned away in disgust to get back to the trail. The Master seemed delighted, and from the way he encouraged him, Copper strained forward happily.

Working along the side of a hill, they came on a mass of sharp-edged rocks lying in the full glare of the sun. Here Copper could not find a trace of the trail. He worked up and down the slope, dragging the Master after him, trying desperately to own the line. He did not give his urinating signal, for he knew that here the man had not simply disappeared—the scent had not abruptly ended, but petered out on the hot, bare rocks. It must be here somewhere if he could only find it.

The Master pulled him off the rocks and for the first time since starting out, unsnapped the leash from his collar as a signal he was to stop tracking. Copper lay down thankfully, licking his bleeding pads, for the rocks were sharp. He was still unhappy over the lost line and prepared to try again after a rest.

The men left him and walked slowly across the rocks. They seemed to find something. Painful as it was, Copper limped over to them and hopefully stuck his nose in the place where the Master was pointing. He was ordered back. He continued to sniff, but there was nothing there, and after a second curt command he returned to the soft earth.

The men climbed the rockslide, stopping frequently, while Copper watched them in agony. He could not understand how they could smell the line when he could not. At the top of the slope, the Master called him. To avoid the rocks, Copper loped around the slide and joined the men. The tracking leash was snapped into his collar, and the Master repeated, "Go on, boy. Go find 'em."

Copper cast around and, sure enough, there was the scent again. How the Master had found it he could not imagine, nor did he try. Human beings had strange powers no dog could understand. Trained never to give tongue while following a man, he could not suppress an eager whine. Then they were off again, the big hound pulling on the leash until the Master cursed him, but Copper was too excited at hitting the line again to pay any attention.

The scent was gradually growing stronger now. It was not too old. As Copper was forging ahead, he was abruptly pulled up short. The men were looking upward. Copper glanced up but could see nothing. The men talked in low voices, and then the Master ordered him on again.

The scent was good now. The eager hound forced his way through laurel tangle and greenbrier so thick the men could hardly follow. They reached a gully in the woods, and Copper smelled water at the bottom. He started down; but the scent was very bad indeed, for there was the circulation of air in the shielded gully to lift the scent above the ground, and Copper was forced to keep his nose almost in direct contact with the earth.

He had raised his head to blow dust from his nose, when suddenly he stopped dead. Ignoring the trail, the hound carefully tested the air. Yes, there it was. The man close—so close the hound could air-scent him. At the same instant, the hound knew the quarry was dead. The heavy, sweet-sick smell of death was strong. There was also blood.

Paying no attention to the trail now, the hound plunged down the steep bank, the men sliding after him on their buttocks. At the bottom of the gully ran a clear stream. Thirsty as he was, the hound did not stop to drink. He splashed through the water and up the opposite bank, the men cupping up quick handfuls of water as they followed. As they climbed, a frenzied rustling came from the bushes ahead. Half a dozen black shapes flushed, and beat their way upward on huge, sooty black wings, leaving a carrion reek as they rose. Copper ignored them. He strained forward, took one strong sniff, and then sat down. The quarry was here.

The Master unsnapped the leash and the men moved forward toward the body. A droning mass of blowflies rose above the corpse for a moment, then settled back. Copper smelled the blood, smelled the birds, and identified the body as the quarry he had been following. Then he smelled something else that made him bound to his feet: a savage, feral scent that made the black hairs of his neck stand up and sent shivers of fear and excitement through his body. Bear!

Regardless of the men, Copper bounded forward and began feverishly to cast around. It was bear, all right. There was blood on his paws and he had been in a frenzy of rage; Copper could tell by the special quality of the scent. His conviction was confirmed when he hit a spot where the bear had urinated in his excitement. The urine was heavily charged with the odor only a furious animal emits.

As he was no longer tracking a man, Copper felt himself justified in giving tongue, and his deep bay rolled out, first in a long howl and then in short, gasping cries. Instantly the Master was by his side. Copper showed him where the line was; but the Master, instead of instantly winding the scent, went back and forth in an exasperating way until he found something to look at on the soft earth. The Master's inability to scent a perfectly clear line, as well as his tendency to stand for a long time staring at pointless marks on the ground, was his most irritating quality, and Copper had never grown entirely reconciled to it. The Master called over the leather-smelling man and they both looked at the ground and talked, while Copper went nearly mad with impatience. Finally the tracking leash was snapped on and he was told to go ahead.

It was no use. The bear had traveled much faster than the man and hadn't dragged his feet as the man had. Copper could only just own the line. After a short time, the Master pulled him off, and even Copper had to admit it was a wise decision. That bear was gone. By the time Copper could have puzzled out the faint trail, the bear would have been too far away to make the hunt worthwhile; besides, neither man had a gun. Copper knew that men always carried guns when they went bear hunting.

After a long, dull journey they returned to the cabin and the cars. While the men, as they always did, talked and talked interminably, Copper slept, licked the cuts on his paws, and slept again. He was intensely relieved when he was ordered back to the car and they started home.

For the next few days nothing happened. Copper, like the other dogs, was bored and restless. He amused himself by lying in front of his barrel and checking the various odors that the breeze brought him. He could just make out the cabin at the foot of the little rise where the kennels were, but beyond that the world fuzzied into a black-and-white haze, although he could barely distinguish a moving figure if it wasn't too far away, Everything looked black and white to Copper even though he could tell a considerable number of shades of gray by their comparative brightness. Copper did not depend much on his eyes, which he knew were unreliable and which had often caused him to make shameful errors. If the Master changed his clothes, Copper would often bark at him until the Master spoke so he could recognize the voice. This was very humiliating, but even while Copper was cringing in disgrace, he liked to get a good sniff in to make quite sure the figure standing over him was indeed the Master.

If his eyes were weak, his nose was quite another thing. Lying on the hill, Copper could tell fairly well what was going on in the world about him. At every moment dozens of distinct odors were pouring into his nostrils; the great majority of them the hound ignored as meaningless. Flowers, grass, trees, the other dogs, activities in the cabin—these meant nothing to him. A distant herd of deer passing through the woods, a stray dog, a human stranger, even a pheasant, goose, rabbit, or raccoon caused his nostrils to twitch as he took pains to separate the important scent from the mass of other odors. He could also tell when it was going to rain by the moisture in the wind, and distinguished between day and night by the different quality in the air almost as much as he did by eyesight.

A few mornings later, he was awakened by the ringing of the telephone in the cabin. It was still pitch black even Copper could smell the dawn not too far away; it always began to cool slightly before dawn. The other dogs moved restlessly and mumbled annoyance at the insistent ringing, but Copper lay awake listening. When the phone rang at night it usually meant a job to do. Perhaps he would be called on again to the further humiliation of the Trigg.

The phone stopped ringing. Then lights went on in the cabin. Even the other dogs knew what that meant, and their chains rattled as they shook themselves and came out of their kennels to stretch, yawn, and relieve themselves. Copper smelled coffee, and was almost sure there was a job on. The Master never made that coffee smell this early unless he was going out.

The cabin door opened, emitting a flood of light, and the Master came out. The wind was blowing to the dogs and Copper could smell his leather hunting boots and the heavy jacket he wore when he started on jobs. Alas, there was no scent of the tracking belt that meant Copper alone was going. But there would be tracking.

The rest of the pack were beginning to leap at the ends of the chains and scream with excitement. The chorus varied from the hard chop of the two gray-and-white treeing Walkers to the deep, sonorous bay of the trail hounds. The Master shouted, "You, Chief! Strike! Ranger! Hold that noise!" The dogs subsided.

With the swift efficiency of long practice, the Master hitched up the dogs' trailer to his battered car while the pack watched anxiously. Then he came up the hill. The dogs groveled, barked, whined, and stood on their hind legs in an agony of anticipation while he made his choice. To Copper's inexpressible delight, he was selected. The Master also took Red, a young heavy-coated July hound, and Ranger, a buckskin Plott who was known as a fighter. Then he took that damned Chief. Chief was a big hound weighing nearly as much as Copper. He was more catfooted than the bloodhound, faster and more belligerent. He was black-and-tan with a white-tipped tail. Because of his habit of skirting, he not infrequently hit by chance on the line that Copper was patiently working out, gave tongue, and took the pack away on it. This was one of the reasons the bloodhound hated him.

Lastly, the Master selected Buck, a long-legged Airedale, and Scrapper. Scrapper's ancestry was uncertain. He had some bulldog, some Doberman, and perhaps a little Alsatian. The inclusion of these two catch dogs meant they were going after dangerous game. Like all the hounds, Copper feared and disliked the catch dogs. He had discovered from painful experience that the catch dogs when excited were more likely to attack the hounds than the quarry. The hounds were put together in the trailer, but the catch dogs were kept in separate compartments.

The white sun was rising in the grayish-black sky as they started. Copper didn't like riding in the trailer; it swayed too much and made him sick, so he lay down and tried to sleep, only growling a little when the other hounds fell across him in their excitement at going out on a job. The ride was not too long, and they made good time because the highway was almost deserted at this hour except for a few night-running trucks that gave off a stench of diesel oil as they passed. They reached a small town, and the car slowed down. A car was parked in the silent street, and the headlights were rapidly switched on and off as they approached it. Though Copper could see the car through the trailer's wire mesh, he could not identify it even after the Master pulled up alongside and stopped. He did know the man who got out—not immediately, but after he had talked to the Master for a few seconds Copper could smell him. This man always smelled of a special grease he used on his gun. There was no doubt about it now: they were going after some potentially dangerous animal. The grease-smelling man appeared only before such hunts.

The two men finished talking and, getting back in the cars, started off. Again Copper dozed. When he awoke, the cars were climbing up a steep grade. The air was fresher, colder, and thinner. Scenting conditions were so good that in spite of the stink of the exhaust Copper could smell pines and even some animal scents, especially deer. The cold air of the mountains made him feel better, and he stood up, swaying in rhythm with the motion of the car.

The cars pulled off on grass and stopped, while the Master came around to let them out. The captives went crazy with excitement, ricocheting off the sides of the van and throwing themselves against the door. The Master had to press the door in with the full weight of his body to get enough play to release the catch. The hounds poured out in an excited stream, and the Master waited while they relieved themselves and checked the new scents. Then he let out the catch dogs, one after another. There was a little trouble between the fighting dogs and the hounds, but the Master was watching closely and at the first growl he spoke so sharply that the dogs avoided each other.

Ahead of them rose a great cliff, painted dead black by the light of the white sun on it. Sheltered beneath the cliff stood a small farmhouse, flanked by a rambling apple orchard and a sheepfold. The air was supercharged with scents here. In addition to the smell of mice, squirrels, rabbits, and grouse on the grass, which interested him, Copper was also conscious of the odor of chickens, cattle, sheep, humans, a dog, and the aroma of food cooking. He also scented water, and hoped they could drink before starting out.

A man came from the house with a dog at his heels. Though the pack paid no attention to the man, they were all instantly fascinated by the dog. Copper could not see the dog plainly, but was quite sure he was a male, frightened, and fairly young. The man ordered him back to the house, and Copper with the rest of the pack went after him to investigate until the Master called them off.

The man took them to the sheepfold. The sheep were bleating, and Copper knew by their scent that they had been badly frightened during the night. They had urinated in their terror, and the pen smelled heavily of the urine charged with the special odor of fear that all animals quickly recognize. Although ordinarily the pack would have been indifferent to the flock, the fear smell made them prick up their hackles and move toward the fold stiff-legged. Even Copper, well broken to all domestic stock, felt a charge of gloating cruelty surge through him. That odor meant the quarry would put up no resistance, but would lie writhing helplessly while Copper buried his teeth in the soft flesh and felt the ecstasy of the victim's death struggles through clenched jaws. That odor maddened him almost like the scent of a bitch in heat. The Master ordered them off, and when the catch dogs seemed inclined to ignore him he took a stick to them.

The man who lived at the farm was pointing to the ground; the Master and the grease-smelling man bent over to examine it. Then the Master called Copper over. As the hound leaped forward, the others tried to follow but were ordered back, to Copper's great satisfaction. The instant he applied his trained nose to the spot where the Master was pointing, Copper burst into a long, sobbing cry. It was bear. It was the same bear he had scented beside the dead man. With his tail wagging frantically, he began to work out the line.

To his surprise, the Master called him off. The grease-smelling man went to the cars and came back with his rifle. Then they started toward the apple orchard, the hounds trotting over the soft gray grass under the dark leaves. By a twisted old tree stood a pile of crates, filled with apples. The heavy boxes had been scattered in all directions, and the round black fruit littered the ground. Copper sniffed at some of the apples. The smell told him nothing.

"Here, boy, here!" called the Master. Copper hurried over. Even before he reached the Master, he smelled the bear scent. Leaping forward, he began to cast about, his tail going madly as he tried to pin down the line. Red, Ranger, and Chief hurried up and also began to cast around. Ranger and Chief had the scent, but young Red was still trying to find out what the excitement was all about.

Then, then it came! Full, strong, and fresh. Copper knew he was on the line and smelled the tracks themselves; not scent blown out of them by the morning breeze. He went a few feet to make sure and then broke into his deep, bell-like bay. Instantly every dog in the pack—even the catch dogs—left whatever he was doing and ran to Copper. Ranger and Chief sniffed desperately and then simultaneously broke into the steady cry of hounds on a scent. Red had more trouble, and then he too gave tongue.

"Go get 'em, boys. Woo-whoop!" shouted the Master. The pack was streaming across the orchard now, swept along by the sound of their own music as much as by the scent that floated in front of them. Copper was following the trail itself, while Ranger and Chief, running on either side of him, were picking up the scent swirls, for the warmth of the rising sun was making the scent rise from the tracks, and a slight breeze distributed it. Red was following Copper to be quite sure of the line. The catch dogs were at the tail, only occasionally getting wisps of scent that made them yelp with eagerness.

The scent held well in the forest, and the pack pressed on, reassuring one another by their rhythmical baying that they were all still on the line. Where the woods were open, the scent lay breast-high and the hounds were able to follow it without dropping their heads—a great advantage. In the deeper woods where the sun had not as yet penetrated, the air was cold and the scent still lay on the ground. Here the hounds were forced to drop their heads, and this slowed them. At times the scent failed completely. At such times the pack stopped their baying and anxiously fanned out, each hound working on his own to find the line. Copper usually found it. He knew all the best places to check: the hollow formed by two roots at the base of a tree, a damp spot where the scent might cling, a protected hollow where the scent might have drifted and could not rise again. Often he was able to take it from bushes that had touched the bear's sides. The scent particles clung to the oily surface of the leaves, while it would not adhere to dead leaves on the ground or to the bare earth. When he was sure, he would speak and the rest would run over and cast out ahead of him. Occasionally one of the other hounds would strike something and speak to it doubtfully. Copper would hurry over to check the spot. The rest would wait until they heard his affirmative deep bay.

Once when the whole pack had been at fault for several minutes, Red, the young July hound, shouted eagerly. No one paid any attention to him, for Red had never opened on a line before. But the puppy kept pleading, until finally Copper went over to investigate, fully expecting to find nothing. Red indicated the spot and stood back anxiously while Copper applied his expert nose. To his surprise, there was the scent. A lesser hound would have gone on and opened on the line farther ahead, as though he had discovered it himself, but Copper would not stoop to such acts. He instantly opened on the line, confirming the pup's yelps. The pack rushed over and soon were in full cry again. After that, whenever Red spoke on a lost line he was awarded the same respectful attention as the older hounds.

Then they came to a blowdown where the wind had knocked down a stand of sharply scented hemlocks. The packs slithered over the trunks until they reached the other side. Here they checked. Somewhere in the blowdown they had lost the scent. Either the bear had turned sharply at right angles and come out at a different spot or the scent would not lie on the sun-baked ground on the far side of the blowdown.

The pack started casting—working out in ever-increasing circles, trying to pick up the trail again. They were still at it when the men caught up with them. The Master tried casting them himself, putting them on at various places where the bear might have come out of the blowdown, but although the hounds worked hard they could find nothing.

Copper left the rest and crawled back through the blowdown to the last spot where he could positively identify the scent. He gave tongue on the old track and then came slowly back toward the blowdown. There was still some dew under the forest timber that held the scent, but the fallen trees in the blowdown were exposed to the full rays of the sun. It was noticeably warmer here, and the heat gave Copper an idea. He stood up on his hind legs. Ah, there it was! Very faint, but detectable. The scent was floating just above his head when he reared up. As the hound could not walk on his hind legs, he would stand up to get the scent, drop back on all fours, take a few steps, stand up again, and so on. Each time he raised himself and caught the ghost of the scent, he would give a low cry. The cries came in a slow, well-spaced *Bow . . . bow . . . bow,* as he advanced. With nose still strained upward he started across the blowdown. His feet slipped and plunged in between the trunks, but he was higher now and his straining nose could barely touch the floating line. His cries slowed yet he kept on. When he reached the hard ground on the other side, he had to stand up again to reach the odor, but he kept on through the still questing pack.

Now the other hounds began to understand what he was doing. They also stood up on their hind legs to test the upper air, some straining up so far they fell over backward. Chief caught the scent and gave tongue. He followed Copper, and they worked their way into the pine forest. Then Ranger began to speak, and finally Red. Under the trees, the scent dropped to the ground again. Here the hounds were able to follow it easily, and burst into full cry.

They quickly outdistanced the men. Now the other hounds had moved into the lead, for the scent was good, and Copper, never a fast dog with his heavy, bloodhound build, was slower. Red was in front, going at such a rate that if the bear had turned off sharply he would be sure to overrun the line. Behind him came Ranger and then Chief. The catch dogs were in the rear, following the hounds, for they could hardly own the line even now.

The scent was getting stronger. The bear was close. Copper dropped back more and more. His legs were stiff, his lungs burned, and in addition he had no desire to come up with an infuriated bear. He knew bears by experience. They were dangerous, and Copper was no fighter.

Suddenly Red began to scream with excitement, and at the same moment came the sound of smashing brush. Red had sighted the bear. Now Ranger and Chief stopped giving tongue and broke into the viewing cry. In spite of himself, Copper caught the excitement and put on an extra burst of speed. The catch dogs tore past him, Scrapper snarling and slashing at him to make the hound get out of the way. Then through the hysterical yells came a deep-throated bellowing. The bear was turning at bay. He had a system of tunnels in the blackberry bushes, and when the pack tried to follow him he turned and charged. The dogs fell over each other trying to avoid him. Copper, mad with excitement, plunged on through the tangle that clung to him and tore at his ears.

Somewhere in the bushes a fight was raging. Hazel limbs were snapping like gunshots. Then Copper heard a yelp from Red as the young hound took a blow. Now the bear growled in pain. One of the catch dogs must have taken a hold. The screaming of the dogs rose in intensity, and Copper rushed on regardless of danger. He saw the red body of the July hound go sailing over the bushes. Copper was warned and slowed down. As he broke through the last cover, he saw the bear.

The great black animal had backed against a fallen tree so the dogs could not take him from behind. He stood there swinging his head back and forth, champing his jaws as the dogs rushed at him by turns. The whole place was filled with his powerful odor, but there was no scent of fear.

The catch dogs had taken up their places one on either side of him while the hounds ran around behind them. First Buck and then Scrapper would leap forward, and the bear would swing his head to face the adversary. Then the other dog would spring in, tear out a mouthful of fur, and jump back to avoid the bear's return blow. While he was spitting out the fur, the other dog would bound forward to pull out another mouthful from the bear's other side. They were making no real attempt to attack— only to hold him.

But how long could they hold him? Twice the bear made an effort to leave the tree and continue running. Once he started going, he could easily outrun the pack in this heavy cover. The dogs knew it and even the hounds rushed in to help the catch dogs snap at his sides and force him back. But if the bear really decided to break, they could not stop him.

The sound of the Master's horn came. He was signaling the pack that help was on the way. At the call, the catch dogs moved into position. When both were ready, Buck gave a quick, sharp bark. Instantly Scrapper rushed in, making a feint at the bear's side that drew him out slightly from the protection of the tree. Buck promptly leaped in and grabbed the bear's ear. Scrapper bounced forward, snapping and barking to keep the bear from turning on his friend, while Ranger and Chief tried to help distract the animal. Buck managed to fling his body over the bear's neck, still hanging to the ear.

The bear stood up on his hind legs, reaching behind him for the Airedale. As he did so there came the stunning crack of a rifle shot. The bear must have been hit, for an instant later came the acid scent of diarrhea as the bear emptied his bowels. The hounds screamed at the odor and flung themselves forward, tearing out mouthfuls of fur. Copper could no longer control himself and joined the attack.

Another shot cracked out. The bear seized Buck in both paws and flung him away into the bushes. Then he turned on the rest of the pack. Scrapper, leaping back to avoid a blow, collided with Ranger. Instantly he turned with insane fury on the Plott, and the two dogs rolled on the ground together, biting furiously and feeling for each other's throats. Copper saw the Master tearing through a mass of honeysuckle with a small gun in his hand. The grease-smelling man was there too, yelling something and waving his rifle. The bear was apparently completely absorbed with the dogs, yet suddenly he whirled and charged the Master.

The Master tried to jump back, but his foot caught in the honeysuckle and he fell. The bear was on top of him. The catch dogs were gone, even at this terrible moment Copper could not bring himself to close with the bear. Then Chief charged in from behind. Closing his forefeet under him, he slid under the bear and seized the raging animal by the testicles. The bear's jaws had met in the Master's shoulder, but this pain was too terrible for the animal to take. He whirled around, but Chief still hung on, although he was lifted off his feet. The Master rose on his elbow and fired into the bear's side with his small handgun. The grease-smelling man also fired. The bear went down, blood pouring from his mouth—the thick, rich-smelling arterial blood that means death. The dogs poured over him, even Scrapper and Ranger forgetting their differences as the smell hit them. Straining in different directions, the pack stretched him out between them while the grease-smelling man fired shot after shot into the body.

When it was all over, Copper lay down with a delicious feeling of satisfied exhaustion. It was much the same feeling he had after having well served a bitch. He was drained of strength and strong emotion. A delightful lassitude filled him.

The Master rose and limped toward them. Copper rose to greet him, proudly wagging his tail in conscious self-esteem for having done a good job of trailing. The Master paid no attention to him. He went over to Chief and, taking the Trigg's head between his hands, spoke to him in the love talk that once he had used only to Copper. Watching them with savage jealousy, Copper knew that his day was done and that soon there would be a new leader of the pack.

2

The Fox

His first memory was that of hearing an eager scratching at the mouth of the den, followed by excited whines. The fox pup was not frightened; instead he was excited and curious, for the noises were not unlike fox noises and he knew of no reason to fear them. His mother reacted differently. In a moment she was on her feet, hissing and snarling, and although the pup had never heard these sounds before he instantly recognized them as danger signals. Then she gave off the terrible scent of fear, and even though this was a new scent to the pup he knew it meant the family was in dire peril.

His brothers and sisters were whimpering and wetting with terror, but the pup did neither. He kept his wits. He had always looked to his mother for guidance and now he gave a plaintive yip meaning "What do you want us to do?" At once his mother spun around and picked him up by the scruff of his neck. Even in her excitement she was careful not to let her canine teeth close over his slender vertebrae, and pushed her jaws far down until she could lift him with her molars. Then she ran down one of the long passageways of the den. This den was a huge affair that had been used by generations of foxes, and some of the passageways were fifty feet long. There were ten boltholes besides the main entrance, and it was toward one of these bolt-holes the vixen ran.

She stopped just short of the entrance. The ground trembled with the stamping of men's feet, and their voices came clearly through the hole. There were other dogs, yelping and barking, half mad with excitement. The vixen backed down the burrow and stood for a moment, tormented by indecision. Then she dropped the pup and ran back for another.

The pup lay cowering as he listened to the sounds around him and smelled the new and terrifying odors that gradually seeped along the tunnel. He heard a dog forcing its way into the earth, and then heard it scream. The vixen had grabbed it by the nose and bitten through to the cartilage. He listened to the gurgling noise of combat as the half-strangled dog tried to tear himself free. Above, the men were shouting and stamping on the ground. Somewhere in the earth he heard a rumbling noise that at first he could not identify. Then he realized it was a second dog that had been put down another hole and was racing to his friend's help. He heard it reach the main den and yell with excitement when it saw the vixen. Then the whole earth reverberated with the screams of the vixen and the cries of the terriers.

The rumbling noise began again and went through the entire system of passageways. His mother was running through the earth with the dogs after her, trying to lead them away from the pups. Then came the most awful sounds he had ever heard: the death cries of his brothers and sisters. A third terrier had been sent down the main entrance, and found them.

His mother suddenly appeared beside him and dropped panting. They lay with their noses touching while the roar of the dogs tearing about through the passageways looking for them echoed through the earth. His mother rose and, writhing around in the narrow pipe, began to dig desperately at the roof. The earth fell in showers around her, gradually blocking up the tunnel. She lay down again, panting, and they listened to the whining of the frustrated terriers.

Coming down the burrow, and separated from them only by the thin earth barrier, they heard the footsteps of one of the terriers. The foxes lay motionless, not daring to breathe. They heard the dog come to the fallen earth and scratch at it. Neither fox moved a muscle. The fallen earth had not only blocked the tunnel; it had also cut off the scent, and the dog abandoned the task, backing slowly out of the passage because he was too big to turn. The foxes resumed breathing.

Above them still came the voices of the men and the drumming of their feet. Now their scent was leaking down to the foxes, and the pup, curious even in this crisis, lifted his head slightly to bring his nose into play. By lying perfectly still the foxes had largely cut off their scent, as the odor was spread by the heat of their bodies when moving; but the vixen's activity in collapsing the roof of the tunnel had filled the narrow pipe with her scent, and that still lingered. With the two animals crowded together in the pipe, the passage grew warm and, as the temperature increased, the scent began to rise out of the bolthole and catch in the tangle of honeysuckle that covered it.

The terriers had come out of the earth now, and the pup could tell by the slower breathing of his mother that she was no longer so frightened as she had been. Also, the fear scent was beginning to fall away. The men had tramped over the entrance of the bolthole several times without noticing it, and they would soon leave.

One of the terriers raced by overhead. As he scrambled over

the honeysuckle tangle, the foxes heard him stop suddenly and begin to sniff. Again they stopped breathing.

The terrier was forcing his nose through the vines until his nostrils were in the bolthole itself. He sniffed louder and then broke into an eager yelping. Instantly they heard the other dogs racing to him. The vixen pushed the pup behind her with her nose and crawled up the pipe to meet them.

Now the men were there and the honeysuckle was ripped away. A terrier started down the hole, but he was too big to make it. A man pulled him out by the hind legs, and another, smaller dog was put in. This dog managed to worm his way in to where the pipe was larger. The foxes heard him coming. There was a narrow shelf along the side of the pipe, and the vixen crawled onto it. She let the little dog pass below her and then suddenly seized him across the loins with her long, pointed jaws. She clamped down with all her strength and had the satisfaction of hearing the backbone snap. The dog screamed in agony and lay writhing in the pipe, paralyzed.

Above them came the furious yelling of men and dogs. Now came a *thump! thump! thump!* The men were digging down to them. At once the vixen slipped off the shelf and, running to the wall of earth that blocked the passage, began digging desperately, but before she could break through another terrier had come down the pipe. He managed to wriggle over his mortally wounded comrade, and the vixen was forced to turn to face him. Wiser than his friend, the terrier made no attempt to attack. Instead he began the chop bark that meant "Here she is! I'm holding her at bay!"

The men recognized the cry and began digging in earnest. There was nothing the vixen could do now. When she tried to break through the wall, the terrier rushed at her, growling and snapping so that she was forced to turn. When she attacked him, he retreated up the pipe, meeting her attacks with open jaws. She could not get past him, and if she had there were the men and the other dogs waiting for her.

The top of the tunnel caved in, splattering dog and foxes with loose dirt. The men had broken through to the pipe. The vixen made one last frantic effort to escape, forgetting in her frenzy even her precious pup. She leaped toward the light and air. Quick as she was, the terrier was also quick. As the fox bounded out, he sprang forward and seized her. Dog and fox came out together.

The pup trembling in the now open pipe heard the horrible sounds of combat above him: the fierce snarls of the terriers just before they took their holds, the hissing screams of his mother as she fought back, and the yells of the men. Then came the guttural sounds of worrying as the terriers made their kill.

The pup never moved. He knew his best chance of safety was to remain absolutely still. He lay in the pipe, a little ball of woolly fur, with only his eyes—just changing from baby-blue to yellow—showing he was alive.

The dogs were still worrying his mother's corpse when one of the men gave a cry and, reaching down into the pipe, picked him up. The pup did not move until the man's hand actually closed over him and he knew concealment was no longer possible. Then he gave a sudden banshee-like screech and buried his little milk teeth in the man's thumb. The man started, and the pup felt himself grabbed by the neck so he could no longer bite. He instantly realized the situation, and promptly relaxed. There was no longer any use in struggling. He dangled limply, watching his chance to make a bolt for it.

He was put in a bag and carried to a car. Throughout the long drive, the pup lay quietly, his mind almost a complete blank. Luckily for him, he was incapable of speculating about the future, and so did not suffer the agonies of apprehension that a human would have endured. At last the drive ended, the car stopped, and he heard voices. The bag was lifted, and he was carried away from the car. Then it was opened, and he was gently shaken out on a floor.

The pup lay there looking up at the man bending over him. The man was talking, but the words and even the tone meant nothing to the pup. He was mainly conscious of odor: the terrifying smell of the man, the strange smell of the room, and the smell of a dog. There was a dog in the room not much bigger than himself who came over and sniffed at him. The pup snarled automatically, but he was not really frightened. The dog's tail was wagging; there was no scent of anger; and the dog's actions were sufficiently foxlike for the pup to recognize that the animal meant to be friendly.

The man spoke to the dog, who hastily retreated. Then the man tried to touch him. The pup twisted himself around to meet the extended hand with bared teeth, for the man had brought his hand down from above in an action recognized by both dogs and foxes as an aggressive movement. Another fox, attacking, would have come down from above in just such a movement to get the neck hold. The dog, on the other hand, had come in on the pup's own level. The man withdrew his hand and then extended it again, this time moving it along the floor. The pup still snarled, but after a few seconds allowed the hand to touch his neck.

The man began to rub him under the chin and scratch the back of his ears. In spite of his fear, a delicious sense of well-being flooded through the pup. He lay in an almost hypnotic state while the hand massaged him, yet at the same time he was tensed to bound away at any sudden movement.

The pup tamed rapidly. He identified with the little dog far more readily than he did with the man, even though the man fed and cared for him. The fox pup and the dog spoke the same language. The language was not vocal, but was made up of signs and gestures, and to a certain degree of scent. The dog smelled more like a fox than did the human, and, more important, he behaved like a fox. When the dog first attempted to play, the pup was suspicious of his intentions. He instinctively swung sideways to the dog, feinting with his brush as a shield and striking at the dog with his flank to bowl him over. When he realized the dog was only playing, he abandoned these tactics. The play resembled fighting as the two animals rolled on the floor together, biting at each other and trying to get the other down, but the tactics the fox used were those he would have used in killing game—the loin grip and the neck hold. Both of these holds are effective in killing a rabbit or woodchuck, but in a fox fight the two opponents are so nearly the same size that it would be impossible for one to get either of these grips on the other except under extraordinary conditions. In using them on the dog, then, the fox was merely playing that the dog was quarry rather than an enemy.

The fox quickly learned his name—the humans called him "Tod"—but he would almost never come when called. He knew quite well he was being called, but he always wondered why they were calling him. Perhaps they had some sinister motive. If the calling became insistent, he would sneak quietly through the house, taking advantage of every chair and sofa until he could see the person calling. If the person had a toy, food, or was even lying on the floor patting the rug, he would joyfully bound in; but if the person had no obvious reason for wanting him, Tod would watch for several minutes and then softly steal away.

At first he had been given the run of the house, but now he was locked up at night in a bare room. Tod hated to be confined and deeply resented this treatment. He learned that after the supper dishes were washed, he would be locked up, so as soon as the dishes were put in the sink, he would quietly steal away. First he hid in the downstairs hallway, which, being dark and seldom used, seemed a good place, but he found that when both the man and his wife went looking for him, they could block both ends of the hall and he was sure to be caught. There were two upstairs hallways, and he tried both of them, one after the other. The same thing happened. He then tried hiding in a room, only to find that when the humans saw him they could shut the door and bottle him up. He tried all the rooms in succession, with the same result. Finally he learned to keep moving. Then it was almost impossible to trap him. As this trick had proved successful, he followed the same pattern rigidly from then on, always going along the same course because the first time he had followed that particular route he had escaped. Tod made no attempt to understand why a certain device succeeded or failed. If it failed he abandoned it, and if it succeeded he meticulously duplicated the same pattern in every detail over and over again.

As he grew bigger, the man did a number of curious acts that puzzled and somewhat annoyed Tod. He would throw some object on the floor, and the dog would bring it to him. Then he would throw it out for Tod. Tod understood what the man wanted him to do, and would pick up the object; but as there was no reason he could see to bring it to the man, he would carry it off. The man would catch him, put the object in his mouth, and close his jaws over it. Tod hated this performance, and fought it so furiously that the man gave up. Tod was willing enough to play, but he saw no reason why he should do something he did not want to do; and as he had no desire to please the man as did the dog, he would never retrieve.

On another occasion the man laid out a series of white metal bowls, each with a small piece of meat in it. Tod went down the line collecting the meat. One bowl had some wires running to it, the wires being attached to a small box that had a strong acid odor. Tod paid no attention to this arrangement, but when he touched the bowl he received a shock that made him jump. Tod carefully avoided that bowl in the future. The man tried placing it in different positions in relation to the others, but this made no difference to Tod, who could instantly recognize it. Finally the man removed the wires, and still Tod refused to go near the cursed thing. Months later, the man offered him food in the bowl, but Tod remembered it and shied away. No matter how the man washed the bowl and mixed it up with the others, Tod could tell it. Although all the bowls seemed identical, each had almost microscopic differences, and Tod with his keen sight could easily distinguish one from the others. Tod would never forget that particular bowl as long as he lived, and wires or no wires he would never go near it again. When the same experiment was tried on the dog, the little terrier got several shocks before he learned to associate that bowl with trouble, and a few months later had forgotten about his experience and ate from it as willingly as from the others. Tod needed only one lesson, and he never forgot.

The man began to take Tod out for walks, at first keeping him on a long lead. Tod loved these walks. He was bored in the house, and there was so much to see and smell outside. After one walk, the man had only to approach the drawer where the lead was kept and Tod was bounding with delight, lying down to wiggle and whine with delighted anticipation, holding up his head so the lead could be snapped to his collar. Getting Tod back to the house was another proposition. As soon as he saw they were headed back, he would fight the lead, lie down, or brace himself with all four feet against the pull.

At last the man tried letting him run free. Now Tod was

perfectly happy. He ran around checking new scents and enjoying the sights. He was fascinated by the farm animals, especially the sheep. They had a heavy odor that attracted Tod, and the first time he encountered the flock he ran eagerly toward them. The sheep scattered in all directions, with Tod bounding joyfully in pursuit. As they scattered more and more, Tod began to herd them, bringing the flock together. Delighted at his power over these stupid creatures, he drove them from one end of the pasture to the other, learning how to keep the flock bunched up and how to change their course without having them separate. When the sheep grew too panicky, Tod would stand still until they had quieted down, often dropping his long nose between his forepaws, with his hindquarters elevated in the same attitude he used when playing with the man or dog. Sometimes he would crawl in among the sheep on his belly so slowly and quietly they would stand motionless watching him. He would worm his way through the flock in this manner, proud of his ability to fool the animals. Then, springing up, he would split the flock and drive one half around the pasture letting the rest go where they would. He was much too small to hurt the sheep, and had no evil designs on them. Yet he had a desire to herd and drive them that he could not explain.

Tod had a remarkable ability to differentiate between various sounds and to interpret even human tones of voice. Once the terrier jumped a rabbit that sprinted down a fence line toward a road where cars were moving. The dog sped after the rabbit; and Tod, although he had not seen the rabbit himself, ran after the terrier. As they neared the road, the man started shouting to them. Both animals heard him, but the dog, intent on the rabbit trail, refused to obey, and naturally Tod kept with his friend—he seldom came when called under any circumstances. When they were close to the road and the speeding traffic, the man's voice took on a new tone. He yelled with fury. The dog continued to ignore him, but Tod stopped short, turned to look at the man in surprise, and then hurried back, fawning at the man's feet apologetically. He knew quite well from the tone that this was no ordinary command; the man was intensely serious.

When autumn came, Tod was delighted to find great new vistas opening. From the top of a hill he could see vast distances, unhampered by tall grass or leafy bushes. Walking was now a real pleasure, for Tod had trouble making his way through dense cover and always preferred open country. Everything had become open country, even the woods that he had hitherto avoided, for the underbrush was gone. He loved the dry leaves, and batted them around with his nimble forefeet, springing up to catch them in the air with snapping jaws or rolling over and over in them. It became harder and harder for the man to entice him back to the house, for being outside was too much fun. Food had no particular attraction for him; he was too well fed, and could quite easily go for forty-eight hours without eating. Also, he was growing bigger, stronger, and more self-confident. Sometimes the man could lure him back with a mechanical toy that always aroused Tod's curiosity, but he spent several nights out, turning up the next morning for his bowl of milk.

It began to grow colder. Tod did not mind the cold; in fact he rather enjoyed it, but in the early morning when the ground was coated with hoarfrost, it upset him not to be able to smell. He ran around sniffing desperately, afraid that something had gone wrong either with him or with the world. He did not relax until the sun started a thaw and scenting conditions were better. Just to reassure himself, Tod would dart around the farm, snuffing at all the old, familiar spots. Then he had a real surprise. Trotting down to the pond for a drink, he found the surface covered with a thin, hard substance. Tod smelled it, patted at it with his paw, and then struck it repeated blows with his pile-hammer nose. The stuff cracked, and Tod got his drink.

One evening Tod refused to return to the house in spite of all the man's cajolements. The atmosphere was oppressive and pressed down on his eardrums. He did not like the smell of the air; it seemed thick, somewhat like the heavy, moisture-charged air before a rain, yet this was different. It was more dense and confining. Tod reacted strongly to anything new; it either fascinated or terrified him. This terrified him. He ran around whimpering until finally the man left him. Then Tod got lonely and went to the back door. He sniffed under it. He could smell the people and food inside, and hesitatingly lifted one paw to scratch; then thought better of it. He was too distraught to think clearly, and ended by running around the farm several times and finally curling up under the woodpile. Scenting was good, and this partly reassured him, as whatever the danger was, he could tell when it was coming by his nose. At last he went to sleep.

When he awakened, the world had turned white. Tod sat up astonished. He was a little frightened but mainly curious. He dabbed at the stuff with one paw and studied the curious way it crumbled. He poked at it with his long nose and was charmed when his nose plunged into the stuff. Now he was thoroughly excited. He bounded out into the snow, diving from one drift to another, knocking it about by quick sideways motions with his nose. When miniature snowballs formed and rolled down the drifts, Tod chased them, biting gaily and then trying to find out what had happened to the vanished spheres. He was still rollicking happily about when the man came out. Tod was so happy he allowed himself to be picked up without a struggle and carried inside for breakfast. As soon as he was through eating, he anxiously scratched at the door to be let out again. This time the man and dog went with him, and Tod had a magnificent time making a complete fool out of them both, for often he could run on the surface of the snow when his two companions floundered helplessly in the drifts. This was exactly Tod's idea of a joke, and he made the most of it.

As the winter continued, Tod grew increasingly restless. His testes began to swell and trouble him so that he sometimes twisted around to bite at them. He grew more and more irritable, snapping at the dog, and several times he bit the man severely when picked up. He stayed away more and more, returning to the farm mainly to pick up food at the garbage dump in the far pasture; but sometimes he still craved companionship, scratching and barking at the back door until he was let in. At such times he would run ardently from the man to the dog, doing everything to show how glad he was to be home. For a day or so he might stay at the farm, following the man everywhere he went, going contentedly to the once-hated room at night and being even tamer than the dog. Then the throbbing would start in his swollen testes again, and he would grow restless and irritable.

His coat, which had been lackluster and shabby, was thicker and so much more colorful that he seemed like a different animal. His back became a burnished red with golden tints. His chest and belly turned a creamy white, while his eartips and the lower parts of his long legs were a rich black. His brush became enormous, until it was nearly half his own size, while a snowy tassle appeared on the tip. A slight but noticeable ruff appeared around his neck that stood out when he was excited. Because of the ruff, his ears seemed more prominent and his thin nose was accentuated. His face resembled an inverted triangle with the apex greatly extended. During the summer he might have been mistaken for a small yellow dog or even a large cat. Now he was unmistakably a fox.

Tod spent hours running aimlessly through the fields or along the edges of woods, looking for something, he knew not what. Occasionally he would catch a mouse and far less frequently a rabbit, half frozen and unable to put forth its best speed. He attacked his quarry with a fury bordering on hysteria, growling as he killed and then flinging it about in an orgy of ferocity. He seldom bothered to eat it, for in killing he was striving to find a relief for the mysterious urge that possessed him. The urge was partly satisfied by the wriggling and squealing of the prey and the taste of hot, salty blood, but within minutes the agonizing restlessness would return and Tod would race on and on, knowing that only by exhausting himself could he rest and sleep.

Occasionally the urge would temporarily disappear, and then Tod was rational again. He would return to the garbage dump to look for food, although he no longer scratched at the door. One winter evening he saw the man on his way to the barn, and Tod ran joyfully to greet him. For nearly an hour they played together as they had often played when he was a puppy—Tod rushing in to bite playfully at the man's outstretched hands, grab any object thrown him, and dash around with it while the man chased him, and once, while the man was kneeling, even jumping on his back and nipping his ear. But whenever the man tried to catch him, Tod ducked away. He did not want to be confined, and his wild life was making him increasingly distrustful of any human.

One night while Tod was sleeping, thoroughly exhausted, under a blown-down pine, he was awakened by a distant scream. It was a shrill, eerie sound, charged with hatred and terror. Tod shuddered at the sound, and lay still. The cry came again and again, growing even more shrill and vindictive. Gradually Tod became interested. He was always interested, if frightened, of anything new, and he had never heard a noise like this. Then, too, there was a quality of fear in the cry that lured him. Tod automatically reacted to the sight or sound of any living creature in distress. When the sheep had run, he had chased them furiously, desiring only to sink his teeth into the frightened animals, but when they had turned at bay Tod had promptly stopped. Once he had heard the scream of a rabbit and run eagerly to the spot, for the hopeless terror in the noise had set his blood pounding. When he found the rabbit in the grip of a great horned owl that clicked at him with its hooked beak and spread its great wings, Tod had hastily retreated. This cry was not unlike the cry of the doomed rabbit, and might well mean some creature was in dire straits. If so, killing would be easy, and killing the helpless always appealed to Tod far more than killing the strong.

He rose and trotted toward the noise. It had stopped now, and Tod hesitated, one foot upraised, snuffing the wind. It was against him, so he made a long circle to get downwind. As he loped along, a scent struck him that brought him up sharply. It was such a scent as he had never known. It was alien, uncanny, alarming, and yet as he inhaled it the pressure in his testes began to mount until it was almost unbearable. Tod ran back and forth, whining, snapping at the air in an agony of pain and fear, yet the odor drew him forward as though pulled by an invisible wire.

Agonized with suspicion, awe-stricken, furious with himself, Tod still crept closer, taking advantage of every bit of cover. The painfully exciting scent was now heavy in the air. There was a little glade ahead, and by the light of the full moon Tod saw something dart from the shadow of a tree into the even deeper shadow of laurel thicket. He dropped and lay waiting for it to reappear. Suddenly the squall came again, so close it made Tod start. The creature had stopped by the laurel, and was crying. Tod lay listening and watching, torn by conflicting emotions.

A night breeze swept through the grove, making air currents eddy. The squalling stopped. Tod knew the creature was aware of his presence; he knew because he could no longer wind it, and when he could not wind something, then the actions of creatures like the dog and the sheep had shown they could wind him. Also, the abrupt stopping of the squalling told him that the creature knew he was there. He was tempted to run, but did not dare reveal his presence or turn his back.

The creature came out of the shadows and approached him. Tod watched it come with apprehension tinged with interest. It was somewhat smaller than he was, which partly restored his confidence, and its motions were not belligerent; Tod's fine eyesight could detect the slightest motion of belligerency even more readily than he could tell the difference between one feeding dish and another. He rose to meet it.

The creature stopped, cringed, and began to whine. Tod studied it critically, checking with both nose and eyes. It had two odors: one was the strange, overpowering scent that had drawn him to the glade, and the other was the creature's personal scent. Tod gradually realized this scent was akin to his own. He was increasingly more interested, and advanced.

Suddenly there was an interruption. Another animal bounded into the glade. This stranger was fully as big as Tod, even slightly larger. It stopped short on seeing him. The vixen ran back and forth between them, whining and cringing.

The newcomer's attitude was surprised rather than aggressive, and he showed no sign of cringing. He approached Tod stiff-legged, and Tod, with many inner forebodings, came toward him in the same attitude. He vaguely realized now that both these animals were foxes and that the vixen was somehow different than he was, but whether this newcomer was a vixen or not, he did not know. Obviously the stranger was also in some doubt, for he kept his brush raised so the identifying scent from his anal glands could spread. Tod raised his brush, and the two gingerly circled each other head to tail, each trying to get a whiff of the other's anus.

Suddenly the newcomer bounded back. As he did so, Tod got a strong whiff of the stranger's anal glands. This was no vixen, but a dog fox like himself. The stranger had gotten his scent a moment before, and now there was no doubt of his belligerency. He snarled, his back humping and his head going down. Tod imitated him. Again they came together, still edging sideways toward each other, each guarding with his brush. The screams of the vixen increased in pitch and excitement.

The stranger hit Tod across the mask with his brush and then flung himself in for a hold, but Tod slapped his own brush into the open jaws and jumped clear. Again they circled each other while the vixen danced screaming around them. Tod tried to knock the stranger over by striking with his rump, but the older fox easily avoided the blow.

Tod was quite willing to retreat. Although the vixen's odor and behavior had attracted him, he was curious rather than lustful, and would have had little idea how to proceed even if this stranger had not arrived. The stranger was bigger and more determined than he was, and had it not been from fear of a rear attack, Tod would have fled. The stranger sensed his uncertainty and did not press home an attack. He wanted only to have Tod depart. Slowly the circling combatants edged away from each other and Tod would have retreated had not the vixen, still cringing, darted in, snapping right and left at both the males. The dog foxes were highly tense and this sudden attack infuriated them. In fact, in their keyed-up state they were not quite sure whether they had been attacked by the vixen or by each other. Screaming and hissing, they came together.

Tod reared up and pushed at the stranger with his forefeet to hold him off. The stranger likewise reared, and the two foxes stood on their hind legs with their forefeet pressed against each other's chests, snapping at each other. They toppled over and rolled on the ground, snapping and trying for a hold. The stranger slid under Tod, his forelegs folded under him, trying to seize him by the testes. He struck a stone, or Tod would have been finished. Tod managed to leap back barely in time. Furious as he was, he did not dare to close again, and ran to and fro, snarling. The stranger ignored him and turned to the vixen. She yielded with only a perfunctory struggle. While the mating took place Tod ran in circles, barking, snarling, and biting at the frozen ground in an agony of jealousy and frustration.

The pair left together, and though Tod followed them a short distance he soon gave it up and turned away. After that, he kept his ears tuned for another barking vixen, and sniffed the breeze hopefully when out hunting, but without results.

Slowly Tod gained a knowledge of the territory. His short height was always a major problem. For that reason, he liked to go from rise to rise, stopping to look around each time. He preferred to trot along the edges of woods where he could see; but because he always felt nervous and exposed in open fields, he followed the fence lines or hedgerows. When he had to cross an open field, he generally ran. He often ran along the top of a post-and-rail fence where he could see a considerable distance; but this did not do him much good in establishing distant landmarks, for when he jumped down again he could no longer keep the faraway objects in view. So he traveled from marker to marker, such as a special gateway, a stump, a knoll, a certain tree, or a large stone, passing close to his marker yet not touching it. When he found a trail, a sheep path, or a wagon track, he followed that for convenience. As time went on, his route became routine and he seldom departed from it. His range was about a square mile, and although when hunting was poor he was forced to extend it, he always left the known territory with reluctance.

In running his route, he knew from experience exactly where all the likely game spots were, and carefully checked them. When he drew a blank and was forced to go into strange country, he ran about aimlessly, yet knowing enough to check each thicket, brush pile, or snowdrift around the base of a tree, as he had learned game often lay up in these places. In the woods he never passed a fallen tree without running along it or a stump without jumping on top. He did this partly so he could look around, but also because he liked climbing on objects simply for the fun of it.

Mice were his staple. Even with snow on the ground, he could scent a mouse tunnel, and would plunge his long nose into the snow to check. At first he dug up the tunnels, hoping to find the mice, but he soon found this was a waste of time. He could hear mice running through the tunnels several feet away, and he would give a great bound, land with his forefeet pressing down the tunnel on either side of the quarry, and bite between his paws blindly. Sometimes he got only a mouthful of leaves or snow, but often he got a mouse. Not only could he hear very faint sounds a surprising distance; he could also pinpoint the exact location of a nearby sound in an instant, but if a sound came from far away, he had considerable trouble locating the source, and was more inclined to depend on his nose than on his ears in such cases, by swinging downwind to smell what was making the disturbance.

Rabbits were his favorite quarry. Mice he could swallow at a gulp, and there was really no great fun in capturing them.

Rabbits were bigger, smarter, and gave him a real run. He liked the flesh better, and there was more of it. One rabbit would last him two or three days, yet he hunted them for the sport quite as much as for food.

One of his favorite rabbit grounds was an orchard where the rabbits came to strip the young trees when there was snow on the ground and other herbage was covered. Tod had first gone to the orchard looking for half-frozen windfalls, and discovered the rabbits by accident. Once he was aware of their presence, he took to circling the orchard first to get downwind and then coming in cautiously, often crawling catlike on his belly. On a straightaway the rabbits could outrun him; however, they usually tried to dodge around the trees, and Tod could turn faster than they could. The rabbits had burrows along the edge of the orchard, and this was another advantage for Tod. When a rabbit went down a hole, he had to hesitate for a split second at the mouth to get his way clear, and in this second Tod could often grab him. It was safer for a rabbit to plunge into a briar patch, for he could hit the brambles at any angle.

One afternoon when Tod was loping along his usual path that paralleled a fence, he saw cattle in the field. Tod stopped short to stare at them. The cattle had been in the barn most of the winter, and this was the first time he had seen them. Curious as ever, Tod trotted over to investigate. The cows raised their heads to look at him. Tod, uncertain of his reception, ran from side to side, trying to make them panic as he had done the sheep. Instead, two heifers charged him. Their attack was so unexpected Tod was nearly caught, and only by rapid dodging was he able to escape. Even so, he returned again, fascinated by the huge creatures. He soon found that by moving slowly and keeping close to the ground he could pass right through the herd without the cattle paying any particular attention to him.

He also found that even though the creatures were dangerous, they charged in a straight line and could be easily avoided. From then on, Tod frequently turned aside from his regular route to torment the cattle, dodging around them, snapping at their legs, and making them chase him. Then, merely to show his mastery of the dull brutes, he would stop, let them quiet down, and deliberately slink through the herd, pausing to lie down in the middle of them, and finally trotting off, his mouth open in his distinctive foxy grin of triumph.

That spring Tod also encountered dogs. They were farm dogs, mongrels without especially good noses, who liked to go hunting in the fields and woods. The first time Tod heard one of them on his trail he stopped, puzzled, and even waited for the animal; but one look at the oncoming cur speedily convinced him this baying creature meant him no good. He ran, mad with panic; and the dog, scenting the odor of fear when he came to the place in the trail where Tod had turned, burst into excited cries.

Tod followed his standard route automatically, even running along a fence rail at a spot where he usually jumped on top of the fence to look out across the valley. He did not stop to look today, racing along two sections of fence before dropping down to continue his wild flight. He started to pant and unconsciously slowed his gait. Then he realized the dog was no longer giving tongue. Tod stopped and, making a circle, cautiously swung around to study his back trail. He found the bewildered dog running up and down the fence line, trying to pick up the broken trail. Tod lay silently watching him for a long time. The dog's behavior was sufficiently similar to his own actions when trying to find a lost line so that he realized what the dog was doing, just as he had been able to recognize gestures of friend-ship or play on the part of the terrier because they were basically the gestures a fox would use under the same circumstances. When the dog finally gave up, Tod trotted off thoughtfully. He knew now that the dog had been following him by his scent, as he followed the scent of a rabbit, and that by fence-running he could throw the animal off. From then on, whenever he was chased by a dog he would follow his usual route to the fence, run along the top rails, and drop off. It did not immediately occur to him that any fence would do as well—he always went to the same spot—but slowly he picked up a repertoire of tricks to throw off dogs. Most of these tricks he learned by sheer chance, like the fence-running. Whenever the dog was at a loss, Tod memorized that particular spot and what he had done. He was not analytical. Once he threw off two dogs by running across a newly plowed field, and from then on he always cut across that field when chased. He could not understand why when wheat started to come up in the field the trick no longer worked and the dogs could follow him easily. However, he still continued to run the field because of the original success.

Tod was not entirely incapable of associating ideas. Once when a dog was after him Tod saw the cattle in the field and had an idea. He knew that the dog was comparatively clumsy, as the little terrier had been, and that the cattle would attack any large animal running carelessly among them. Tod turned off his usual route and ran across the field toward the cattle. When he drew close to them, he dropped and slunk forward among the grazing cows, worming his way into the middle of the herd. Then he turned so as to be able to watch his back track, and waited. In a few minutes the dog came racing along in full cry. Intent on the trail, he never lifted his head, and charged blindly toward the cattle. The cows bawled and turned toward him with lowered horns; nevertheless the dog kept on. A cow charged him. The startled dog was barely able to avoid her horns, and as he sprang aside another cow caught him and rushed him against the fence. Tod, sitting up to see better, watched the dog go flying into the air, yelping with pain and fright. Another cow caught the dog as he tried desperately to escape along the fence line. He finally managed to get away, and departed crying with pain while Tod bounded in the air to watch, dancing with delight and grinning until his jaws nearly met at the back of his neck. He was perfectly safe, for the cattle were watching the dog. Tod was so proud of himself and in such ecstasy at the success of his trick that he deliberately went looking for dogs thereafter to lure them into the field. He kept it up until every farm dog in the neighborhood learned to avoid the herd, to Tod's great disappointment.

Tod followed his beat with such regularity a man could almost have set a watch by observing when the fox passed a certain point. Part of his run was along an embankment where a train ran twice a day. Tod had originally climbed the embankment because it was high and gave him a better view. He soon learned to trot along one of the rails, for the cinders hurt his pads, and he would run the rail for a few hundred yards before turning off to take a footpath through a juniper tangle that, in turn, led him to a culvert under a highway and thence up a hill to the fallen pine under which he usually denned for the day. He always reached the embankment an hour before dawn, but one morning he was late, having been delayed by an opossum that played dead so successfully that even Tod with his educated eyes and nose had been fooled. As he trotted along the rail shortly after sunup, he heard the whistle of an oncoming train.

Tod paid no attention to the sound, and kept on. He felt the rail vibrating under his pads, and stopped to stare down at it in wonder. Then he heard the train itself and, looking over his shoulder, saw the monster racing down on him.

Tod ran for his life along the rail, but the train was faster. It never occurred to Tod to leave the rail until he came to his familiar turning-off place at the juniper thicket. The cowcatcher was almost touching his brush when he reached the place and made a hysterical bound off the embankment. Hitting the ground with all four feet, he continued racing along the path, positive that the train was after him. Gradually he realized the monster was still on the embankment, rushing by. Tod stopped and stood watching it, gasping for breath. A week or so later, the fox was again delayed and again heard the whistle and felt the vibration while running the rail. This time he was prepared. He started running instantly and reached the jump-off spot in plenty of time. After a few more such experiences, he learned that the monster always continued in a straight line, not unlike the cattle when they charged, and therefore could be easily dodged. He even made a game of the business—as he did of everything—and would deliberately jump on a rail and race ahead of the engine, jumping off whenever it got dangerously close.

Autumn was a great time for Tod. Food was plentiful, and there was enough of a snap in the air to give him added vigor. He was bored, for hunting was easy and he had no friends. He left his usual range and roamed afield with memories of the vixen in his head. On one of these trips he passed a cabin on the slope of a hill, and smelled dogs.

It was just before dawn, and Tod hesitated. Curiously he circled the hill and then crept closer. To see what would happen, he gave an experimental bark. Instantly dogs burst from their barrel kennels, screaming with rage. Tod turned to run and then saw the dogs were chained. He had been chained himself, and understood the situation perfectly. He loped off, grinning to himself at the animals' rage.

A few nights later, he passed the same spot. This time Tod slunk over to the nearest barrel, taking care to stop just outside the circle of hard-packed earth that showed the limits of the captive's chain. Then he began barking. He was rewarded by seeing a big hound burst out and rage at him. The other dogs instantly erupted from their kennels, and Tod sat in the midst of his hereditary enemies, enjoying their futile fury. Then the headlights of two cars swept the hill, and he hurried away.

It was nearly two months later when Tod again happened to pass the hill shortly before daylight. He stopped in front of another kennel and barked tauntingly. The results were gratifyingly predictable. The hound burst out, standing on his hind legs as he forced himself against the collar, and within seconds the whole hillside was a madhouse of raging, thwarted dogs.

The cabin door was thrown open, and a man came out. Tod instantly whirled to run. At the sight of his fleeing figure, the pack really went frantic. Tod had almost reached the cover when he heard the cry of the hound he had been goading take on a note of triumph, and sound nearer. Tod glanced back. To his horror, he saw that the hound had broken his collar and was after him.

Tod sped for the woods, confident he could easily outdistance the hound as he had the farm dogs. To his growing alarm he heard the savage, eager baying rapidly getting closer. Out of the corner of his eye Tod saw that the hound was gaining on him He turned loose his top burst of speed. As he did so he heard the man shouting, "Chief! Come back here!" The hound paid no attention to the voice, and as Tod dived into the woods the hound was right behind him.

Once in the woods the hound could no longer see him and was brought to his nose. Tod headed straight for the familiar home range where he knew the country so intimately. He expected the hound to drop far behind him like the farm dogs, but the baying continued steadily. The hound was not gaining, but neither was Tod lengthening the distance between them. This was not good, not good at all. Tod decided not to play with this animal, but get rid of him as fast as possible.

He had reached his home range now, and thankfully Tod bounded up the slope of the well-known embankment. The dawn was coming up, and he heard the whistle of the train at a distant crossing. The sound gave Tod an inspiration. The train behaved like the cattle, just as the cattle had behaved like the sheep. He had gotten rid of the farm dog by taking him in front of the cattle. He could get rid of this animal in the same way. Tod looked back and saw the hound struggling up the embankment. The scent was poor on the rail, and the hound was at a loss, so Tod slowed down to wait for him. The hound finally picked up the line and loped along between the rails, checking with his nose at intervals to make sure his quarry had not jumped off. Tod felt the tingling of the rail under his pads. The train was coming.

The hound checked the scent again and as he lifted his head from the rail he saw the fox running ahead. At once he burst into the cry that meant "In sight! In sight!" From somewhere there came the bleat of a hunting horn, blowing demandingly and insistently, but with the quarry in view the hound disregarded it. He tore along the ties and Tod had to stretch himself to keep ahead.

The pulsation of the rail increased. The train was bearing down on them. Tod could see that the hound was right behind him. He waited as long as he dared, and then flung himself off the rail and down the embankment. As he did so he heard the desperate call of the horn, the frenzied whistle of the train, and then a single scream of agony from the hound. The train swept past while the panting fox made his way to the juniper tangle and dropped, dead beat.

Silently he watched while a man came along the tracks with a big hound on a lead. The man stopped and stood looking at the dead hound a long time. Then he knelt and gently lifted the body. Tod heard him make a peculiar sobbing noise he had never heard before, and cocked his ears to listen.

The man turned and looked out over the cover while Tod froze, afraid that he would be observed. The man held up the dead hound and shouted at the top of his voice. Tod could tell by the man's tone that he was filled with hatred and making some threat, much as Tod could tell that the vicious barking of a dog constituted a threat. Slowly the man turned and started back, carrying the dead hound while the hound on the lead followed him. When they were well gone, Tod rose stiffly and walked along the footpath, crawled through the culvert, and went up the hill to his pine-tree den. For once in his energetic life, he had had enough. He hoped never to see the man or any of his dogs again as long as he lived.

3

The First Hunt—Shooting at a Crossing

For the next few days, Copper was supremely happy. His hated rival, Chief, was dead, and every time a current of air brought him the stale whiff of the Trigg's scent from the empty kennel, Copper knew a thrill of satisfaction. Yet this was only part of his joy. Every day now the Master came up the hill and picked him—and him alone—to go out. The other hounds screamed their frustration and jealousy, but little did Copper care. He was again top dog and the Master's chosen companion.

True, he could have wished that the Master would do some real hunting rather than the boring, routine work required of him. The same day that Chief was killed and the Master had buried him in the dog graveyard up in the woods behind the cabin, the Master had gotten Copper and taken him back to the railroad tracks where the fox had jumped off. Although the scent was now cold, Copper had had no trouble following it through the junipers and to the culvert. Copper's educated nose told him the fox was not in the drain, so they had crossed the road to the other side. Here Copper had gotten a distinct air-borne scent from the hillside ahead. The fox was lying up on the slope, probably watching them at that very minute. He had promptly thrown his deep voice and strained at the lead, but the Master was strangely obtuse and held him back. Instead, the Master had studied the hillside carefully for some time and then dragged the reluctant Copper back to the car.

From then on, the Master had picked up Copper every morning at sunrise, put him in the car, and they had driven for hours over the rough back roads. From time to time, the Master would stop the car so suddenly that Copper was nearly thrown from his rack behind the front seat. Then the Master would get out and stare at the road, sometimes walking back and forth slowly and sometimes bending over to stare at marks in the soft dust that apparently told him something, although Copper could not imagine what. Then they would go on, only to repeat the process again and again.

But sometimes after such a study the Master would call Copper out of the car, snap on the lead, and take him over the fields to a point where two fence lines crossed, a fallen log over a stream, or a gap in the hedgerow. If the ground was muddy, the Master was content with his own observations, but if it was hard or there was grass, he would call on Copper. Copper would apply his marvelous nose to the place indicated, and if a fox had passed that way within the last twenty-four hours, he would throw his tongue.

In such cases, the Master would let him follow the line to a soft place where there were marks. Then the Master after examining them would often pull him off, saying, "No!" For a long time, Copper could not understand the difficulty. He had long ago learned not to speak on the trail of a gray fox. For some reason, grays were useless to the Master. Copper never smelled their hides with the stretching boards inside hanging on the side of the cabin, and so he was scrupulously careful to make sure the scent was that of a red before giving tongue. Even so, for some time the Master clearly did not find what he was seeking. Copper was eager to help, and felt that somehow he was being remiss in his duties, yet he had no idea what was the matter.

Then one morning where a power line ran between a multiflora hedge and a wire fence covered with honeysuckle, Copper hit a fox scent he remembered. It was the fox who had run the rails and had been lying up on the hill that day. Copper spoke on the line without much enthusiasm, as he was now convinced that everything he did was wrong. As usual, he was ordered to track, and he followed the line to the banks of a little creek where the fox had trotted across fresh mud to drink. As soon as the Master had examined the mud, his whole attitude changed. Copper sensed the excitement in his voice as he ordered, "Go get 'em, boy!" Copper wagged his thin tail, expecting to have the lead unsnapped, but the Master repeated the order and the astonished hound realized he was supposed to track while still on the lead. Disappointed but obedient, he set off. He was still tracking when night came and the scent grew no warmer, but the Master seemed pleased.

For the next few days, Copper tracked the fox until he knew the animal's regular route almost perfectly, even though the Master always stopped him when they approached the culvert and the hillside. Copper had not the slightest trouble in distinguishing between this particular fox and other foxes, just as he could easily tell the scent of an individual man from man scent in general. After a few errors, Copper learned that the Master was interested only in this especial animal, so the hound ignored other fox trails and concentrated on the now familiar scent. Except for the unusual concentration on an individual scent, Copper perfectly understood what the Master was up to now, for he had played this game with him many times. Yet never before had the Master been so determined to trace out the entire nightly run of a fox, and Copper grew heartily tired of the business and eager for the climax that he knew was coming.

There had been a cold spell and every morning the ground was covered with frost; so scenting had been difficult, if not impossible, until after the sun rose and the frozen earth released its odors. Then came a warm night. Copper was still sleeping when he heard the Master's footstep and his name spoken. At once the old hound wormed his way out of the barrel and jumped delightedly on the Master, for he knew this must be the day.

It was. The Master had no lead and was carrying his shotgun. There was a fog; but this did not bother the hound, as he made comparatively little use of his eyes anyhow. Scenting conditions were perfect and Copper happily sucked in lungfuls of the air, noting and separating the multitudinous odors that came to him. After the long freeze he felt as happy as though he had been locked up in a dark cellar and the light had finally been turned on.

They started off, stopping and picking up two men at different farmhouses on the way. Both men carried guns, and Copper recognized them by their odor as old hunting friends of the Master's. The men made much of Copper; and he enthusiastically responded, for now there was no doubt whatsoever about the purpose of the expedition. When these two men went with the Master, they always came back with a fox.

The sun was up now and the fog was breaking up into rags of mist, lifting like steam from the warm earth. As they drove past farmhouses, Copper could smell smoke from the chimneys, always a good sign, for it meant the smoke was lying low instead of going straight up and the scent would also hug the ground instead of rising over his head. In spite of his eagerness,

Copper made it point to lie quietly as the car bumped over the washboard roads, for he knew he had a long run ahead of him and would need all the rest he could get now.

The car stopped and Copper shook himself and prepared to rise, but the Master was only dropping off one of the men. Copper recognized the spot; it was the crossing where the multiflora hedge and overgrown wire fence intersected. Copper watched with a professional eye while the man took up his position in a sassafras thicket. He was well placed, at least fifty feet from the crossing where the fox could be expected to run. Copper had seen men so stupid they had taken up a stand at the crossing itself, where, of course, the fox winded them as he came in. Copper checked the breeze to make sure the man was also downwind of the crossing. Everything was all right, and Copper settled down with a contented sigh.

After a few miles they stopped again, and this time Copper did not bother to move. He knew they were dropping off the second hunter, and Copper watched him go down toward the log over the stream. This was another crossing that he and the Master had carefully worked out. Then the car went on with only him and the Master left, so Copper knew well their destination.

They stopped near the railroad tracks and Copper jumped out as soon as the door was open. The Master followed. Copper ate some grass to make himself vomit so he would be lighter for the long run ahead. Then he hit the well-padded trail through the juniper, checked the culvert briefly, and crossed the road, where he stopped to sniff. The wind was against him but Copper did not worry. The fox would surely be lying up on the hill ahead as he had that morning a week ago. Copper knew foxes.

They started up the hill, Copper running ahead. The Master spoke to him and he slowed his gait. Up and up they went, Copper constantly testing the breeze, but it was blowing from behind them and told him nothing. They were close to the crest now, so surely something had to happen soon.

The Master gave a sudden yell. Copper could see nothing, but he knew the fox was running, and dashed forward. Casting about frantically, he found the fallen pine and the heavy smell of fox hit him full in the face. Copper screamed with excitement, but the scent was so strong he could not at once pick up the light trail made by the fleeing animal.

"Here, boy, here!" shouted the Master. Copper was so excited he did not respond until the second call. By then he realized that he could not hit the trail right off, so he ran to the Master, who was pointing downward. Coming in at an angle, Copper crossed the fox's line higher up and instantly stopped as though he had run into a brick wall. He ran up and down briefly to make sure of the direction the fox was going—the forward trail smelled slightly different from the heel because of the position of the scent glands in the fox's pads—and then tore downhill, baying at the top of his great voice.

The scent was breast-high, so there was no need to drop his head, and he saw the fox cross the road ahead of him, a brief flicker of dark gray. On the road he lost the scent momentarily— it was covered with dry dust that got in his nose—but Copper made no attempt to follow it here. Knowing the fox had crossed straight over, he rushed on, holding his head up to avoid fouling his valuable nose with the dust. On the other side were grass and weeds, so here the scent held and Copper resumed his baying. As he ran, he heard the sound of the Master's car starting up and then pulling away with a rapid acceleration from one gear to another. Copper was delighted at the sound, for he knew from many past experiences that the Master, now he saw how the fox was running, would speed to the next crossing and wait for the fox there.

The fox was now on his regular route and, barring unforeseeable accidents, would stick to it, as he knew the path so perfectly he could make better speed along it than across country. Copper knew it too and pressed hard. The fox could of course run his route either way, but as Copper expected, he ran it upwind so he could smell anything ahead of him. Copper understood this principle perfectly, for he disliked running downwind himself—it was like running blind not to know what was ahead of you. There was a north wind blowing and it was so strong, damp, and cold that occasionally Copper got whiffs of scent from the fox himself as well as the scent from his tracks.

The fox was not bothering to exert himself; he was running easily only a few hundred yards ahead. Copper could tell, for when the quarry puts forth its full efforts the scent is much stronger and more distinctive as the energy forces more odor from the scent glands. The knowledge outraged the hound, and as the scent was screaming hot, he charged on ahead recklessly. In spite of his heavy build, the half-bloodhound was capable of putting on a surprising burst of speed for short distances, and Copper noted with satisfaction that the scent grew gratifyingly stronger and that there was even a wonderful trace of the fear odor mixed with it. That exciting odor caused him to redouble his efforts.

They were approaching the first crossing now, a windbreak of evergreens that ran beside a road. The route led along the trees and then made a sharp turn to the right across the road and through some locusts to an open field. The Master would be behind the evergreens, waiting. Copper's baying took on a triumphal note as he anticipated the boom of the shotgun.

Then he heard a sound that filled him with shame and foreboding—it was the noise of the Master's car coming up the road. At once Copper slowed down. In his excitement he had committed the unforgivable crime, unworthy of even an inexperienced puppy, of pressing the fox too hard and not giving the gunner a chance to get to his stand. One of those stupid Walkers or Triggs might make such a mistake, but that he, Copper, would so forget himself was inexcusable. Remorsefully, he fell into a trot and almost stopped baying in hopes the fox would slow his pace, but he knew it was too late. The sound of the car was too far away and the fox was still running strong; he could tell by the hot scent. There was nothing for it now except push on. Copper ran the line of evergreens, crossed the road, and followed the line through the locusts. Then, safe from possible punishment by the Master, he resumed his baying.

Beyond the locusts, the fox had left his usual run to cut across the open field. Copper was so surprised that he checked carefully, suspecting some trick, but the trail was plain and distinct. The rising sun was warming the ground, making little currents of air that swirled the scent around the tufts of grass, and Copper followed the line from tuft to tuft to save time. The fox had run a zigzag course across the field as though looking for something, and Copper took advantage of this to cut straight across, following the fox's general drift rather than trying to unravel each of the loops. The field was heavy with the foil of cattle, but none were to be seen. At this hour they were all in the barn being milked, and Copper could hear their lowing and smell their sweet breath and the hot, fresh scent of the milk. At one place the fox had stopped to roll in some half-dry manure before going on. The manure neutralized his body odor and would have caused Copper real trouble if he had been forced to take the trail from leaves or tall grass that had rubbed against the animal's body, as was often the case in cover or in overgrown fields. Here in the short-clipped pasture he could smell the scent from the pads where they pressed the grass, so the manure hardly bothered him at all.

The fox left the field and cut across country, completely ignoring his regular run. By so doing he missed the next crossing where, Copper knew, the Master would probably have gone. There was nothing to do but continue on the trail, baying as loudly as possible so the Master could tell what had happened. The fox was now running in an almost perfectly straight line, clearly headed for some definite objective, and Copper apprehensively increased his pace. The fox might be planning to go down a hole. Copper knew from the fox's smell that he was a young animal, hardly more than a pup, and pups were more apt to go down holes than older foxes.

The trail led into another field with grass as short as a lawn. Here the fox had made a number of spy-hops—leaping high in the air to see about him. These spy-hops made a series of breaks in the trail that puzzled Copper until he realized what they were. Then the fox had turned off at a sharp angle. After running a few yards, he had dropped down and started to crawl on his belly. Here the scent was so strong Copper burst into full cry, lifting his head as he ran in hopes of seeing his quarry ahead of him.

Instead he ran into a flock of sheep that exploded in front of him. A belligerent ram refused to move, and stood threatening with his head down. As the trail led right under him, Copper grabbed the stupid beast by the wool around his neck, dragged him to one side, and then continued on. But the panicky animals had virtually obliterated the line with their sharp hoofs and pungent odor. Copper could find only the faintest ghosts of scent, and these were too scattered to form a continued trail.

After a few minutes' effort, Copper left the trampled field in disgust and made a long cast around the fence line. Behind the sheep there was nothing, and Copper had to turn and go the other way. Here he finally picked up the line again where the fox had gone under the fence. The fox had backtracked—just like one of those sneaky creatures! He had crawled in among the sheep and lain there, watching Copper come up. He had probably still been there while Copper was having his fight with the ram. Then when he saw Copper start out to make his cast, he had run back through the flock, ducked under the fence, and was now headed back toward his regular run. Copper began to bay again, in indignation at the trick that had been played on him as much as in satisfaction at hitting the line.

As Copper had suspected, the line led back to the regular route, and he picked it up beside a post-and-rail fence surrounding a plowed field where winter wheat had been planted. The plowed earth completely absorbed the scent, and Copper would have been hopelessly lost had he not been able to pick up occasional ends of odor blown into the furrows by the wind. Copper paused to clear his nose by sniffing loudly and long before going on, but even so the bits of scent were so few and far between he would have been defeated had the fox not kept along the fence. As soon as he realized how the fox was running, Copper simply followed the fence. Had the fox turned and cut across the field, the hound would have been at a hopeless loss, but the fox had here kept to his regular run, and at the end of the fence where he had turned at right angles to go up a path leading to a small woods, the hound was able to pick up the line again and follow it.

As he approached the trees, Copper smelled where the fox had jumped a rabbit from its form and turned off the route to catch and kill it. In spite of his careful training, Copper could not resist the temptation to make a quick cast to see if the fox had left the rabbit lying there, but he had carried off his quarry. Clearly the fox thought he had lost the hound in the sheep field, and was no longer worried. Copper would show him differently. The hound pushed on, hoping to find the fox eating his kill. Just before he reached the woods, he came upon the body of the rabbit. The fox had not broken into it and had dropped it when he heard or smelled the hound coming. After a quick sniff at the dead animal, Copper plunged into the cover.

The trees were pines, and their resinous odor tended to mask the scent. Even worse, the ground was heavily carpeted with dead needles that carried almost no scent in the deep shade, especially as the ground was still frozen here. Copper went on by taking the scent from branches that had touched the fox as he passed. He came to a place where the fox had run along a fallen tree, the roots still in the ground. Copper jumped clumsily on the trunk and followed the scent along it until he came to the end five feet above the ground. Here the fox had apparently jumped off and continued his flight, but Copper did not even bother to make the jump himself and check. He knew this fox trick. He turned and carefully retraced his steps, sniffing carefully. Ah, just as he had suspected, there was a double track. The fox had run to the end of the log, turned, and backtracked. Copper followed the double line to a point where there was only a single trail and then jumped off there. After a quick cast he came to where the fox had landed and continued running. With great satisfaction, Copper took up the trail again.

Scenting conditions were especially bad here, and the pines grew so far apart Copper could not get any scent from the twigs. He was forced to stop and scratch with both paws among the needles to stir up what scent there was. His loose upper lip spread as he sucked up the faint hints. Then to his infinite satisfaction he came to a place where the fox had obviously run around in circles, hoping to leave such a tangle of trails the hound would be hours unraveling them. Copper made no attempt to follow the line. He simply left the mess and made a long cast around it, knowing the fox would have to come out somewhere. He struck the fresh, straight trail and went right away on it. As he ran he burst into a little clearing and heard a crackling in the frozen ferns ahead. When he reached the spot, the smell of fox hit him like a blow. The fox had been lying in the ferns, confident that the hound could never read the riddle of the log and the tangle. Now the quarry was right ahead of him and Copper drove hard.

At the edge of the cover, Copper came on fresh dung. The fox had emptied his bowels, both from nervousness and a desire to lighten himself for a long run. He was not nearly so confident as he had been at the beginning of the hunt. He had probably been chased by cur dogs who had been easily fooled by such tricks. Very well, this fox would now learn the difference between a cur and a hound.

Out of the cover, the fox had run along a slash made by a high-tension line and then through a hole in a fence so over-grown by honeysuckle and grape that no trace of the original wire could be seen. The fox had been running just ahead of the hound, but now he suddenly put on speed, as Copper could tell by the scent growing distinctly fainter as the fox outdistanced him. Copper knew what that meant—they were coming to a crossing. The fox wanted to leave the hound well behind so he would have time to stop at the crossing, look about him, and test the breeze before going over the road. The fox's path lay along a hedgerow that fenced a farm, and as Copper reached it, he recognized by both sight and smell the multiflora hedge where one of the gunners had been stationed.

At once, Copper put forth his utmost speed, at the same time changing his rather perfunctory baying to a loud cry in order to alert the man ahead, just as the volume of his baying changed when he wanted to notify other hounds that the quarry had changed its course and was headed toward them. It was crucially important for the fox to be pressed as hard as possible coming into the crossing, as otherwise he would have time to detect the presence of the waiting man. Although his feet felt heavier now than they had at the beginning of the run, and breathing was harder, Copper flung himself forward, shouting as loudly as he could.

The thorny, unclipped stems of the hedge hung down in a veil, and between them and the hedge itself the fox had made a run that was almost a tunnel. Copper was too big to follow him here, and also the thorns tore the hound's long, soft ears, so he ran across the field, paralleling the hedge and still throwing his voice until the baying echoed from the side of a nearby barn. Copper knew well the fox was heading for the crossing, so there was no need to follow the trail exactly—simply press hard and notify the man that they were coming.

Two farm dogs rushed out of the barnyard and ran barking toward Copper. The hound was annoyed at these yapping idiots and kept on, but the dogs refused to let him go. Thinking that he was running from them they rushed in, dividing to attack from both sides. To his amazement and rage, Copper found himself involved in a dogfight with two ignorant curs who did not recognize a professional hound at work when they saw one.

Copper had never been a fighter, leaving that to the catch dogs, but in his indignation he turned on the two curs with a fury that caused them to withdraw, fighting on their home ground though they were. Copper tried to go on, but as soon as he turned the farm dogs rushed in again, snapping and snarling, their crests raised, their lips curled back to show the white teeth, their tails high. Copper was forced to defend himself, and the three furious animals spun around in a circle, rearing up as each dog tried to get higher than the other for the back-of-the-neck grip, and then falling to roll together on the grass.

Copper did his best, but he soon realized he was outmatched. Disengaging himself, he ran with the curs barking victoriously on his tail. They chased him across the field and under a barbed-wire fence. This was the limit of the farm, their home range, so they stopped at the fence, barking as loudly as possible and threatening all sorts of punishments if the hound ever dared return. Finally they trotted off toward the barn, shoulder to shoulder, feeling very proud of themselves and extremely companionable as brothers-in-arms.

Copper had not been seriously mauled, but he felt stiff and shaken as he went on. It took him some time to recover from the shock of the unexpected assault and get his mind back on the business at hand. He finally managed to orient himself, and returned to where the fox's line paralleled the hedge. Then he went on.

As he approached the crossing, he winded the gunner in the sassafras. That he could do so worried him, for it meant the wind had shifted slightly during the morning and the fox could do the same. Copper dropped his nose to the trail and followed it with a sinking heart. His worst suspicions were confirmed. Yes, here the fox had come to a sudden stop and there had been a slight spurt of urine. Then the fox had turned off sharply. Copper followed the line with scarcely enough enthusiasm to bay. The fox had avoided the crossing and gone over the road a quarter of a mile farther down. If only those damn curs had not interfered and Copper had been able to press him hard at this critical point, the hound would be worrying the body right now.

There was nothing for it but to keep on and hope for the best. After all, there were two more posted crossings, and at one the Master was sure to be waiting. The thought gave Copper confidence, and his baying rang out clear and true.

Copper knew from experience that from now on the fox would be doubly cautious at all crossings, determined to lose him, so the hound followed the line with meticulous care, alert for tricks. At first, there seemed to be nothing to worry about. The fox returned to his regular route as soon as possible and kept to it. Here the route led across some open fields, going from rise to rise in typical fox fashion, and although the strong light of the noonday sun was beginning to kill the scent in the open—as strong sunlight always did—enough of it lay in the shaded sides of the mounds to enable the hound to press on at a fast lope. There was also a little breeze here that made the scent swirl so it was more readily detected.

Copper came to a circular mound some fifty feet across with a deep depression in the center. The fox had run up the side of the mound, but here the scent ended. There was limestone under the grass, which always killed scent, and the rim of the mound was all in the full glare of the sun. Copper circled the mound, working the lip carefully to find where the fox had left it, but his nose told him nothing. He then made another cast, going over every foot of the outside slope. Poor as the scent was, he could not believe that the fox could have run down the mound again without leaving some trace. The fox must still be there somewhere, possibly in a hole.

Copper returned to the lip of the crater and then worked out the inside slope as systematically as he had the outer incline. Again he drew a blank. Copper was baffled. There were some outcroppings of limestone in the crater, and Copper wondered if he could pick up some scent in the shadow of one of these. He started to check them one after another.

Nothing—nothing—nothing. Copper was getting discouraged. Looking around with his nearsighted eyes, he saw one last rock lying in the bottom of the hollow. Without hope, and merely as a routine, final gesture he walked over to it and extended his muzzle.

To his astonishment, the rock suddenly darted away. Copper was so surprised he jumped back with a growl. Then the odor of fox hit him. Bellowing with excitement, he rushed forward, but not until he passed the spot where the fox had been lying did he realize that the fox had been crouched there curled up like a ball all the time he was casting to and fro in the crater, often not ten feet from the motionless animal. When he lay still the fox gave off virtually no odor, and to the color-blind hound the grayish limestone rocks were the same color as the fox.

They were off again. The fox was running through a hollow now, and the soil was moist. In spite of the sun, the grass was damp, and the scent from the fox's pads spread so rapidly the hound no longer had to follow the tracks themselves but a scent path several feet wide. Ahead lay a plowed field, and the fox cut across it. Copper approached the dark-colored earth apprehensively, but to his gratification the scent held well. The dark earth absorbed the warmth of the sun so the ground was warmer than the air and the scent rose, hanging an inch or so above the furrows. At dawn, at sunset, or on a warm day, scenting conditions here would have been impossible but now they were just right.

On the far side, the fox returned to his regular route, and now Copper sensed a subtle change in the scent. It was weakening. For a moment he thought the fox had speeded up for another crossing, but the scent was not stale. Nor were scenting conditions bad, for they were in the shadow of a line of maples. Copper felt a thrill of exultation. The fox was weakening and scent fades with a fading fox. Heretofore his baying had been low in the scale, and prolonged. Now it increased in tempo, key, and volume.

The fox ran along a snake fence, which bothered Copper not

at all, tried his backtracking trick again, and then put on speed. As he ran, Copper began to note familiar landmarks, although he had been over this portion of the route only once before. Copper had a remarkable memory for certain details, and he began to recognize the touch of a pokeweed stalk that brushed his shoulder at a certain angle when he had run this way earlier, the smell of an individual rusty iron post, and the clear, moist odor of flowing water ahead. They were coming to the log over the stream crossing where the second gunner had been posted. This was a "low" crossing in the bottom of a little valley, and scent would be bad. Copper increased his pace to keep the scent as fresh as possible, as well as to push the fox.

Here the fox's route crossed the stream twice: first across some stones in the creek, then along a line of scrub willows, and then back across the log. Copper threw his voice, but the scenting grew so bad that he was forced to concentrate on the line. He came to the creek where the fox had bounded nimbly from stone to stone without wetting his feet. The heavy, tired hound floundered through the water and up the other side. Here the scent stopped. Copper searched the clay bank in vain. He wondered if the fox could have turned and waded down or up the stream—foxes often did. He must be sure.

He turned and ran upstream, forded the creek again and tried the other bank. Scent would not lie on the running water, he knew, but if the fox had waded . . . bits of scent were often carried by the stream into little bays and backwaters. Copper checked them all and then tried downstream. Nothing there. He returned to the stepping-stones, went up the bank, and worked out the line of willows. At long last he found the line again. Baying loudly, Copper tore on.

There was the log, and the trail ran straight for it. Copper had almost reached it when he saw the gunner stand up from his ambush with the gun in his hand. Copper's nose told him the fox had already passed—why hadn't the man shot him? After several hours of his lonely vigil in the intense cold, the man must have relaxed to stretch, yawn, or scratch himself. He had taken his eyes off the log for a moment, and of course it was in that instant that the fox had slipped past. Copper had been too busy working out the line to warn him by baying. Raging, the hound crossed the log and kept on.

Well, there was still the Master. Copper knew the Master would not relax even for a second with a fox running. And he never missed. Copper had no idea at which of the remaining crossings the Master had posted himself, but he would be somewhere; that the old hound never doubted. Then all his efforts would be rewarded.

They were on good humus and the scent was clear although fading. The fox must be weakening, and Copper deliberately held back, for he did not want the fox to go to ground. The fox took advantage of the lead to make for a swamp, and there he left another maze of trails. This was more of a problem than the other tangles had been, for the swamp was too big for Copper to circle it and pick up the trail where the fox had emerged. He had to work it out. The job was not as hard as he had feared, for the sun had melted the frozen mud and there were puddles of water that held the scent beautifully after the fox had splashed through them. The fox had also jumped from hummock to hummock, and the dry swamp grass held his body scent. He had doubled in and out, crossing his own trail constantly; but Copper could perfectly well tell the difference between a trail made a minute before and one made two minutes before, and he was never confused. The fox would have to come out sometime, and come out he did. Copper even got a glimpse of the gray shape drifting across a meadow as he emerged from the rushes, and for a few wonderful seconds the hound was running by sight, telling the whole world of his triumph.

Now the fox tried what were obviously his last tricks. He ran along the bank of the stream for some distance and then down into the water. Copper needed to go only a few yards to be sure the fox had not gone downstream. A dam of driftwood had formed that the fox would have had to cross, and there was no scent on the dam. Upstream, then, it had to be. Copper waded up the stream, smelling each rock and watersoaked log in case the fox had rubbed against them, but he found nothing. Then he tried the banks. Still nothing. This was a puzzler. Copper begrudged every second these casts cost him, for any delay made the fading scent grow still colder and also gave the fox a chance to rest.

As usual in such a situation, Copper returned to the last place he had a sure scent: the spot where the fox had gone down into the stream. Yes, although the scent was now dead the quarry had certainly run along the bank and then gone down the bank. But wait a minute. There was something peculiar about the scent. Could it be—yes, it was double! The fox had run down to the stream and then backtracked. But where had he then left the trail? Copper had been conscientious about checking for jump-offs to one side or the other ever since the fox had started his series of tricks.

The hound backtracked along the trail. He went some distance before the double trail stopped, but the fox had not jumped to either side. Ah, the stream! He could reach that. For the second time Copper waded into the stream, but now below the dam, and began checking. The creek was so fast-flowing there were no little backwaters that might hold the wash from the fox's body, but mulberries overhung the stream and from their trailing limbs Copper was able to pick up the scent he sought. Yes, the fox had come this way. Copper followed him from the twigs until he came to where the fox had left the stream and resumed his run.

This had been a long check and the scent was growing cold, so Copper hurried on. He came to where the fox had run a hardtopped road—a common trick and annoying rather than puzzling. Unlike moist grass, the scent from the pads would not spread on the hard asphalt, but remained in little patches that made tracking difficult. Still, the fox had to leave the road somewhere, and Copper followed until he found the place. Several times he was nearly hit by passing cars, but Copper remained indifferent to them in his concentration on the elusive line, merely regarding the vehicles as a nuisance because their exhaust fumes and stinking tires further confused the line.

The fox cut through some woods where the scenting was easy and then down a long slope covered with orchard grass where the scent was even better. For the first time since the log crossing, Copper threw his voice in the full, rich bay of a tracking hound, and galloped on eagerly. There was something about this place he remembered. Yes, there was the cherry with the rotten limb lying beside the trunk. Yes, there was the patch of mint, and here was the stone wall covered with poison ivy and wild roses. They were coming to another crossing. Copper felt a sudden surge of confidence that here the Master would be waiting. It was a "high" crossing; if possible the fox always crossed a road where it ran over a little ridge. The fox liked high crossings as he could see in all directions and get the wind blowing straight across the valley unhampered by trees or hills.

There was, however, a good sumac tangle here that made a perfect ambush. Right in front of it ran the rutted dirt road and from the tangle the Master would have a perfect shot at the fox as he crossed. Once before in this same place the Master had shot a fox running before Copper just as this one was doing; in fact, this fox had taken over the dead animal's range, including most of his former route. Copper inhaled the fading scent and knew the fox was putting on his usual burst of speed before a crossing. Baying with the full force of his great lungs, Copper threw all his powers into catching up and preventing the quarry from hesitating at the road.

Men had been timbering, and the hauled logs had pressed down a long, wide swathe in the tall grass. As he rounded a bend in the wall, Copper saw ahead of him the lithe form of the fox speeding toward the road. Instantly he broke into his viewing cry that meant the quarry was in sight. The Master waiting would know what the change of pitch meant. The fox could not turn or stop now with the hound only yards from his brush. The Master would not be scratching or yawning, but waiting with his gun trained on the open patch of road that the fox must cross. Already Copper could feel the taste of soft fur in his mouth and the stench of the body as he worried it. The fox had almost reached the road now.

Down the road came an ancient, rattling farm truck, its driver indifferent to the baying hound or the fleeing scud of the fox. Copper saw the fox hesitate. For an instant he thought the animal would dodge in front of the truck and continue on his route, but instead the fox swung off to one side.

Bang! The half-frozen ground shuddered as a charge of shot struck under the white-tipped brush. The fox leaped convulsively, his hindquarters twisting at right angles, his brush shooting out sideways to act as a counterbalance as he swerved. Then the brush spun around and around, as though giving him momentum, and he was off. Until now, the fox had not been running; only keeping ahead of the hound. He ran now. The slim form seemed to shoot over the ground without touching it. In seconds, he was out of Copper's sight.

Laboring hard, Copper plunged after him. If only he had been hit! He smelled the torn earth and the odor of the shot mingled with the spurt scent of urine and fear. No blood, but there might still be some. Copper kept wildly on. It was useless. The sudden fright had scared the scent from the fox, the shock temporarily paralyzing the scent glands so they were inoperational. One drop of blood—just one little drop every few feet and Copper could still trail that fox across a desert, but there was no blood. Tracking was impossible, and Copper turned sadly back.

On the road, the Master had stopped the truck, and Copper could hear him yelling the driver. Copper could not understand the words but he recognized the tone. On a few occasions the Master had spoken to him like that, so he knew how the driver must feel. The thought gave him some slight satisfaction.

4

The Second Hunt—Jug Hunting

Tod learned three valuable lessons from that terrible day which had climaxed with a sting of shot in his hide that itched him for a long time afterward. First, he made it a point never to use the same lying-up place twice in succession so his enemies would not know where to find him. Second, especially when being chased by a slow hound who made no attempt to press him, he took care never to cross at a crossing; instead he made a detour around such places. Last, unless so hard pressed he was forced to take the easiest and therefore most familiar route, he did not stay on his regular run when hounds were on his trail, and made it his business to learn a number of alternate runs he could use when hunted. When hunting himself, he generally stayed on his regular route because the run had been laid out to enable him to visit the best game areas where mice, rabbits, and other quarry lived; but at the first cry of hounds he switched over to one of his secondary routes as quickly as possible, usually alternating between them, particularly if the hounds were forcing him to run downwind.

Tod had not acquired the bag of tricks he had played on Copper simply by being chased by farm dogs, and even less through any process of abstract reasoning. For several months before that well-nigh fatal day, he had been chased, often three or four times a week, by packs of experienced and determined hounds. These hunts always took place at night, and followed a predetermined pattern that Tod had learned to expect.

The first time Tod heard the pack on his trail, he stopped to listen in astonishment, for he had no idea what the sound was. He even turned and trotted back toward the cry, a victim of his all-consuming curiosity. Still, bewildered, he waited until he caught sight of the hounds—huge, bounding ominous shapes in the darkness—and heard their cry grow shriller and more bloodthirsty as the night breeze carried his body scent directly to them. Now at long last Tod realized that these creatures were deadly enemies. Not only were they terrible to see but the tone of their voices was clearly aggressive. Tod turned and ran for his life.

He kept to his regular route from habit, and luckily for him, within a few yards his route took him under a gate. The hounds were too big to squeeze under the bars, and lost time finding an opening in the hedge through which they could force their way. This gave Tod a few precious yards' lead, but unaware that he had temporarily lost the hounds, he continued running wildly. When he realized that the pack was no longer speaking on his line, he slowed, but when the strike-hounds found the trail again and threw their voices, he continued his panicky flight. Coming to a road, he was turned back by the sight of some cars whose owners on hearing the pack had stopped with lights on and engines running. Spinning around, Tod ran back over his own track and then turned off to one side, making a long leap to avoid a muddy ditch. Still running, he heard the pack come roaring along and cross the road at full speed. Here their voices soon died away. Thoroughly winded,

Tod crouched in a patch of bunchgrass and listened. He heard the hounds coming back along his old trail, whimpering with frustration in their efforts to find where he had turned off. They passed the spot where he had made his sideways jump over the ditch and continued on. He heard no more from them that night.

Shortly before dawn, Tod recovered from his fright sufficiently to double back and start tracking the hounds. Although he seldom bothered to track quarry—there were far easier ways of obtaining a meal than that—he had often tracked other foxes and even humans merely to see what they had been doing. As these animals had given him such a fright, he was curious to find out where they had gone and what they had been doing on his range.

He found where they had chased another fox, and followed the dual lines until the sun was up and it was time to go to his lying-up spot. By now, Tod vaguely realized that the hounds must have tracked him and the other fox by scent; after all, he was using exactly the same technique himself. He still did not know quite what to do about it; but when a few nights later he heard the pack on his trail again, he promptly headed for the gate, ducked under it, ran to the road, turned, made his jump across the ditch, and then, after running a few yards, stopped to listen. Again the hounds were baffled. Exactly how Tod did not fully understand. He only knew that as this device had worked before, he had duplicated it—just as in the house he had duplicated whatever technique had kept him from being caught and put to bed.

Tod, however, was quite capable of associating certain ideas, and after several hunts he learned that the hounds could not follow him when he broke contact with the ground, regardless of whether he ran a fence line, ran along a stone wall, or climbed a sloping tree, went out along a branch and then dropped down. Backtracking also puzzled them, and this was generally the first trick he tried because it was the easiest. He had already learned from the cur dogs that he was safe among cattle, and if no cattle were available he could play the same trick by running among a herd of deer. The best trick of all was to foul his line with that of another fox and then jump sideways to make a break in his trail. The hounds were almost certain to take off after the other fox. Virtually every trick Tod was ever to use was based on one of these principles, although he showed such ingenuity in combining and varying these basic rules that he gave the impression of having an unlimited repertoire of techniques each more puzzling than the last.

The hunts usually took place on dark, moonless nights when there was a north wind blowing—or at least not a south wind that tended to deaden scent with its heavy humidity. While going his nightly rounds, Tod would hear the baying of three or four hounds. He quickly came to recognize the cry of each individual hound—the hornlike cry of a Travis, the chop of a Helderberg, and the turkey voice of an old Spaulding. After waiting awhile to make sure they were on his trail, Tod would start running. Before long he would catch the scent of woodsmoke from a campfire and often see the bright eye of the fire itself on some knoll. With the woodsmoke came the odor of men, cars, hounds, coffee, and a stinging sweet odor reminiscent of apples that had lain on the ground long enough to ferment. Once Tod had visited one of these camping places the next day from curiosity, and found, in addition to the smoldering remains of the fire, an empty jug broken and lying on the ground. There were a few drops of liquor in it, and Tod, always fascinated by the unusual, had lapped them. His tongue had stung so he leaped back, shaking his head and wiping the sides of his mouth between his paws. He knew well it was from these camping sites that the hounds had been released.

Once the original three or four hounds were running strongly and throwing their voices in full chorus, he could soon expect to hear other hounds. The men held these other hounds until the first hounds had struck the line, and Tod could tell by the way these first strike-dogs followed the trail and by the confidence in their voices that they must be old, experienced animals, while from the eager but often disorganized cries of the next lot he knew that they were either young or second-rate animals without the scenting powers or know-how of the strike-dogs. When the pack came to a check and the baying ceased, it was nearly always one of the strike-dogs who found the line again.

On dark nights, Tod tended to keep to the top of ridges, for he disliked the intense shadows of the hollows, so the cry of the hounds running on the high ground, unstifled by trees or valleys, rang out strong and clear. This was an advantage to Tod, as he could tell where the pack was and how close they might be. Tod hated to be run by a silent dog, as occasionally had happened, for then he had no idea where the animal was. He could not smell it because he always ran upwind if possible so he could tell what was ahead of him, and naturally the dog was behind. Tod never ran faster than was absolutely necessary to keep ahead of his pursuers and save his strength; so a hound that ran mute was a real menace to him and he got rid of the brute as quickly as possible. With baying hounds, as long as there were no men involved, Tod had no worries. In fact, on a good clear night when he was bored and had finished his hunting, he even rather enjoyed the hunt. He liked making fools out of the pack, and regarded the affair more in the light of a game than that of a danger. Of course, if he were hungry or tired, the whole business was an exasperating nuisance; and Tod would fence-run at once, as this usually left the pack so confused that by the time they picked up the line the scent was cold. If there was no fence handy, he would run to a little covert he knew and bolt a couple of gray foxes who lived there. The grays always ran from him on these occasions, and the pack were almost sure to take out after one or the other of them. Tod had learned this trick by accident while cutting through the covert one night, and never forgot it.

There was, of course, always the outside chance that something might go wrong and he would be caught, but for Tod this only gave the sport a zest. Very rarely was he ever in any danger. One of his favorite tricks was to run under a gate into the apple orchard, dodge around among the trees, and then escape by means of a hole under the woven-wire fence that surrounded the orchard to keep out rabbits. Naturally the rabbits knew all about this hole, and Tod had caught a number there, lying in wait beside it like a cat by a mousehole. He had played this trick so often that an Adirondack hound had caught on to it. While Tod was busy making his tangles in the orchard, with the pack trying to follow his twists, this long-legged son of a bitch had ceased giving tongue and run silently to the hole. He had waited there in the darkness for Tod just as Tod had waited for the rabbits. All unsuspecting, Tod had trotted over to the hole, enjoying the futile cries of the pack behind him. He would have been a dead fox then and there if the hole had not been upwind. At the last instant he smelled the waiting hound and, spinning around, had run for his life with the Adirondack after him screaming for blood. To his horror, Tod now found himself trapped in the orchard, for there were only two exits—through the hole and under the gate, and the pack was between. Actually, Tod could have gone over the wire like a cat, using his long dewclaws to help him, but in his panic he never thought of that, for he was a creature of habit and had always used the holes. Instead he ran hysterically around while the pack tried to follow him through the maze of cross trails. At last he collapsed exhausted in some tall grass and lay there panting while the hunt raged around him. He was saved by the farmer's coming out with a shotgun. At the same time, the hounds' masters drove up a road outside the fence. A noisy interchange followed between the farmer and the hound men that ended in the men coming through the gate and taking away their hounds. Tod made sure they were well away before he rose and limped to the hole. He never tried the orchard trick again.

Tod soon got to know each hound, not only by his voice and smell but also by his personal traits. There was a Hudspeth who never followed Tod into a covert. Instead, while the other hounds were drawing, the Hudspeth would run around outside. After confusing the pack, Tod would lope out of the cover confident that his enemies were all questing about among the trees, and twice he nearly ran straight into the waiting jaws of the Hudspeth, who, unpleasantly enough, could put on a surprising burst of speed for a short distance. Then there was a Birdsong who when the pack came to a check would always run to the top of the nearest hill and wait until one of the strike-dogs got the line. Then he would race down the hill and with the momentum it gave him pass the strike-dog and take off on the line ahead of the others. Once, after a neat backtrack and jump-off, Tod had sat down to enjoy the discomfiture of the pack and also to get his breath. The Travis finally hit the line, and Tod was preparing to lope away when down a hill came charging the Birdsong, coming at such an unexpected angle and going so fast Tod was hard put to avoid the rush. On the other hand, the hounds' individual eccentricities were often a help to the fox. The Spaulding and the Travis disliked briars because their ears were especially tender, and when Tod got into a briar patch they would stick to well-marked trails or stay outside. As these two hounds had the best noses, by staying in the thickest part of the patch Tod could throw the rest off. Best of all, the hounds were all fiercely jealous of one another and never willingly cooperated. If one hound found the line, he frequently would not give tongue, but follow it a quarter of a mile or more before throwing his voice, to get a head start on the rest. But then when he came to a check, he had to work it out alone while the rest toiled to catch up. This naturally gave Tod a tremendous advantage.

The men did not stay in one place. When the hunt passed outside their hearing range, they would get in the cars, drive to a new spot, start another fire, and bring out the inevitable jug. Often they went to a dozen spots in one night as Tod widened his range and took the pack into new country. As they had no guns and took no part in the chase, Tod ignored them; but once he was nearly run over on a road by one of their cars. He had been running the hardtop to throw off the hounds, and the headlights struck him so suddenly he was blinded and confused. He fled unseeingly in front of the car and could have easily been run down had not the driver slammed on the brakes. As Tod ducked into the underbrush, he heard the call of a horn from the car, bringing up the pack.

Tod got to know these horns well, and their wailing calls generally came as a relief to him. When the men had had enough of their sport, they would get out their horns and call in the hounds. Each hound knew the sound of his master's horn, and could distinguish it from the others, and after a few hunts so did Tod, although naturally he could not have cared less. All he cared about was that the horns recalled the pack and left him in peace. Of course, all he had to do when chased by hounds was go down a hole to escape, but Tod did so only as a last resort. He was always afraid of being bottled up in a hole even if there was an escape hatch, and he much preferred to lose the hounds in a straightaway run. And perhaps there was even a certain feeling of pride in shaking off the pack fair and square. The grays had no such pride and when hunted nearly always climbed the first tree, leaving the pack raging futilely and hopelessly below. Once Tod had even seen a gray go up a telephone pole. Those grays weren't really foxes at all; they were cats.

Owing to the jug hunters, Tod acquired an encyclopedic knowledge of hounds; in fact, after a few months he knew far more about the hounds than did their masters. He knew exactly what a hound could do and what he could not do. As, except when there was a black frost, scenting conditions were much better at night than in the daytime—this was largely the reason Tod did most of his hunting at night—tricks that only temporarily puzzled a hound at night usually completely baffled the same animal during the day when sun tended to kill scent. Even a cold-nosed, highly experienced hound like Copper could not stay on Tod's trail during the day if the fox was determined to lose him. Both Copper and his Master soon discovered this fact, so Tod was no longer bothered by attempts to shoot him at crossings.

Autumn was Tod's favorite time of year. He hated the heat of summer, disliked the wet spring, and in the dead of winter food was so difficult to obtain that hunting was no longer a sport but a grim need for survival. But in autumn food was, if anything, more plentiful than in summer, it seldom rained and the weather was cool. Tod was no longer a pup, but a full-grown fox with all his physical powers and enough wilderness know-how never to have to worry where his next meal was coming from. He had reached his full weight of twelve pounds and was three and a half feet long, including his fifteen-inch brush. He had no natural enemies, for man had exterminated the wolves, coyotes, lynxes, and eagles in his district long ago. Only the foxes remained, and they actually benefited by man's presence. Red foxes disliked heavy timber, and man had cleared the fields, making ideal country for field mice, rabbits, woodchucks, and pheasants—all excellent fox food. Also, the pastures and hedge rows grew an abundance of vegetables such as succulent grasses, blackberries, raspberries, blueberries, wild grapes, and other eatables on which the foxes largely depended. As a climax, the farmers had thoughtfully stocked their property with fat, helpless chickens, ducks, and geese just in case the foxes' hunting was unsuccessful. Tod and his brothers would have been hard put to survive without human aid, so they did not move to wilder country where there was a lack of good foraging. Although he seldom bothered the farmers' livestock, he was so dependent on cleared land for his style of living that Tod was virtually a parasite on man.

Tod usually slept during the day, generally selecting some knob or high hillside from whence he could look out over the surrounding country so he could see any enemy approaching. It never occurred to him that the enemies could also see him and that his russet coat showed vividly against the dry autumn grass. He liked to lie with his long, thin nose resting on his black outstretched forepaws and with his brush straight out behind him. If it were a sunny day, he would turn occasionally to bask luxuriously from side to side in the warm light. Even when he was fast asleep, Tod's nose continued to function, and at the first hint of an alien scent he was instantly alert. His hearing was incredible—he could detect the squeak of a mouse at three hundred yards—and he could hear a car a mile away. He never slept long, dozing in a series of quick catnaps, and constantly awakened to open one eye and check the terrain around him on the remote chance that his ears and nose might have missed some possible danger. It was almost impossible for a man or dog to sneak up on him; yet one day after a rain, when the grass was soggy and gave off no sound, a farmer cutting across lots happened to approach Tod from downwind and got within six feet of the sleeping fox. Luckily for Tod, the man had no gun and thought the animal was dead. It was not until he leaned over to pick him up that Tod scented him and made a flying leap away that startled the man quite as much as he had startled the fox.

As the sun sank, scenting conditions steadily improved, as Tod's nose told him even when he was fast asleep. What had been a dead world with only a few odors now gradually became alive with scents. Tod's nose twitched as his sleeping mind unconsciously sorted and identified them as easily, and often far more accurately, than his eyes identified objects when awake. He automatically discarded scents that were meaningless just as when awake he took no interest in trees, clouds, or buildings unless they had a special significance for him. Anything alive, whether it was eatable or not, had a special interest for him, although the odor of ripe apples, sarsaparilla, or pokeberries were almost equally interesting. Tod was quite as much a vegetarian as he was a meateater, although it would have been hard to convince the chicken farmers in his range that this was so.

By dusk, Tod was fully awake. His first act was to stretch, extending himself at full length, shooting out his claws almost like a cat, while his dewclaws stood out nearly at right angles to his slender forelegs; then he yawned until his pink tongue curled between his long white canines. He stood up, cocked his head on one side with a typical "foxy" look as he gazed out across the valley and the fields of winter wheat. Anything moving caught his eye immediately, but he could not readily distinguish between a motionless living being and an inanimate object. Unlike Copper, Tod had excellent vision, but he was not able to interpret the details of what he saw through reason. A human seeing a motionless cow could still immediately identify it as a cow, for he could not only recognize the horns, head, body, and legs but could also realize that these details made up a cow no matter whether the animal was moving or motionless. Tod could see the cow as well as the human, and knew what a cow looked like, but until the animal moved he could not connect the details he saw with the animal he knew. Furthermore, because he was color blind, he saw the world in varying shades of gray, so that a black cow standing in a field of green grass was black against black. On the other hand, Tod could distinguish between odors in a way impossible for a human. A skunk had been killed by a car on a nearby road, and the air was so full of the potent musk a human could have smelled nothing else. Tod could not only smell the musk but dozens of other scents also, and easily distinguished between them. So although he had good eyesight he depended on his nose and keen ears more than on his eyes.

This evening Tod trotted down the hill to where he had cached a woodchuck the day before. He had not killed the chuck; a hunter had shot the animal and it had managed crawl down its hole before dying. Tod had smelled it there and dug it out. Tod could kill a chuck if he had to, but an old groundhog is an experienced and determined fighter, and Tod had a great deal of respect for his own hide. Young chucks in spring were fine if he could catch them away from their hole, but a big boar chuck he left alone. He had eaten part of the animal and tried to bury the rest, but the task was too much for him and he had covered the body with loose dirt and dead leaves. To his disgust, Tod found that crows had located his cache and eaten most of it. Tod set to work to finish off the remainder. It was not gamy enough for him; he liked his meat so decayed it was soft and fell apart easily, yet he was hungry and went to work with a will. Although he liked tender meat, he felt a deep satisfaction in chewing through the tough hide and feeling the bones crunch under his rattrap jaws. He lay at full length, his eyes half closed with bliss as he chewed and chewed, indifferent to the meat in the ecstasy of crunching. When he was tired he played with the carcass, tossing it up, catching it, pretending it was alive so he could jump and worry it, and rolling it about with his long forepaws, which he used almost like hands. When he was tired of the game, he buried what was left, making sure this time the remains were completely covered. He excavated a large hole, his forefeet going like pistons as he dug, and then pushed in the dirty, stinking carcass with his long muzzle. He filled in the hole, using the side of his muzzle to sweep the loose dirt in place, and afterward tamped it in with repeated blows of his nose, delivered with such force it was amazing he did not hurt himself. Lastly, he urinated on the spot to mark it as his personal cache.

Tod then continued on his regular route. He was headed for the orchard, but on the way he passed a honeysuckle tangle and heard the squeakings of two fighting mice. In a flash Tod made a six-foot bound and landed in the middle of the tangle, his forefeet striking the vines on either side of the exact spot from which the noise had come. He stood there motionless, watching intently for any motion, but the mice wisely remained quiet. Tod patted on the vines to make them move and then thrust his long nose through the mat. He located the mice's runway and plowed it up with his nose, turning his head from side to side so he could see if the mice tried to make a break for it. Even though he quickly became convinced that the mice had escaped along the tunnel, he continued his excavations for some time, more as a game than with any hope of catching the mice. Finally he stood up, shook his head to get rid of the dirt, sneezed, and continued on his way to the orchard.

He made a brief detour to pass under a black walnut tree, and was lucky enough to find a squirrel collecting the nuts. Tod made a dash for him, and for a few seconds the two animals dodged around each other, moving so rapidly they became a blur. Tod was not really hungry, and did not put forth all his efforts, so the squirrel succeeded in outdodging him and tore up the trunk with Tod snapping at his great banner tail. From the safety of the lowest branch, the squirrel cursed Tod while the fox ran around the trunk looking up at him. Convinced that there was no way of reaching the furious little animal, Tod loped sway, ducked under the gate, and entered the orchard.

There were several windfalls around, and Tod bit into the most luscious. He then tumbled them around with his nose, patted them with one forefoot to make them roll, and amused himself for nearly half an hour with the delightful toys, making graceful, curving bounds as he came down on them and, stopping to seize one in his mouth, running with it as though looking for a good spot to bury his prize, and then dropping it and returning for another.

Tiring of the sport, Tod went over to the edge of the orchard where there was some saw grass, still fairly green. He grazed there until the patch was cut down to the roots. Tod was very fond of grass, and ate a surprising amount of it. When there was snow on the ground he seriously missed this important item of diet. When he was full he dived through the familiar rabbit hole under the fence and picked up his route again by a grove of locusts.

Customarily Tod's route ran along the edges of fields, partly because Tod tended to feel exposed in the open and partly because by keeping close to the hedgerows he could often cut off rabbits feeding in the open fields. Tod's typical method of progress was to go some twenty yards with his nose to the ground, picking up any stray trails, then lift his head to look around, and then return to his trailing. Even when he crossed a fresh rabbit trail he seldom followed it, for he had learned by experience there was no point in trailing a rabbit; it took too long, and even when he caught up, the rabbit was almost sure to be aware of his presence and go down a hole or into a briar patch. Tod checked the trails merely as a matter of interest. He liked to know what was going on.

He did leave his trail several times to visit scent posts. These posts could be an isolated tuft of grass, a piece of dead wood, a large stone, a tree, or a fencepost. Tod always approached these scent posts with keen anticipation. Generally there was nothing there, and after smelling carefully Tod would lift his leg and leave a spurt of urine on the post to establish the boundaries of his range and also so any passing foxes would know about him. Although Tod was not a social animal, still he was curious about his kin, and always made a point of leaving his scent indicator so other foxes would leave theirs.

When another fox had been to one of the posts, Tod became so excited he forgot his usual caution. He would sniff the urine scent long and critically, his nostrils distended as he sucked in the deeply significant odor. The caudal glands at the root of a fox's brush heavily impregnated the scent, and often a visiting fox would drop his feces as well, and these droppings were especially charged with information. At one post, Tod noted that the visitor was a this year's pup, probably looking for a range of his own. The pup was nervous, underfed, sickly, and a male. Tod decided that if the youngster hung around, he would have to be driven away. A young vixen had also been there, squatting to leave her scent on the ground. Tod had no interest in her, but no great objection, either. At another post, an adult dog fox had left his sign the night before. He was clearly a full-grown animal in prime condition—the urine was plentiful and carried the scent of rabbits, showing he was eating well—and the visitor had taken pains to scratch thoroughly around the post as a sign of defiance, as well as to sink the odor of his pads well into the ground so there could be no mistake. The odor from his caudal glands had been extremely powerful, too. Tod felt the hairs on his neck lift as he smelled around this post, and he also experienced a feeling of apprehension. Checking, he saw where the stranger had come up to the post and where he had departed. Tod trailed him nearly a mile. Then, satisfied that the stranger, in spite of his arrogant behavior, was merely passing through, Tod returned to his run. He was still nervous, and went out of his way after that to check not only all his posts but any other outstanding bush or tree that the stranger might have marked. This fellow could be dangerous.

Tod did not welcome other foxes, male or female, on his range, but he did not violently object to them, either. There was plenty of food, and he did not begrudge a stray rabbit or a few mice to visitors. Of course, if another dog fox deliberately took over his territory, using his runs, hunting on his special preserves, and scaring away the quarry every night, that was a different matter. But Tod was curious rather than belligerent toward his visitors, and after all he had many times trespassed on other foxes' territories either when he was searching for an unoccupied range as a pup or simply from wanderlust.

Between checking his posts, Tod put in some time hunting. In the open, he systematically worked the areas where he knew he could expect to find rabbits, mice, or pheasants. At this time of year, the pheasants roosted in great numbers in a stand of pines, and although they usually roosted too high for him to get them, he always checked the stand on the chance a young bird might be sitting too low. In timber, he was more haphazard, but he did take pains to check each thicket and brushpile. He also examined all clumps of grass, especially those growing around the base of trees, and invariably stuck his nose down every burrow to take a good sniff. Whenever he came on a fallen log, he always ran along it. The thick undergrowth of the forest annoyed him, and even the respite of a few feet given him by the smooth surface of the log was a comfort.

Tod never stayed in the woods longer than necessary to do a little routine checking. He hated having to force his way through the tangle, and despised the gray foxes who rejoiced in such places. As soon as possible he returned to the open country.

When winter really set in, Tod extended his range so greatly it might almost be said that he no longer had any real range at all. He went where the food was. On bad nights he depended on his caches, which he spread all up and down his runs. During the golden autumn days he had often killed half a dozen rabbits a night, and as he never ate more than one, he buried the rest. True, Tod was careless about burying his quarry deep enough, and the caches were frequently found by raccoons, opossums, skunks, and even the sharp-eyed crows; but enough had escaped to give him an almost endless source of supply when his hunting failed. Tod made no attempt to economize on his caches; he would often dig up a field mouse he had buried, chew off the head, and leave the rest for scavengers. Tod was not above doing some scavenging himself. He investigated the garbage dumps in the vicinity, checked roads where animals might have been hit by cars, and knew where the carcasses of three deer lay that had been shot during the gunning season and escaped to die later of their wounds. He seldom let a night pass without visiting the orchard, for he knew rabbits went there to strip bark from the young trees. He also went to barns and outbuildings, looking for rats. He was always cautious when near human habitation, for when raiding chicken houses he had learned that humans regarded chickens as their personal property, and resented poaching on their territories more than he did.

On his rounds, he never overlooked a scent post. To humans, Tod's selection of scent posts would seem to have been done at random, but this was because humans did not live in a world of scent. A scent post had to be isolated, as slender as possible—never more than three feet in diameter—and near a run. (If it were larger, something might be hiding behind it; and besides, Tod had to be able to go around and around the post easily to get all the special odors.) In addition, it had to be in the paths of air currents and have a surface that held scent. Occasionally Tod would make an exception. There was an old dried tortoise shell that fascinated him, and even though it made a most unsatisfactory scent post, it was one of his favorites.

When snow came, Tod had a hard time of it, but not so hard as might be thought. He could scent mice in their tunnels under the snow, and now that the ground was frozen the mice had to stay in their tunnels and could not dodge off through the grass or under vines. The morning after a snowfall he always checked drifts around thickets for grouse, and sometimes pheasants would lie there covered by the snow but shielded by the twigs. Tod would locate them by his nose, steal up to the spot, taking elaborate precautions to make no noise, and then stand motionless like a bird dog pointing, except when he swayed himself back and forth, building up momentum for his leap. He could jump ten feet, landing on top of the concealed bird and instantly plunging his long muzzle into the bank, biting at random. Sometimes he would get nothing but a mouthful of feathers, but sometimes he got a meal that lasted several days. Tod buried the surplus in the snow; and if a sudden thaw came he was always bewildered when he discovered his carefully hidden cache lying exposed on the ground. He would run around it several times, suspecting some trick, often retiring to the top of some little mound the better to look around in case some enemy had unearthed it and was waiting in ambush. Often it took him an hour to go down to the quarry, and sometimes he abandoned it entirely.

By late November, Tod felt the remembered pulsating in his testicles. The sensation began gradually and did not disturb him, yet he took an increasing interest in the trails and scent of vixens at the posts. Often he would follow them, taking care to step exactly in their tracks where the tracks were visible so it would have taken an alert woodsman to see that two foxes rather than one had passed. He became increasingly more vocal. Heretofore, Tod had seldom uttered a sound, but now during the long winter nights he would mount to the top of a rise and give a call in four notes, repeated over and over. Sometimes he would stand with his muzzle pointed upward like a dog baying at the moon; more often he would drop his head almost between his forelegs as he called. With increasing frequency the call would be answered by other dog foxes, and rarely by the sharp double yap of a vixen. When the males heard that note they would stop their calls and stand listening intently. Then they would all begin together, hoping for another answer, but the vixens rarely called twice.

By January the vixens began to answer more frequently, and their cries took on the squalling note that Tod remembered. The throbbing beat in his testicles had now become a driving urge that made Tod call more than ever. The other dog foxes must have felt the same urge, for the night was full of their anxious calling. The vixens' squalling became more tortured and urgent;

the males' voices also changed, and they yowled almost like tomcats. Now they began to seek the vixens' company; but the females were not as yet quite ready to receive them, and there was still not the odor that maddened the males and drove them on in spite of their natural reluctance to associate with others of their species.

One night as Tod lay among some frozen weeds, his magnificent brush covering his delicate nose—the only part of him not warmly covered by his thick pelt—he heard the agonizing call of a vixen. Tod pricked his ears. The call came again and again. Tod trembled with excitement as he listened. Then he sprang up and raced toward the cry.

He had not realized how far away the sound was—not that it would have made any difference to him if he had—and he ran on and on through the night, going into increasingly unfamiliar country. As he topped a rise, the night wind hit him full in the face, and with it came the exquisite, torturing odor he remembered. Tod flew. He no longer seemed to touch the ground; he shot over it.

He found the vixen trotting down the side of a little stream, closely followed by two other dog foxes. They both stopped and looked at Tod, while he ignored them. He ran eagerly toward the vixen. She looked him over and then darted away, Tod racing after her with the other two males furiously following. He caught up with her in a deadend gully, and the vixen ran toward him, crouched, and presented her throat while squealing hysterically. Tod could tell by her scent that she was considerably older than he was, but he cared little, for the burning, intoxicating odor from her banished all other considerations.

Tod had no idea what the proper procedure was in such cases, and sprang back, but the other two were more experienced. They rushed forward, jostling him to one side. Tod whirled, snarling and slashing left and right, but they ignored him in their determination to reach the vixen. Instantly she sprang up, hissed and snapped at them, and then ran. For nearly a minute the four animals ran wildly about the gully, so close together a blanket could have covered them. Then the vixen broke out and tore through the woods, a gray shape in the blackness, with the three males after her.

They threaded their way at top speed through the woods until the vixen stopped again and, running to Tod, dropped and resumed her wild crying. Again, the other two males tried to shoulder Tod aside, but this time he whirled on the nearest, fastening his teeth in his neck. Both foxes rolled on the ground; Tod lost his grip, and they struggled together, their screams rising to a savage crescendo. The other fox was the more experienced fighter; but Tod was younger and stronger, so they were evenly matched.

The vixen had stopped, but when the other male tried to approach her, she viciously fought him off. She was watching the fight, and kept turning each time the male tried to mount her. The fighters broke apart and stood with humped backs and lowered heads, snarling at each other. Promptly the vixen started to run, with the attendant male at her heels. The sight was too much for the fighters, and they followed. As soon as they were running free, the vixen turned and ran to Tod again, cringing and crying.

This process was repeated time after time until all four foxes were so exhausted they could hardly move. At last one of the rival males remained lying on the ground when the vixen started running. Now there were only Tod and the remaining male. Tod was so tired he was prepared to abandon the entire project, especially as he had only the vaguest idea what part he was supposed to play, and had the other male turned on him he would, after a few perfunctory snarls, have vanished into the night. But again the vixen ran to him, cringing and screaming hysterically. Puzzled what to do, Tod shrank back and then reared and drummed on her with stiff forelegs. The vixen lay motionless, still crying. The other male tried to approach, but the vixen rushed at him and bit him savagely on the foreleg. Unwilling to fight back, the male tore himself free and then disappeared.

Still giving her piercing, overwrought cries, the vixen returned to Tod and flung herself on her side, her teeth bared in a paralyzed grin like an opossum playing dead. When he stood staring at her in bewilderment, she ran to a cache she remembered, unearthed part of a squirrel, and tore it to pieces, still squalling. She made no attempt to eat the meat; instead she flung it around wildly, biting into the pieces again and again.

She seemed to be waiting for Tod to make some move, but the tired, puzzled, and somewhat frightened male had no idea what she wanted. Suddenly the vixen charged him with bared fang. In self-defense Tod bared his own, and at once the vixen collapsed, cringing and presenting her throat. Uncertain what to do, Tod struck at her again with his rigid forefeet. She submitted; and then, seeing he would do nothing else, sprang up and attacked. This was too much, and Tod furiously returned the attack. She promptly collapsed, head thrown back to expose her throat.

By now, Tod was half frantic with anger, bewilderment, and some all-consuming urge he could not understand. He threw himself on the vixen, grabbing her by the back of the neck and shaking her as he would have shaken a rabbit. The vixen squirmed under him, forcing her rump against his hindquarters, screaming continually. She began to move her rump convulsively, and the action drove Tod mad. Releasing her, he frantically licked her, and the action seemed to calm the vixen.

She stood quietly straining her hindquarters, and then slowly writhed under him. Now at long last Tod's instinct asserted itself and, clinging to her supple body with the full grip of his forelegs, he bred her.

When it was over, the foxes lay side by side, thoroughly exhausted. Half in play, half in affection, Tod threw one of his long legs over her back, and the vixen turned to lick it. She whined and cuddled closer to him, thrusting her long nose under his leg. Tod looked down in awe at this half-crazy, puppy-like creature and felt a strange sense of proprietary affection toward it—not unlike the feeling he had for the tortoise shell where he had so often known the satisfaction of relieving himself. Vaguely he sensed that this remarkable creature that behaved in such unreasonable, unpredictable ways was putting herself under his protection and he would have to defend her, much as he had to defend his range from intruders, once he had established it by urinating on the scent post. The realization worried and somewhat frightened him, and as the throbbing in his testicles was now relaxed, he decided it might be best to leave. He rose and began to trot away.

The vixen promptly sprang up and trotted at his side. Tod had no idea what to do. In a way, he liked to have her companionship, yet his native desire to be alone was still strong. Obviously the vixen had no such doubts; even when he quickened his stride she loped along beside him as though this was her predestined place. Tod was too polite to drive her away, yet it was clearly impossible for him to perform his regular runs and hunts with this curious creature running with him.

They left the woods and started out across the open fields toward Tod's home range. Now the vixen started to show signs of nervousness. She whimpered and tried to turn back. When she saw that Tod was not turning with her, she darted in front and tried to turn him back by snapping at him. Swinging his muzzle from one side to the other, Tod avoided her bites, and kept on. When she persisted, he broke into a run. The vixen soon realized she could not keep up with him, and in a determined manner spun around and headed back to the safety of the woods she knew and away from the haunts of man. Glad to be rid of her, Tod kept on, slowing to a walk.

He had gone nearly a mile and was close to his old range when he realized the vixen was following him. She had made her defiant move in the belief he would not desert her, but when it became obvious Tod would not yield to her wishes, she had, after a struggle, decided to follow her new mate to whatever place he preferred. Far from being flattered, Tod was distinctly annoyed. He thought he'd gotten rid of her at last.

Ahead, the stars were taking on a washed-out look, and Tod could smell the coming dawn as the early-morning breeze flowed over the fields, bringing with it innumerable new scents. Tod realized he was ferociously hungry. The exertions of the night had given him a ravenous appetite. He wanted rich meat to stay it—not the thin, stringy flesh of rabbits but the luscious, nourishing meat of birds. The farmers' hen roosts were dangerous at this hour, but Tod remembered the stand of pines where the pheasants roosted. There had to be one bird roosting too low this morning—there had to be! He swung away toward the pines, the vixen padding silently a few feet behind him.

The sun had risen by the time they reached the pines, and the pheasants were awake, to Tod's disappointment. As soon as he saw the birds, he dropped flat on his belly, and the vixen dropped beside him. Both foxes lay motionless, only their bright eyes moving as they watched the pheasants mantle—stretch one leg and one wing together as they prepared to fly down. All the birds were too high for the foxes to reach, although that made no difference now they were awake. Not even the craftiest fox could steal up to the pines without the birds seeing him.

Tod lay regretfully watching the pheasants, so near, yet so far out of reach. He could smell them now, and the delicious warm odor made his nostrils twitch. Wistfully, he thought of every trick he knew. None would work.

To his amazement he saw the vixen rise and deliberately trot past the pines in full sight of the pheasants. At once a chorus of cackling call went up, interspersed with the shrill warning cry of the cocks. The vixen paid no attention to the flock and continued on her way, utterly indifferent to the birds. The ground was hilly, and as the vixen passed behind a little rise so that she was hidden, several of the pheasants flew to higher limbs so as not to lose sight of her. The vixen passed the flock and, still without glancing in their direction, turned and entered the pines a few yards from the roosting place.

The pheasants watched her suspiciously, although they knew that they were perfectly safe. A young hen flew from one pine to another, watching the fox and crying constantly, afraid to let the predator out of her sight. To follow the progress of the fox among the trees, the hen had to fly lower and lower so that her vision would not be cut off by the broad fans of green needles Yet she was careful never to get too near the fox while still giving her alarm call.

The entire flock was standing with upcraned necks, trying to see the vixen. Now Tod slunk forward, belly to the ground. Like a cat he crawled through the pines, watching the hen pheasant. As she flew from limb to limb, screaming at the fox almost as a jay would have done, all her attention was concentrated on the vixen. Now she was only a few feet above the ground.

Tod balanced himself, swayed back and forth, and then made his rush. In seconds he was under the tree. As he sprang upward, the rest of the flock saw him, and from a dozen throats went the shrill danger scream. The hen stopped her scolding and looked stupidly around for the threat; as she did so, Tod had her by the leg. Bird and fox crashed through the dead twigs to the ground, the pheasant beating desperately with her wings, the fox holding on for all he was worth. She might have gotten away with the loss of a leg had not the vixen spun around at the first sound of struggle and sped to help. With the skill of long experience, she hurled herself at the thrashing bird and with one nip broke its neck. Then she leaped lightly back and sat down, having no wish to be struck by one of the lashing wings, and knowing the end was sure. Tod, not being certain what had happened, continued to maintain his grip, and got unpleasantly kicked and beaten during the bird's dying struggles. After all, Tod was not much bigger than a large house cat, and to him a pheasant was as formidable an adversary as a swan would be to a man. A man can overcome a full-grown cob, but it is not a pleasant experience.

When the pheasant ceased struggling, Tod prepared to feed. To his indignation, the vixen raced in, snapping at him in a fury. Tod stood back, whereupon she seized the bird and, still snarling, dragged it away. Whenever Tod approached, she hissed at him, pulling the pheasant out of reach. As Tod regarded the bird as his property, he considered such conduct an outrage, but when he tried to assert his rights the vixen attacked him with such a frenzy of rage he gave way. This was not the half playful snapping and squalling she had shown previously, she really meant it. Not until she had eaten her fill was Tod allowed to approach the bird.

After gorging, Tod retired to one of his lying-up places. The vixen accompanied him, but to Tod's relief, picked her own spot some distance off. He was already beginning to grow accustomed to her presence, and even took a certain satisfaction in having her around, yet he still insisted on privacy. Obviously she felt the same way, so although they kept within scenting range of each other, they maintained their distances.

To Tod's surprise and pleasure, the vixen turned out to be a most useful hunting companion. When hunting by himself, Tod went along the edges of the bramble patches in the hope of cutting off a rabbit feeding in the open as it made a dash for cover. Now the vixen accompanied him on his rounds, and as soon as she got to know the country she would leave him to make a swing around any likely territory and drive the rabbits to him. This maneuver was especially effective with pheasants who, if not pressed too hard, would run a long distance before taking to the air. Tod had almost never been able to catch a pheasant, no matter how carefully he stalked them, until the vixen showed him how it was done. When their noses told them pheasants were feeding in cover, the vixen would circle around behind them, leaving Tod crouched in ambush. She was amazingly dexterous in herding the flock toward him, cutting them off when they tried to turn to one side and, if the flock showed signs of too great alarm, dropping flat on her belly and waiting until they calmed down. These were the same techniques that Tod had used to herd the sheep in play, and now he saw their value. Working as a team, the pair of foxes did considerable damage to the pheasant population. They also, unwittingly, saved many of the young apple trees in the orchard from being girdled by rabbits and mice. Tod had long ago discovered that an excellent place to look for mice was around the roots of the apple trees, and nearly every tree showed where he had dug up the mice during the nocturnal hunts. Rabbits had been much harder to get, but the vixen changed all that. Once he had shown her the hole under the wire fence, she would lie there while Tod went into the orchard after the rabbits. When the rabbits dashed for the hole, she was ready for them. They also used the same trick at runways in the hedges where formerly Tod had been forced to wait for an hour or more before a rabbit happened to use the hole.

Thus, based on habit and mutual assistance, a bond grew up between them that slowly ripened into a deep affection lasting long after the vixen had passed her period and the rut was over. It was even possible that for this vixen whom he had sought out in alien territory and brought to his own range, Tod had a special feeling that he would not have felt for a local female even though he would have equally readily mated with her. He had, so he thought, defeated two powerful rivals for her affections and rescued this weak, helpless creature from her dismal land of thick timber and little food to bring her to the pleasant open farm country well stocked with provisions. The old vixen on the other hand, had immediately known that Tod was young, inexperienced, and would be easily molded. He was also big and strong, two factors that strongly appealed to her female instincts. So she had deliberately selected him from the two older, more sophisticated males, although it would never have occurred to Tod that the whining, abject female was actually dominating the whole affair.

They were well mated; the older, more experienced vixen, the powerful, enthusiastic young male in the full glory of his youthful prowess. The vixen had been mated three times before, her last mate dying only a month before under the blows of a club as he writhed helplessly in a trap. Even though they had been mated for three years and had always been faithful to each other, the vixen had at once set out to find a new mate once she knew he was dead. Tod had been her choice, and she had every intention of molding him into a model mate. Tod, in pride of possession over this poor, weak female, would have been greatly surprised if he could have known what she had in mind.

5

Third Hunt—Gassing

Spring was raw and wet that year, and the vixen, used to living in the protection of heavy cover, suffered especially. While Tod was content to lie out in the worst of weathers, the vixen sought the shelter of overhanging rocks and during especially heavy storms even went down holes. This conduct bothered Tod, as he regarded it not only as most unfoxlike but also dangerous; if you were under the overshoot of a rock you couldn't see what was coming up behind you, especially as heavy rain killed scent, and going down a burrow was even worse—you might be trapped down there by terriers. Tod remembered his own childhood experience vividly. None of these considerations bothered the vixen, as she had been brought up in a wilder district where men were scarce and dogs nonexistent. If Tod had been an older, more decided male she might have followed his example. As it was, she went her own way.

Tod became far more conscious of his territorial rights than ever before, and in this he was amply abetted by the vixen. The growth of sperm in his testicles during the rutting season made him combative; and instead of regarding visiting foxes with good-natured curiosity, he now considered them thieves and invaders. For a while foxes without a territory of their own could avoid him by checking the scent posts and seeing when Tod would be on a certain section of his range at a given time, for with their marvelous sense of smell they could tell when a post had been used within an hour or so. As it took Tod three or four days to make the complete round of his range, they hunted before or after he made his tour. Now, however, the thought of poachers so infuriated Tod that he altered his once rigid schedule to catch interlopers. Even though the trespasser was bigger and stronger than Tod, he would seldom put up even a token resistance, but fled at once, for he recognized Tod's property rights as laid out by the scent posts. In his fury, Tod would often pursue the stranger off his range, but as soon as the interloper was well clear of the marked territory, he would slow down and eventually turn to fight. When that happened, Tod, who had been blind with rage, would suffer a change of heart. The two foxes would slowly revolve around each other, side to side and head to tail, ready to feint with their brushes or knock the opponent over with a flank bump. Nearly always the duel ended with both combatants gingerly edging apart, scratching contemptuously with hind feet, and defiantly urinating before going their separate ways.

It was the vixen who goaded Tod to keep poachers off his range. From her actions at the scent posts, Tod knew she violently resented trespassers, and he tried to observe her wishes Tod's anger was directed toward other males; he had no feelings toward females, and whenever he came upon a visiting vixen he was polite to her—if she was still in season, more than polite. He soon discovered that his mate viciously resented this chivalrous attitude he considered so natural. Once she came upon him sniffing courteously at the hindquarters of a cowering, squalling vixen, and at once attacked the husband-stealer with an insane frenzy that horrified Tod. The strange vixen, nothing loath, went at her with equal fury. Tod watched aghast while the two vixens tore at each other, screaming at the top of their voices and observing none of the etiquette of fox fighting. The strange vixen soon went down before the murderous intensity of his mate's delirium, and Tod expected to see her give the formal token of surrender by presenting her jugular—a signal that was always acknowledged and respected among males. Nothing like this happened. His mate got the foreigner by the back of the neck and shook her until the victim's eyes rolled up, her hind legs kicked convulsively, and she finally lay limp. Even then the maddened vixen did not give up, but worried the body until all sign of life was gone. Finally she dropped the corpse on the bloody snow and limped stiffly away with the awestruck Tod following behind her. Tod could not know that she was not fighting for prestige or simply for sport, as did the males, but for her mate; and the mate was now all-important, for new life would soon be stirring within her and she had to have the male to hold the range and provide food for the pups when they were born. Under these conditions, she would kill anything that stood in her way.

As March came on, Tod was well past the rut, and his belligerency declined while the vixen's increased. There would have to be plenty of food on the range for the pups as they grew, but she savagely begrudged every mouse taken by poachers. Tod had never before known what hatred was; he had never hated the quarry he killed any more than he hated the apples he ate, nor did he hate the hounds that chased him or the men who tried to kill him—he feared and dreaded them as he might fear a bolt of lightning striking near him, but he did not hate the lightning. Now he learned to hate other foxes with a deep, fanatic intensity of purpose that would last until autumn when the pups were on their own. He did not know why he hated these strangers except that it was his nature to do so, and the vixen encouraged him.

Coming from an area where food was scarce, the vixen wanted him to maintain a range some five miles square; but as Tod soon discovered, there were several other dog foxes in the district who were mated to vixens with similar expansive ideas, and good hunting preserves were limited. Fighting broke out all along the boundary lines, and even though the combats never had serious results, the males soon became tired of the business. By an unspoken agreement they reduced the ranges to areas of about a square mile, which in a land flowing with mice and rabbits was ample. The vixens did not approve of this compromise; but after all it was the males who had to do the fighting, so they were forced to accept the limited ranges.

So far, the vixen had kept her slender shape and was as active as ever, although she no longer liked to play with him. Tag had been their favorite game, and they would chase each other for twenty minutes at a time over the fields and through the open woods. Now she began to grow heavy and inactive. She also became increasingly quick-tempered. The growing pups were draining the calcium from her system to make their bones, and the loss made her weak and irritable.

She started to show a remarkable interest in burrows, investigating and often enlarging every one she found. In one such burrow she encountered a large woodchuck, just emerging from his winter's sleep. Tod could have told her that such an animal was best left alone, but in her overwrought mood the vixen attacked him. She was so far down the burrow that only the white tip of her brush was showing, and Tod, dancing around eagerly outside, heard her screams of anger followed by the grunts and teeth-chattering of the chuck. As the underground battle raged and the inflaming odor of adrenaline rose, Tod dug desperately through the half-frozen earth to squeeze down and get at the chuck himself. To his astonishment, the vixen turned on him. Both foxes burst out of the burrow, screaming at each other, rearing up on their hind legs, their teeth clashing together. For once Tod was in the same blind passion as the vixen, and grabbing her by the loins, he clamped down until his long canines drew blood. Instead of being cowed, the vixen continued to fight. The taste of fox blood brought Tod to his senses. He turned and ran, pursued by the screaming vixen. He could easily outdistance her, and kept a few yards ahead of the hysterical termagant until she dropped, panting and exhausted. Tod stopped and stood regarding her gravely until she recovered from the fit and they could resume normal relations.

After enlarging and then abandoning what seemed to Tod innumerable burrows, the vixen at last settled on an empty woodchuck hole in a cover of scrub oaks on the extreme northern edge of the range. The burrow was small, but the vixen dug it out to suit her needs, loosening the earth with her forefeet and then kicking it out with her hind. Even when finished, the den was a modest affair. The main room, the highest part of the den for drainage purposes, was only two feet square; there was only one entrance, and the passageway was a little more than ten feet.

Tod highly disapproved of this whole arrangement. His home den had been much bigger and more elaborate. It had comprised a network of passages, some fifty feet long, and the main room had been twenty by thirty feet. Also, it had been located on the side of a hill, as all proper fox dens should be, so the occupants could see for miles around. Tod's home den had been inhabited and enlarged by generations of foxes, and this new, cramped den struck him as a regular death trap. He hated cover anyway, and the vixen had deliberately picked the densest cover she could find. However, there was no arguing with a female, as Tod had discovered, and he was forced to accept the vixen's choice.

The vixen spent a great deal of time remodeling the den and even on occasion allowed Tod to help her, although quarrels became so frequent she preferred to do most of the work herself. Both foxes had begun to shed their winter coats, and while the long outer hairs came out easily, the thick undercoat matted and clung to them in gray, cotton-like tangles that could not be bitten free. The itching annoyed them and did nothing to steady their already volatile tempers. The vixen was now so swollen she had trouble getting in and out the narrow entrance, and finally she made it clear to Tod his presence was unnecessary. Tod was too curious about what was going on to leave the den area entirely, so he fell into the habit of lying up some fifty yards from the entrance during the day. Before going out on his nightly rounds, he would stop by, sniff at the hole, and cock his head to listen; but neither scent nor sound told him anything except that a very irritable vixen was within.

One evening as Tod walked toward the den, he stopped suddenly in his usual attitude of alert: head up and one foot raised. He had heard a series of whining yelps coming from the burrow's opening. After a brief hesitation, Tod trotted closer, and sniffed. Yes, there were strange new smells there, and the whining was distinct. Neither the sounds nor scents were foxy, and if Tod could have gotten in, he might well have made short work of the new arrivals, not knowing what they were. He was saved from such infanticide by the vixen, who thrust her nose partway out of the burrow, hissing and snarling. Tod leaped back, landing on all four feet at the same time, and hastily withdrew. Hunting was good that night, and Tod caught a superabundance of rabbits. Knowing the vixen must be hungry, he carried one back to the den with him as a peace offering. Dropping it a few yards from the den entrance, he called her, hoping she would come out and play, for in spite of his independence Tod was growing a bit lonely. The vixen stuck her head out, but refused to leave the burrow even when Tod tempted her with the rabbit, yet he could tell by the way she sniffed that she was ravenously hungry. At last he was reluctantly forced to bring the rabbit to her. She snatched it without any of the usual friendly byplay both indulged in when sharing food, and dragged it into the den with her. Listening, Tod heard an outburst of the yelping cries, and wondered more and more what was down there.

Even though he brought her food faithfully every night, it was not until two weeks later that she allowed him to come even partway down the passageway to inspect her treasures. There were five of them, covered with mouse-colored fur, blind, squirming, and helpless. They were not much bigger than mice, and probably equally eatable, but from the actions of the vixen it was obvious she considered them the most remarkable crea- tures ever to inhabit the earth. She walked over to them, nudged them with her nose (an act that produced a storm of excited yelps), and then lay on her side with her feet toward them so they could nurse. The blind pups crawled toward her, throwing their heads from side to side, mewing loudly, and clearly guided by the warmth of the vixen's body rather than by sight or smell. As they came within reach, she moved them against her with swipes of her long nose. One little fellow got headed in the wrong direction until at last the vixen had to rise, pick him up gingerly in her mouth, and bring him back to the others. Then she lay down again, spread her legs until each of the babies found a teat and started sucking. The pups nursed by pushing on either side of the teat with their tiny paws and sometimes jerking back with their heads to make the milk flow. The mother watched them with an expression of utter delight as their tiny mouths nursed the milk from her swollen glands and relieved the intolerable pressure that had been tormenting her. When they finished, she lay back reveling in the blissful feeling of relaxation, as though a throbbing pain had been suddenly eased.

Now that Tod had been allowed to see the miracle that she had wrought, he was again forbidden the den, but Tod had seen enough to make him wildly proud and excited. He realized that these tiny, helpless creatures belonged to him, and he wore himself out bringing food to the den, often far more than the vixen could eat. Feathers began to accumulate on the yellow earth that had come from the hole, and formed a half-circle in front of the den's entrance. There were also the hides of woodchucks, neatly turned inside out; rabbit legs and some lambs' tails. Tod had not killed the lambs; he had collected the tails from the pasture after the lambs had been ringed and the tails had fallen off. Both foxes always kept an eye out for a lambing ewe, not because they had designs on the lamb but because they liked to eat the afterbirth. Afterbirths were impregnated with fetal fluid for which all mammals have a passion, and it was to obtain the fetal fluid that mothers licked their newborn offsprings so carefully. Tod found several afterbirths, but he always ate them himself, bringing other food back to the vixen. There was a limit to masculine devotion.

In spring, game was so plentiful that Tod had no killing all he needed for both himself and the vixen; his main trouble was transportation. Tod carried all his kills in his mouth—even with comparatively large quarry like a pheasant he never slung it over his shoulder—and when the results of a night's hunting was a mixed bag such as ten mice, a pigeon, a starling, and a muskrat, it would have required several trips to get them all to the scrub-oak patch. Tod hit on an ingenious solution to the difficulty. Once when he was returning with a mouthful of four mice, he came on two cock pheasants fighting. This was too good a chance to miss, and dropping the mice, Tod slunk up on the birds, crawling on his belly through the bunchgrass. He got one bird, and then came the problem of transportation, for Tod refused to leave the mice. After some thought, he neatly tucked the mice under the pheasant's wing—two mice under each neatly tucked wing—and then triumphantly carried the whole load to the den.

It was nearly a month before the pups' eyes opened, which was lucky for the vixen, as they were such restless little things they would have crawled out of the den in spite of her best efforts and in their helpless state would have fallen easy victims to any passing predator, even a crow. When their eyes did open they were a blue-gray, only slowly turning to the yellow amber of the adult fox. They were still in their baby wool, and except for their long noses and triangular heads, looked more like baby lambs than foxes. Instead of being black, their noses were flesh colored, and they still had their baby teeth. They were very clumsy, and fell over themselves rather than walked, but at the end of five weeks they could scamper around. From then on their progress was rapid.

The vixen now began the process of weaning them. She was running out of milk, and the constant nursing that had at first given her such exquisite satisfaction and made her adore the pups was now becoming more and more of a nuisance. When the constant pushing and worrying at her teats became too irritating, she would turn on her stomach; if the pups insisted, she would walk away and leave them. Now that the first flush of delight in them was passing with the end of her milk, she became more of a disciplinarian. When the strongest and most aggressive of the pups rushed at her to demand his right to nurse, she whirled on him with a sudden snarl that made him fall over on his back in astonishment. She allowed Tod to approach the litter and even permitted him to clean out the pups' anuses with his tongue, a right she had always reserved for herself. Without the cleaning, the pups' rectums would soon have become clogged and they would have died. As the pups exercised more and gained more control over their body functions, their feces became harder, so the parents abandoned the cleaning practice that was now no longer necessary.

As the litter could not as yet eat hard food, the mother fed then by regurgitating food already digested in her own stomach. The pups soon learned to like this stimulating diet more than the plain milk—in fact, they would never lose their taste for it and would eat vomit more readily than any other food. At first the vixen gave them only well-digested food, then partly digested, and finally regurgitated it only a few minutes after eating. When the pups were able to eat that, she brought them freshly killed prey, carefully ripped open, for the pups' milk teeth could not bite through tough hide, and besides, they still had no idea that eatable flesh lay under the hard skin.

By now the pups were strong enough to leave the den and scramble about outside. Their active minds had become bored with the dark, uninteresting den and they were delighted, if a little alarmed, by the world outside. Even the dried, hard-packed earth at the den's opening was a source of wonder to them. They sniffed at stones, nudging the strange objects with their noses, and then leaped back, terrified, when the stones rolled. Feathers were safer. They could bat them around with their paws, grab them as they fluttered down, roll on them, and steal them from each other. The strange smell of the woodchuck hide and rabbit legs—quite different from the odor of the fresh meat their mother had fed them—at first made the pups suspicious, but as they grew older the rabbit legs made even better toys than the feathers. They staged tugs-of-war with the legs, pounced on them and shook them ferociously.

During these sports, the vixen would lie on the earth mound, watching her children with obvious pride and love, her usual wary look erased by a maternal smile. So entirely did her expression change, she seemed like a completely different animal from the alert huntress, the crawling sycophant, or the furious virago of her former moods.

Tod was nearly as delighted with the pups as his mate, but she was still suspicious and somewhat jealous. If the pups ran to him, she called them off with a quick, hard bark that the pups seemed to recognize instantly as a warning, for they turned away at once, tumbling over themselves to reach either the vixen or the mouth of the burrow. By degrees she relented and let him play with the pups but if any of them seemed too pleased with the game, she would rush in, grab the offender none too gently by the neck and carry him squawling and kicking back to the den.

Mostly the pups played with each other and learned how to use their teeth, how to jump forward and backward in their mock fights, and how to employ their long forelegs. They also learned from their toys how to grab a moving object, how to get the best purchase on it, and how to hold it steady for a bite. One of the pups was bigger, stronger, and more aggressive than the others, just as one was small and weak—the runt of the litter. As the pups grew older, their playful fights became more serious and real battles raged among them until the biggest pup was able to convince the others that he was the dominant one. Since they were not "pack animals," the issue of who was to be leader was not so serious a consideration as it would have been among dogs or wolves, and everyone was glad when the problem was solved and they could relax.

The biggest pup was the first to make a "kill." While turning over a rabbit skin, he uncovered a burying beetle that tried to scuttle away. The pup regarded the scurrying creature suspiciously, his black nose between his forepaws. Then he knocked it over with one deft pat. The beetle lay kicking its legs in the air, while the pup put his head next to the ground and regarded it sideways, not sure what to do next. Ultimately he summoned up enough courage to dispatch it with a nip. Then he ate his first quarry proudly. It was much juicier than the dead food his parents brought him, and he went looking for more, deftly turning over the other skins with his nose after first sniffing under them. The other pups soon got the idea and went beetle hunting on their own. The quest took them off the earth mound and among the oaks, where they knocked the dead leaves about and pulled pieces of bark off trees when their noses told them something was underneath, and a little vixen had a moment supreme triumph when she found a white-footed mouse with squirming young clinging to her teats, hampering her escape. This was the first warm-blooded quarry any of them had seen alive, and the scent of it drove them all wild. The vixen had hard time keeping her quarry from her rapacious siblings, but she managed to tear it to pieces and swallow it while they were picking up the dropped babies.

The mother had been watching this exploit, and the next day she brought them in a live mouse and dropped it in the midst of the litter. The pups never hesitated; they tore it to bits in an instant. After a few more mice, the mother brought in a live rabbit paralyzed by a bite across the loins, yet still able to kick. This was more fearsome quarry and none dared to do more than sniff at the monster until the biggest bravely rushed in. The rabbit gave a frantic kick that sent the pup running in terror, at which the mother promptly sprang in and dispatched the rabbit with one scientific neck nip. Even so, it was some time before the pups would break into the corpse. They got dead rabbits after that until they had overcome their fear. Then Tod brought in another wounded rabbit. This time the biggest pup was able to kill it. He dragged his prey away and stood guard over it, snarling at the others, refusing to eat for fear they might get some too. He was so excited at his victory that he forgot his hunger and ended by eating only the head.

The biggest pup was a bully, and whenever either of the parents brought in food, alive or dead, he would charge forward, grab it as his right, and then if he was not especially hungry sit on it to keep the others away. Having learned that rabbits and small birds could not hurt him, he rushed in recklessly, seizing the quarry wherever was easiest and often not bothering to kill it after he had carried it off. The big cub was the vixen's favorite and she indulged his antics, but one day when she was not around, Tod brought in a muskrat with a broken leg and dropped it on the earth mound. The big pup rushed vaingloriously in, only to receive a bite that sent him away screaming. Not until the rest of the litter had worried the crippled animal until it was too exhausted to resist did he return to deliver a death bite. After that, he was much more cautious about how he blundered in blindly, and always killed the quarry as quickly as possible.

The pups seldom came out in the daytime. When the sun dropped, a head would appear at the den's mouth with huge ears pricked for the slightest noise and the big baby eyes eager and curious. After a careful check, the pup would emerge and start foraging. He would first examine the remnants of food left around the den, grab a bird's wing and shake it ferociously, and then roll on his back, steadying the wing with all four feet. By now another pup would appear and take a flying leap on his brother. Both pups would roll around, growling and pretending to bite. Such mimic fights could still lead to real combats, but the rest of the litter would come out to join the fun. Then there were games—hide-and-seek, king of the castle, tag, and follow the leader in which the parents often joined. The whole family would race through the woods, Tod leading, then the biggest pup, then the vixen, and then the rest of the family strung out in a long line. They seemed held together by an invisible string, and no matter how Tod dodged and ducked through the cover, the rest followed him, nose to brush, until all were tired. Then they played hide the thimble. The parents had left dead mice, birds, and rabbits in the cover, some in plain sight, others under leaves. The pups had to find them. The litter spread out while the parents watched how they used their noses and eyes to find the caches. When it was time for Tod to check his scent posts and do some hunting on his own, he would lope away while the vixen called the pups to her with the single shrill bark.

The pups learned by imitating their parents, since, except for a few calls, the adults made no sound. The pups were instinctively cautious—they were afraid of every new object, be it a stone, a toad, or a new type of quarry brought in by their parents. Watching the adults, they learned what creatures in this strange new world were dangerous and which were not. A screaming mother robin diving at your head was not dangerous, but a great horned owl drifting by on silent wings was—the instant reactions of their parents told them as much. The scent of cattle meant nothing, but the scent of a passing dog did. Left to themselves, the pups would have been more alarmed of a cow than of a dog—they would probably have regarded the dog as another fox—but the tensing of their parents when dog scent was in the air taught them differently. They were highly imitative, even following exactly in the vixen's footsteps when she took them out for their first hunting lessons, the whole family walking in single file. Their reflexes were lightning quick; and at first they had no idea how to control them, so they were constantly "jumpy." As they grew in confidence, they kept their alertness but tempered it with knowledge. They could be quick as red flashes when necessary, yet they seldom made an unnecessary move.

The parents were amazingly shrewd in some matters concerning the den and young, yet surprisingly stupid in others. They always approached the den from downwind to detect the presence of any enemy, and checked the cover to see if any humans had found their home. If so, the vixen was prepared to move the pups instantly to another burrow that she had already selected to use in emergencies. On the other hand, they made no attempt to conceal the den entrance, and as the pups grew older they left a series of trails through the cover and on the adjacent hillside all pointing toward the den entrance like the spokes of a wheel. The refuse of the prey they left lying around immediately marked the entrance as an occupied fox den, yet this never occurred to the pair. They did not kill near the den and the farmer's roosters, who could be heard crowing every morning from a nearby farm, were quite safe from the parents. This was not from fear of retribution—there were several rabbits and low-nesting birds in the cover who shared the same immunity—but rather because they did not like to call attention to the den by hunting near it, and slipped away from the sacred spot as quietly and inconspicuously as possible.

The pups' first hunting exploits were directed mainly against insects, with a rare mouse. They learned to catch May beetles and June bugs, making graceful, sinuous observation leaps to clear high grass while watching the progress of their prey. Later, the vixen took them to the cow pasture and showed them how to turn over cow flops to get the dung beetles underneath. They could sneak up on crickets, spotting the insects' position by their chirping or by slight noises with marvelous accuracy. They also learned how good fresh grass tastes, new buds and berries. They discovered that a skunk was not such easy prey as he seemed—although the biggest cub required a personal demonstration of this fact before he was convinced, and had to roll in a mud wallow afterward—and that a nest of yellow jackets are not to be dug up as casually as an ants' nest. The pup who made this mistake also had to take a trip to the wallow. The pups were perfectly content to live on these easily obtained food sources, and reluctant to exert themselves to catch other prey. In fact, so reluctant were they to learn the strenuous and occasionally dangerous techniques of hunting big game that few if any of them would have survived the winter when neither insects nor plants would be available. The parents knew this, but they had no way of conveying their knowledge to the cubs except to encourage them by example to hunt warm-blooded quarry. As the pups would rather play than hunt, the parents' efforts were not noticeably successful.

Much as they loved them, the pups' irresponsible behavior often drove Tod and the vixen half mad with exasperation. The pups insisted on regarding rabbits as animated toys rather than as quarry to be caught and killed as expeditiously as possible. The older foxes knew only too well that there was a definite relationship between the amount of energy obtainable from a quarry and the amount of energy necessary to catch it— for example, there was no use spending half a winter's night tracking down a rabbit even if you got him in the end, for the amount of strength you used up would not equal the amount of strength you obtained from the rabbit. Both the adult foxes carried a sliding scale of such values in their heads, gained from many a long winter's hunt when they had discovered they felt weaker after a prolonged though successful stalk than they had when they started. Yet lacking a system of vocal communication with the pups, there was no way they could pass this knowledge on. Perhaps this was just as well; otherwise the countryside would be thick with foxes, whereas even if a pair of foxes lived for fifteen years and had an average litter of five cubs a year, probably only two of the pups would survive—enough to take the place of their parents—unless some source of easily obtained food appeared to tide them over the winter.

The Tods, however, were interested only in the survival of their pups, and so it was maddening to see the half-grown idiots gaily chasing rabbits they could not hope to catch, and refusing to learn the skills of stalking, waiting by holes, or hedge-running. The pups soon learned the rabbits' warning signal— a reverberating stamp on the ground with the hind legs—that sent every rabbit within hearing tearing for cover. Instead of realizing that this meant they had been clumsy and made their presence known, the cubs knew only that it meant rabbits were about, and would lightheartedly run to the noise in hopes of an exciting chase. If any rabbits were to be caught, that was their parents' job—what else were parents for? It did no good for the Tods to refuse to feed them—they tried that early in the game— for the pups could exist very nicely on insects, grass, and an occasional mouse. As far as the pups were concerned, it would always be summer, and their parents were stupid old codgers to work so hard catching large and difficult quarry. The pups loved to chase birds—when the birds flew away they turned to some other sport—but acquiring the stiff-legged slink, head high to see over the grass, tail straight out, taking advantage of every speck of cover and learning the final bound, not only leaping a good ten feet forward but going high enough to come down on the bird from on top as he rocketed into the air, were all a waste of time. If their parents chose to bring them birds, well and good. If they didn't, there were always helpless baby birds fallen out of the nest, the eggs of ground-nesting birds, and sometimes you could find starlings and other hole-nesting birds sufficiently close to the ground so the holes could be torn open or the young scooped out with an agile paw.

The biggest pup was the first to kill large quarry. When the farmer planted corn, he had left a strip of plowed but unplanted land running parallel to the tall green rows. The chickens liked to scratch in the soft soil, and it was perfect for taking dust baths. The biggest pup soon discovered that these birds could not fly, and in the first flush of excitement, chased them wildly around the barn. Their frantic squawks brought the farm dog, a smallish cur, racing to the scene, and the fox pup had to run for his life. The nearest cover was the corn, and as scent would not hold on the plowed earth the dog was brought to his indifferent nose. He was unable to own the line, so the pup escaped.

After he had recovered from his fright, the pup was determined to get one of the chickens. Both his parents did all in their power to lure him away from the farm—Tod because he knew the menace of man from experience, the vixen because she instinctively distrusted human habitation. Overconfident, the pup refused to be diverted.

Through what he considered great cunning, he learned to crawl through the corn and wait in ambush at the edge of the rows in early morning when the hens were being released from the chicken house. Before long they would make their way to the plowed land and start scratching. Gathering himself together, the pup would make a lightning rush and his long, thin jaws would close over the back of a hen before she knew what was happening. One crunch, and the hen died almost instantly, both lungs crushed. The pup would be back in the corn and on his way to the den almost before the rest of the flock had recovered sufficiently from their shock to start cackling. Knowing that the dog could not trail him, the pup felt confident he had an unbeatable system, and the anxiety of his parents merely amused him.

One morning Tod and the vixen were lying out in front of the den with the other cubs when they heard the frenzied cackling of guinea hens from their nightly perch on the barn roof in the valley below them. Both foxes cocked their ears to listen, Tod especially, for although the guinea hens often cackled when the pup made his morning kill, they were keeping up the noise, which meant they could continue to see the danger. Both he and the vixen with one accord rose and stood sniffing the morning breeze. An eddy brought them the information they wanted—the biggest pup was running and the farm dog was after him: Tod knew exactly what had happened. This was a day when scent held well, for it had rained during the night and the moisture still lay thick on the ground. Under these conditions, the farm dog had been able to trail the pup notwithstanding his poor nose. A fox well understands the difference between good scenting days and poor, as any huntsman knows.

The vixen gave the bark that sent the rest of the litter running for the den and then she and Tod hurried toward the farm. They were guided by the baying of the dog, who had started to throw his tongue. They ducked under the stake-and-rider fence and galloped to the top of a hill. A fearful sight met their eyes. The pup, still holding the chicken in his mouth, was running wildly only a few yards ahead of the dog, who was rapidly gaining on him.

Neither fox hesitated. Together, they charged down the slope and went for the dog. Fast as Tod was, for once the vixen was faster. She hit the cur so hard she rolled him over, and when he sprang to his feet, rolled him over again. He turned on her but now Tod was on him. The fight raged up and down the pasture while the guinea hens went mad from their post on the barn. The dog snarled, growled, and yelped when the foxes' teeth went home, but they fought silently and even when he ripped their red coats made no noise. The pup had fled, at long last dropping the chicken in his panic.

The vixen and the dog were rolling together on the ground, and Tod had sprung back for a fresh hold when a movement by the barnyard caught his eye. There stood the farmer with a gun in his hands. Tod waited for nothing else. Regardless of the vixen or the cub, he turned and bolted for the fence—a flicker over the close-cropped grass. He heard the report of the gun and instinctively flinched, expecting to feel again the sting of the pellets, but the shot hit ahead—the farmer had led him a little too much. Still going at top speed, Tod swerved to avoid the tainted ground reeking with gunpowder, and flung himself under the fence. As he did so he heard the second barrel go off, but it was not aimed at him, for he was now out of range of the shotgun. The farmer had fired at the vixen, who was also running. Afraid of hitting the dog, he had again aimed too high and she also escaped.

Tod was too wise to go directly to the den with a dog involved, and took care to tangle his trail before heading for the cover. When he got there he found the exhausted pup and vixen already in the earth. He and the vixen licked each other's wounds they had received from the dog, but Tod refused to stay long in the earth. He hated being underground anyhow, and ran about through the cover, constantly testing the wind and listening for distant sounds.

Two hours later, he heard the noise he feared more than anything else in the world except the crack of a gun—the deep, bell-like voice of Copper. Tod stopped frozen, one foot upraised. Then he ran to a hill where he could overlook the valley. He saw that Copper was on a trail, the trail of the pup. He must have been put on by the fallen chicken. With him was Copper's Master—even at that distance Tod recognized him by his movements. He had a gun. The farmer was also with him and had another gun, but for him Tod cared little.

Watching how the hound ran, Tod saw he was heading directly for the oak cover. Of course the frightened pup had made no effort to confuse his trail. The hound was well away from the men now, who were following leisurely. Tod waited until the hound was hidden from the hunters by a line of wild cherries, thickly overgrown with grapevines, and then ran toward him.

Beyond the cherries was a gravel road, and here Copper was brought to a momentary check. Without breaking his stride, Tod plunged down the high bank on the far side of the road and ran in front of the hound. When Copper did not lift his head, the fox gave a quick bark as he swung away.

Tod had deliberately crossed upwind of the hound, and now Copper got the full scent of fox—and not only fox, but the accursed fox he and the Master had been after so long. He instantly burst into the "view-cry" and rushed after the fleeting form. Tod knew well that the clumsy half-bloodhound—unlike the fast Trigg or Hudspeth—could not possibly overtake him, and he ran just ahead of Copper, luring him away from the oak.

They had gone only a few hundred yards when from the road behind them came the commanding call of what seemed to be a horn. The Master had broken open his shotgun and was blowing across one of the barrels, producing a deep note with great carrying powers. For a little while Copper, with the fox still in full view, ignored the summons, but as the call was repeated insistently he reluctantly turned away and went back to the road. Frustrated, Tod circled back to try again. As he approached cautiously from downwind, he heard the trailing call of the hound and saw Copper once more following the pup's line. The men were keeping with him this time and Tod dared not go in again.

Instead, he ran for the den. When he arrived panting, the vixen and the pups were outside, listening to the baying of the hound. Tod made a swing around his family and started away. Some of the pups tried to follow him but the frightened and hysterical vixen called them off. They obeyed her. Tod tried to show the vixen by his actions that their only safety lay in flight, but she ignored him. She had never been hunted by hounds and to her, Tod was little more than a pup himself and she had no confidence in him. Instead, she sent the pups into the den and when one did not go, angrily shoved him in with her nose. She had always found safety underground. Tod, with his childhood memories of the ravaged den, knew better.

The cry of the hound was growing nearer. Now came the terrible man scent, together with the stench of the hound. The vixen was frantic. Tod knew it was too late to save the litter even if they all started running down, the hound could overtake the half-grown pups. He and the vixen would have to save themselves. He tried to entice her away, but she refused. She was utterly bewildered, running into the den to be with the pups and then bursting out again to sniff and listen.

Copper had reached the oak cover. At last the vixen made up her mind. Ignoring Tod, she dashed off recklessly in the hope of luring the hound away. Tod made a last effort to get the pups out of the den and start them running. He made a circle through the cover, keeping downwind of the dog. There might still be something he could do.

He heard Copper lead the men to the den, sniff at the mouth, and give the bark that meant the quarry had been found and brought to bay. One of the men stayed with the hound while the other went away. Tod heard the vixen running back and forth among the oaks, trying to decoy the hound away. At last she succeeded. Not even the Master's iron discipline could control the hound, and he took out after her, filling the cover with his baying. Slowly the noise faded away. There came the sound of a farm truck toiling up the hill. The farmer drove it as far into the cover as he could. Then the two men ran a long hose from the truck's exhaust to the burrow, thrust the end into the hole, and padded it with old clothing. The engine of the truck was started and allowed to run. Soon the stink of the car fumes seeping up through the ground filled the cover.

Tod left and went to find the vixen. He barked from several hilltops, but there was no answer. At last, faint and far away, he heard the baying of the hound and ran toward the sound. Copper had checked momentarily where the vixen had run beside a stream and the cool water had sucked the scent out of her tracks down the shelving banks. Tod was able to cut ahead of him, and found his mate crouching in a ditch, absolutely exhausted, covered with mud and with a matted brush. He licked her face, but she was too beaten to respond. Tod ran back, easily taking the hound off her line, for she was so tired her scent was very faint and Copper switched to his fresh scent at once. Then Tod baffled the hound by running a wall and leaping into tree that overhung it. Copper followed the line along the wall but was unable to find the fox curled up in the crotch over his head, for there was a complete break in the trail and no scent clue of any kind.

After nightfall, when the hound had given up and returned home, Tod sprang down a little stiffly and went back to the oak grove. The vixen was there. She had dug up the bodies of the cubs and laid them out in a row. Their coats were damp where she had licked and licked, trying to restore them to life. Beside the biggest pup was a fresh-killed chicken she had gotten from the barnyard, hoping the odor of his favorite quarry might bring him back to consciousness. All night she worked over them, and it was not until morning and the blowflies came that she would admit the tragic truth. And even then, for days afterward she returned to the den, hoping upon hope that a miracle had happened and that the cubs would once again run out to greet her.

6

Fourth Hunt—Trapping

There was almost no autumn that year. Winter struck early and hard. The frozen ground hurt the foxes' pads and they had few caches to fall back upon. The scent world had changed. At night, the intense cold "froze" scent so it could not evaporate, and the foxes were forced to hunt after daylight when the sun's warmth thawed the oily scent particles sufficiently to allow them to rise.

The habits of the game also changed. Rabbits were no longer found in open fields but crouching in brushpiles or sometimes in drainpipes. Quail, grouse, and pheasants went to roost deep in honeysuckle tangles, as they would have frozen to death in trees. The foxes might not have survived the winter had it not been for their teamwork. They nearly always hunted in couples now, the vixen either following Tod and often stepping in his footprints, or else running parallel to him some fifteen yards to one side. When they came to a brushpile, they would separate and approach it from both sides so that if a rabbit darted out, one or the other would be ready. If they passed a drain pipe running under a road, one fox would take up a position by one end of the pipe while the other ran through it to chase out any rabbits. On these expeditions, Tod would follow the ridges where he had a good view, while the vixen stopped in whatever cover was available. When Tod came to the highest point, he would sit down like a dog and study the surrounding country both with eyes and nose. If either brought him word of game, he would swing around and try to herd it toward the vixen waiting in ambush. So by keeping together they were able to exist, whereas either alone would have grown too weak to hunt.

The intense cold had given both foxes magnificent rich, deep pelts dyed burnt orange, lemon, ebony, and ivory. As the foxes were color-blind, they could not see their own glory, but the coats kept them warm except on the very worst days when even Tod had to take refuge in a burrow.

One morning while Tod was running along a high ridge, he saw the Man who had hunted him with Copper following his route along a fence line. The Man was alone and had a pack basket on his back, but Tod recognized him both by smell and by his manner of walking. Tod stopped at once to watch while the vixen, thinking he had found game, glided into a rhododendron thicket to wait. Curious as usual, Tod watched to see what the human would do. The vixen grew tired of waiting and ran up the ridge to find out what was going on, but when she saw the Man she turned away at once. The vixen had no curiosity about humans, only a deep dread. Tod, on the other hand, had been brought up by a human and lived near them all his life. He knew they were potentially dangerous, as were hounds, but he was confident of his ability to outwit a hound and equally confident he could outwit humans, whom he regarded as a kind of a hound but capable of killing at a distance. As the Man had no gun, he was temporarily harmless.

Seeing he was absorbed with the distant figure, the vixen went about her own business while Tod, after waiting until the

Man was out of sight, trotted down the hill and began to trail him, stepping in his tracks. Tod enjoyed the game of stepping exactly in footprints just as when a pup he had followed in his mother's footprints to make sure not to get lost. As the length of the Man's stride was so different from his own, Tod made poor time. When he found that the Man had left the route along the fence line and gone out into a field, Tod followed in his marks, still playing his game. Then he stopped suddenly. He had caught the strong odor of fish oil.

Tod recognized the scent, having occasionally caught chub and sunfish during summer droughts when pools were low. The smell was very powerful indeed—there even seemed to be some skunk mixed with it—and it exerted a strong attraction. It was not so much that Tod liked to eat fish as it was that he enjoyed the smell for its own sake. Some smells fascinated Tod, such as well-rotted manure, and he liked to roll in them.

Still following the Man's trail, Tod hurried on, thus making a wide swing as the human had done. Now he caught two more odors—the scent of fox urine and the delicious smell of nicely decayed woodchuck. Looking up, Tod saw ahead of him the unmistakable cache of another fox.

Tod was outraged. This was his hunting grounds. Fearful that the intruder might still be about, he approached slowly and cautiously, sniffing at every step. The stranger had left his urine scent mark on a thistle to establish property rights, and Tod's nose told him the woodchuck cache was right by the thistle. He could easily see where the other fox had scratched up the ground in front of the cache with his hind feet after leaving the scent marker, for there was a V of torn earth, the apex at the thistle and the sides stretching away from it toward his fence-line trail. Tod was hungry, and there was also the satisfaction of teaching this interloper a lesson by stealing his cache.

Ordinarily, Tod would have scented the fish-oil lure while walking along his usual route and cut directly over to it, thus approaching the V through the open end. But because he had been following the Man, he came in from behind the thistle. With no trouble, be dug up the piece of woodchuck and bolted it. The fish-oil scent was strong and attractive. Although most of it was concentrated in the cache, a few drops had fallen in the open V. Thinking there might be another cache hidden there, Tod began to dig. The ground was surprisingly soft, and he made it fly.

Suddenly there was an explosion. The earth under his nose flew in all directions. Something leaped up through the loose dirt, and two jaws lashed together with a terrible snap. Tod went straight up in the air, landed on all four feet, and fled like a flicker of light. Then, seeing he was not pursued, he made a long swing and came slowly back.

The thing was lying on top of the ground, motionless. After circling it for half an hour, Tod inched in and smelled at it. The thing smelled of butternut wood and smoke, the odors combining to smother all other smells; but now that it was aboveground Tod could get a faint scent of iron. Tod had no fear of iron. On his hunts, he had often run across iron horse-shoes in pastures, crawled under iron manure spreaders, and used iron fences as scent posts. Iron meant nothing to him, and even if the thing had smelled to high heaven of iron and been left lying on the surface of the ground, Tod would have stepped into the middle of it without a second thought. The forest-bred vixen would have avoided it as she would have avoided anything connected with man, even a dropped handkerchief or a mislaid spoon, but Tod had no such feelings.

Very carefully, he extended one paw and poked the thing. It moved slightly, and Tod sprang back. After watching with his head on one side, he poked it again. By now he was convinced that the thing was lifeless in spite of the way it had moved. A chain was attached to it, and by pulling the chain Tod tried to drag it off, but the chain was fastened to a stake that held it. After trying to pull the stake up, and failing, Tod ended by contemptuously urinating over the whole affair.

Curious rather than alarmed, Tod continued to track the Man. Half a mile farther on, he smelled the fish oil again and, following the odor, came on another of the curious caches. This time a burdock had been used as a scent post with the same scratch-mark V in front of it. Profiting from his previous experience, Tod swung around and unearthed the cache from the roots of the burdock, but his constant curiosity prompted him to see if there were another of the iron things in the V. With a careful paw, Tod dug in from the side of the V; and sure enough, within a few inches he touched a hard, curved edge. At once Tod pulled back, expecting to see this one also leap into the air with a snap, but nothing happened. With fantastic delicacy of touch, Tod reached under the object and gave it the same flip he occasionally used to toss a mouse out of its tunnel. Then he got his explosion. This time Tod felt so proud of himself he not only urinated on the object but covered it with his feces as well.

Tod had now acquired two fine pieces of delicious wood-chuck, well seasoned, and was beginning to enjoy this business. Hurrying on, he found several more of the caches, each with one of the iron objects buried beside it, and he conscientiously sprang them all. Then that evening he came on one that had quite a different smell—a heavy, skunklike odor—and trotting over to it, Tod found a mink caught by one foot.

The tortured animal had torn up the ground in a circle around the central stake. It lay there panting, watching Tod.

Tod's impulse was to spring in and kill the helpless captive; but he was fearful of some trick, and ran around the fatal circle. The mink was too exhausted to do more than turn its head. Then as Tod came closer, the mink writhed to its feet, hissing, and tore at the trap. Crazed with pain, the prisoner rolled on the ground, his teeth scratching on the iron, and then in his agony tore at his own foot. Tod felt no sympathy for the mink, yet the whole business frightened as well as fascinated him. He could only vaguely realize what had happened, and kept running back and forth, approaching the mink as closely as he dared and then leaping back to run wildly about, half hysterical with excitement and bewilderment. When the mink lay on its side at the edge of the circle, gasping and snarling, Tod crawled in on his belly until their noses were almost touching, and crouched there, snarling back. Then he sniffed at the mink inquisitively until a fresh spasm of the animal made him retreat.

Tod stayed by the mink until the sun was so high that he decided to return to his lying-up place. The stench of fright, the odor of blood, the tortured thrashings of the animal all had made a profound impression on him. Tod was able to understand that somehow these iron things could grasp and hold anything they caught even though they were not alive. This was a new idea to Tod, and difficult for him to connect with his past experiences, for to Tod anything that could seize a living creature was alive.

Tod was profoundly puzzled. He had been able to adjust to being hunted by hounds, as the method used by the hounds to track him was not fundamentally different from the manner in which he himself tracked quarry. The efforts made to shoot him at a crossing had not unduly alarmed him—once he realized the danger of firearms—for he could understand how a human would wait in ambush for him while a hound drove him past the spot; after all, this was not too unlike the way he and his mate herded game to each other. These iron things presented a problem totally alien to his way of thought. Still, they could not chase him nor could they kill from a distance. He decided to find out more about them.

From then on, Tod made a circuit of the trapline every night. He invariably sprang each trap after eating the bait. He gained no advantage from springing the traps, he simply enjoyed doing it. Except for the brief rutting season, he took no interest in sex, and generally obtaining food was so simple it had become routine. Tod was bored and he had an active mind. His catholic diet caused him to develop techniques not only for catching game but also for devising means of getting grapes (he did this by climbing into a sloping tree and then jumping down on the grapevines from above) and learning how to get the lids off garbage cans. He had become intensely curious about everything he encountered, and delighted in experimenting with unusual objects to see what would happen. Much of his hunting was play rather than a desire for food. He would go out of his way to stalk a squirrel because he knew how difficult squirrels were to catch. If he succeeded, he often did not bother to eat his kill—the satisfaction of the hunt was enough for him. He enjoyed springing the traps because it was a difficult thing to do, coupled with just enough danger to make it exciting.

He tried taking the vixen around the trapline with him, but she was terrified of the whole business and could not imagine why he found this dangerous sport so pleasurable. She had a deathly fear of man and all his works, and once he showed her that there were traps in the V's before the nice-smelling baits, she refused to go anywhere near them. Being more cautious, she ran fewer risks, but she also learned nothing about traps.

Tod became so expert at springing them he grew cocky and overconfident.

Occasionally Tod would find another animal caught, often another fox, for the trapline was not confined to his range; and because it was winter, Tod had no hesitation about trespassing on adjacent properties. When the captive was a fox, it was usually a this-year's pup. The sight of the trapped fox invariably drove Tod half mad with anxiety. He would run around crying, in his frenzy occasionally charging at the victim as though about to attack him, and then later digging up a cache of food and bringing it to him. Tod did not precisely feel sorry for the doomed fox—even if he could have released him it is doubtful whether he would have done so, although in the case of a pup his parental feelings might well have been strong enough to cause him to save the prisoner. The scent of fear that poured from the captive like a stinking mist affected Tod's mind, just as the odor of a vixen in heat made it impossible for him to behave normally. He seemed to go temporarily insane. Yet the fact that he would bring the prisoner food (which was never eaten) showed he was not entirely indifferent to the captive's fate. He was especially attentive to pups, and would often stay with them until his nose told him the Man was coming. Then, and not until then, he would slip away.

One morning while Tod was lying up in the lea of a stand of hemlocks, he heard a jay screaming in the valley. There was a standing feud between Tod and jays; many a time they had spoiled some of his most elaborate stalks by flying down and screaming at him, thus warning his quarry. Even so, Tod used the jays as sentinels, for if they screamed at him they also screamed at anything else dangerous or unusual.

Tod lay for some time listening to the jay. The bird might be yelling at an owl who had not been able to make it back to the woods when daylight overtook him, or even at another fox. Still, there was a special note of insistency in this bird's voice that made Tod suspect he saw a man. Finally Tod rose, stretched, and made a swing downwind to investigate.

There was a good breeze blowing, and as Tod glided along through the cover—for in broad daylight he never exposed himself if he could help it—he caught the strong smell of the Man. If he had been on one of the farms where men were supposed to be, Tod would have paid no attention to him; nor would the jay have screamed. But the Man was on the overgrown slope of a hill, one of Tod's favorite hunting grounds, where men never went if they were attending to their own affairs.

Still keeping downwind of the human, Tod snaked through the cover until he could see him. He was making one of the caches. For the first time, Tod saw how the iron thing was put in the V.

When the man finally left, Tod went over to investigate. Everything looked as usual, but he circled the spot for a long time. He could smell the fish-oil lure and the bait—it was muskrat this time. At long last, he edged in cautiously, alert for any new device that might be awaiting him. With his nose he checked every inch of the ground as he progressed, not only for the smell of iron but also for the odor of freshly turned earth. He also used his eyes, studying the ground ahead before putting his foot down to see if anything had been disturbed. His whole body was tense, ready to leap instantaneously if the ground moved beneath him. Occasionally he would pat the ground lightly with one extended forepaw before putting his weight on the spot.

He reached the edge of the V. Sniffing, he could easily smell the iron thing under the loose soil. Always heretofore the traps had smelled of butternut wood or balsam, which hid the odor of iron, but there was no scent here except that of the trap. Tod could tell exactly where it was. Delicately he scooped out earth to one side of it until he could insert one paw underneath. Then he gave his flip.

Instead of leaping up, the trap went off under the ground, and Tod to his indescribable horror felt the jaws seize his paw. The trap had been set upside down. Even as the jaws closed, Tod threw himself backward. His foot tore free. Tod was so amazed and startled he stood staring at the partly exposed trap. Then in a blind fury he tore it up by the chain and shook it like a rabbit. The jaws were still slightly open, for a small stone had wedged between them. In his relief and anger, Tod defecated on the thing until he could force nothing more from his straining bowels. He left the trapline alone for the next couple of days because his foot was still sore; but the temptation to outwit the human proved so strong that on the third morning, he went back to checking the line.

So exquisitely sensitive was Tod's touch that after a little experimentation he could tell by feeling the edges of the traps how they were set. If they were set in the normal way, he flipped them up from below. If they were set upside down, he dug down from the top until he reached the release catch and jarred it loose. For two nights he systematically sprang all the traps along the line, confident now that he understood the whole system. These traps were not chained to a stake, but to a drag that moved with the trap so a fox could not free himself by a quick jerk as Tod had done before.

The next night he found a cache freshly baited, and located the trap without trouble. He dug under it. It was upside down, so Tod began to dig in from above. The trap jumped to meet him. The jaws flew shut on his paw. At the same instant there was another explosion under the trap. Two traps had been set, one above the other, the bottom one upside down.

In his fear and agony, Tod ran blindly, the drag bumping behind him. Going at top speed, Tod tore between two rocks. Here the drag caught. There was a sudden racking jerk that flung Tod down, but when he got up again he was free. The trap had been torn from his paw.

Tod limped for many days afterward. It would seem incredible that after such a lesson he would again return to springing traps, yet he did. Tod needed excitement almost as much as he did food. The jug hunters with their nocturnal hunts had provided it for a while, but the country was getting built up now, and the jug hunters came no more. When Tod was playing with a trap, little spasms of delightful ecstasy trembled through him as the threat of imminent danger set his adrenaline gland pumping fluid through his veins. After such an experience, Tod could eat the bait with a satisfaction impossible under any other circumstances; and when he rejoined the vixen, he would even try to mount her in play as he never did otherwise. He could no more forego the divine emotion that only danger induced than he could forego the sexual drive. It was to those pulsing shots of adrenaline that Tod owned his quicksilver reflexes, and his whole being revolved around them. He was prepared to run great risks to obtain that thrill, and besides, he had not been really seriously hurt—as yet.

Tod now worked out a new trap-springing technique. Using the side of his paw and employing delicate, surface strokes, he would brush away the loose dirt covering the pan of the trap. Tod usually lay on his side when performing this operation. Once the trap was uncovered, Tod could then see how it was set and how best to deal with it.

Tod began to notice a new odor to the traps—the acrid scent of filed steel where the rough edges of the pin and release catch had been filed away to give the trap a hair-trigger set. But he had developed so fine a touch at the ticklish operation of uncovering the pan that no matter how lightly the trap might be set, he did not spring it. Now Tod was sure he was safe; man had nothing more to show him.

One evening as Tod lay brushing the loose earth from a trap's pan, he felt something prick his paw. When Tod tried to jerk his paw away, the thing's curved tip clung to his fur for a fraction of a second—only a fraction, but enough to set off the trap. A fishhook had been soldered to the pan, and this time Tod was caught full and fair.

Tod spun around and ran. For a wonderful moment he thought he could escape even with the trap fastened to his foot, as he had before, but when he came to the end of the chain he was thrown down with a force that sent spasms of torture up his leg. This time the chain was not fastened to a drag, but to a stake. Now it was Tod's turn to rave and tear at the iron jaws, to bite at his own leg, to tear up the ground in a circle around the immovable stake, and finally to fall exhausted and panting on the snow. He fought in silence; no sound escaped him in spite of his pain. Time and again he rushed the full length of the chain, only to be brought down again.

He tried to chew his foot off, but it was not numb enough yet to be anesthetized. He knew well what would happen to him when the trapper returned. He had smelled the fate of other foxes caught in the bloody snow. Frantic, Tod made another rush, racing from one side of the circle he had made straight across to the far edge. Again he was pulled off his feet, but the abrupt yank had jerked his foot a fraction of an inch clear.

Tod collapsed gasping. Spasms of pain ran up his leg, and he wanted to do nothing but lie still and suffer. Still, he forced himself to stand, and then made another rush. The fearful tearing jerk was almost more than he could bear, but again his pad was pulled slightly through the trap's jaws. Again and again he made the effort, until his tortured brain refused to function and he fought in a haze of suffering without purpose or hope, yet always running the full length of the long chain to build up momentum for the final yank. How many rushes he made he did not know; yet finally, after one rush, he pitched forward and somersaulted on the snow. He struggled to his feet and charged on again. This time the chain did not yank him back, and he went on and on, falling, recovering himself, and still making wild rushes, unable to realize that at last he was free.

He could see nothing and smell nothing, yet he fought his way forward, caroming off trees and plunging through brush. Then he felt himself falling, and hit ice-cold water. As he went under, the shock brought him to his senses. Too weak to struggle, he let the current carry him downstream. He was drowning but he did not care. A bridge of ice had formed across the stream, and here he was stranded. For hours, Tod lay there barely conscious. The deep black of the shadows faded into gray as day came under an overcast sky. Still Tod did not move.

Then he heard it—Copper's deep-mouthed bay. The sound was far upstream where the trap was. The Man had brought the hound to trail him. Dimly Tod heard the hound triumphantly throwing his voice on the well-marked line, and then the baying ceased. Copper had come to the stream and was checked.

He would not be checked long, and Tod knew it. He had learned from experience that the hound understood well how to run the banks until he picked up the trail again. Tod dragged himself up the shore. Whenever he tried to stand, his leg buckled under him, and he was too weak to run on three legs. Foot by foot he wormed his way along through a pine plantation planted for a watershed. Of course the hound would find where he had crawled up the bank; still, he had to go on.

Raindrops began to leak through the mat of needles overhead. The drops came down more and more heavily until, as the full force of the storm broke, rivulets formed, pouring past and around him toward the stream. Soon the whole hillside was awash. Tod had been pulling himself forward with the dewclaw of his good leg, but that could no longer hold in the rush of water. He was finished. Tod collapsed and waited for the end.

He heard the Man and Copper coming along the far bank of the stream. Then came the sound of splashing as they crossed. Now they were on his side. It would not be long now.

Automatically, Tod's nostrils twitched, trying to smell them, but the torrential rain had washed all scent away. The Man and Copper passed within ten feet of him, the Man calling encouragement to the hound. Then they went on. Tod lay still, not believing his good luck. Surely they would return. They never did.

The rain stopped shortly before noon. Tod was sufficiently recovered to limp to an old woodchuck hole he knew and crawl down it. Here he lay for two days.

It was the vixen who found him. Several times during those two days Tod had heard her bark, calling for him, yet he had not answered. He was too despondent to care. On the evening of the third day he was so desperate for water he crept down to the stream for a drink, and the vixen, casting about through the woods, hit his trail. She followed it to the woodchuck burrow.

Having found him, the vixen had no idea what to do. She seemed more annoyed than sympathetic, snarling and hissing at the burrow's mouth, although when she wriggled down the hole she licked his injured foot assiduously. Then she went hunting for herself. She brought him no food that night, but the next evening she arrived with a rabbit. Apparently she had not brought it as food; she had killed the rabbit on her way and carried it with her, not finding a good place to cache it in the frozen ground. Tod was now furiously hungry, and when the vixen crouched down by the burrow and started to eat the rabbit, not knowing what else to do with it, Tod pulled himself out and attacked her. After a hissing, snapping, screaming session the vixen retreated while Tod bolted the still-warm flesh. Afterward, he felt much stronger. The vixen stood watching him, and from then on, brought him food regularly.

A fierce cold spell set in that actually benefited the foxes, although Tod had to lie on his injured foot to keep it from freezing. After dark, the vixen canvassed the plantation, stepping lightly over the guano six inches deep left by thousands of grackles, cowbirds, and starlings that used the pines as a roost. Every few yards she would find a bird frozen to death, and after eating her fill she would bring the rest to Tod. She could carry three birds at one time, lining them up side by side and then carefully running her long lower jaw under the trio and lifting them together. Gradually Tod recovered. Luckily for him, no bones had been broken, although he would always favor that foot, especially after a hard night's run.

At long last, Tod had learned his lesson and from then on he stopped playing with traps. The very odor of the fish-oil lure was enough to cause him to make a wide detour. He even sedulously avoided the caches of other foxes, not knowing for sure if they were genuine or a trapset. The most luscious woodchuck or delightfully "high" muskrat could be buried temptingly a few inches from the surface, and it was safe from Tod. He no longer ran casually over horseshoes or bits of old iron; the mere scent of such things alarmed him.

In spite of her innate fear of man, the vixen was more indifferent to danger than Tod. She had neither Tod's terrible experience nor his knowledge of traps, and as long as the presence of man was not too obvious she felt that she was safe. Although she was routinely cautious, she did not adopt the elaborate precautions that Tod did now that he had some understanding of how a trap and a man worked together.

There came a severe blizzard, and for once the foxes were hard put to find food. Territorial boundary lines were forgotten as all foxes roamed the countryside indiscriminately in their search. In a pinch, they could dig up corncobs in the fields, find a few forgotten windfall apples, or even chew the bark of branches; but the craving for meat grew increasingly intense. It was not simply hunger: the meat provided protein their systems craved, and the fur or feathers of their quarry gave them oils they needed. Even a mouse became a valuable catch, and every morning there were fresh tracks around the farmers' chicken houses, which were seldom bothered in better times.

Then one evening Tod and the vixen came on a bonanza. In a slight depression half a mile from a farm, they found a dead sheep. Crows had already been feeding on it, and four-footed scavengers, for the snow around the carcass was polka-dotted with tracks.

Hungry as they were, the foxes did not go in, even though all signs showed that the carcass was innocent enough and not even their trained noses could detect the odor of man scent. They circled the carcass, testing every wisp of breeze from every angle, still not daring to approach within fifty yards. They returned the second night, and this time dared to come within twenty yards. A dog had been feeding on the sheep, tramping down the snow all around the body and leaving his heavy scent. Obviously nothing had happened to him. Even so, the foxes were not yet entirely convinced.

On the third night most of the sheep had been devoured, and the foxes could resist the odor of the meat no longer. The dog had been back, going straight into the carcass, as dogs will.

Yet the foxes refused to go straight in. After circling the sheep several times, they headed for a little mound that overlooked the depression. From this eminence they could study the situation before making the final decision.

Wind had kept the top of the mound clear of snow. As they bounded up the slope, Tod abruptly checked. Something about the look of the bare earth bothered him. He had a feeling it had been disturbed. He stopped, rigid and sniffing. There was no man scent, yet could he or could he not detect the faintest smell of turned earth? Tod swung around to get the full strength of the night breeze. He still could not be sure, but he did not like the look of things. There was a certain quality about the bare patch that reminded him of the deadly V's. He continued to hang back.

Unhesitatingly, the vixen ran to the top of the mound. She was too wary to approach the sheep, but the mound was isolated and safe enough. Tod saw the earth leap up, and even though he was twenty feet away he bounded back. He was rigid, his hair standing up with fright until he looked twice as big. The vixen went straight up into the air, fell, and tried to run, but the trap had her. Frantically she rushed to and fro; this time the stake chain was shorter, and she could not get up enough momentum to jerk free. She rolled on the snow, tore at the steel jaws, pulled and strained. It was useless.

Tod ran about helplessly. There was, indeed, nothing he could do. As the night went on, half a dozen other foxes came in, drawn by the fearful odor of terror and despair that went from the doomed vixen. Like Tod, they rushed around aimlessly They made no attempt to dig up the stake, help the vixen chew on the chain, or try to release her. Perhaps they were too afraid of the strange device. Even Tod, who understood traps well, was incapable of solving such a problem. Clever as Tod had been in learning how to spring traps, it had never occurred to him to pick up a stick in his mouth and hit the pan or even to roll a stone onto the pan with his nose—a simple feat for him. Tod could "reason" in a sense, but only in certain ways and in certain combinations of circumstances. He could not deduce by reason how a trap worked or the logical way of coping with one.

When dawn came, all the foxes left but Tod. He stayed with the gasping, beaten vixen until he saw the distant figure of the Man plodding over the light crust on snowshoes with his pack basket on his back and Copper at his heels. Then he slipped away. He returned that night, but the vixen was gone and the smell of death was heavy on the mound.

In December, Tod felt the old pulsing in his testicles, and once again he began to listen for the sound of a barking vixen and snuff the night winds. His old, reliable guides, the scent posts, were now largely useless to him, for he was suspicious of the smell of strange fox urine, which he associated with a trap. Although he spent hours barking from hilltops, no vixen answered him. Indeed, he heard few dog foxes. Several times Tod had found foxes in traps or come on a trap that held nothing but a chewed-off foot. The winter's trapping had decimated the fox population until there were only a few left. As a result, foraging was much better and finding food had again become a minor consideration for Tod.

By January, the few remaining dog foxes were in full rut, and desperate. Several of them drifted away to search for mates elsewhere, yet Tod stayed on. He hated to abandon his beloved range, and his nose told him there was no vixen in heat within a radius of fifteen miles.

Trotting down a well-padded trail by a laurel thicket, Tod suddenly smelled the odor he had been longing for—the scent of the urine of a vixen in heat. Instantly he burst into a wild run. The vixen had obviously squatted by a scent post only a few yards ahead, and the odor was so fresh she could not be long gone. Trailing her would be easy. Even as Tod broke into his full stride, he was knocked to one side, and another dog fox, maddened by the odor, tore past him. Raging, Tod sped after the white tip of his rival's brush. Only a few feet apart they shot along the trail.

Ahead, in a narrow part of the trail between two bushes, was a small tuft of meadow grass. This was the scent post, for the odor came from it. The vixen had crouched here to leave her mark before going on.

Even though Tod was doing his utmost to pass his rival, the other fox kept ahead of him and reached the narrow section of the path first. Two sticks, a little more than a foot apart, had fallen across the path on either side of the tuft, and Tod's rival bounded over the first one. As his forefeet hit the ground, there came the now all too familiar sound of clashing jaws.

Tod twisted sideways and ran. Behind him he heard the other fox running, and this frightened him even more. The fox was running on three legs and Tod could hear the rattle of the chain and the bumping of the drag. He redoubled his efforts and found himself running alone. A thrashing in the laurels told him the drag had caught and the trapped animal was flinging himself about among the tough stalks. Tod circled downwind and stopped to listen. Then he hurried away.

Toward dawn, Tod's ever-present curiosity made him return. His nose told him that there was a second dog fox in still another trap by the treacherous tuft of grass. Still wistfully hoping that a vixen might be involved in the business somehow, Tod lay up in the laurels, if only to sniff that thrilling perfume. Shortly after sunrise, he smelled the Man and Copper and then heard the hound's bay as he tracked down the two prisoners, both entangled by their drags in the bushes. After the Man and hound had gone, Tod returned to the fatal spot and examined it from a discreet distance. The vixen's urine had been replenished and the torn ground was now smooth again. Tod made no attempt at further examination. He knew well what lay beneath the innocent-looking earth and that there was no chance of finding a new mate here—only death.

A few nights later, Tod did scent a vixen. He followed the odor swiftly, yet not with the wild, impulsive speed he would once have shown, for he was now suspicious of everything. He found the vixen crouching in abject terror while a dog fox tried to mount her. She was young, and so starved her coat seemed to hang on her in folds. Her brush was ragged; her pads were worn and sore, her flanks hollow, her eyes hot. Even so, she was a vixen, and in season. Tod began to circle in his usual fashion, but the dog fox rushed him. At first Tod tried to hold him off with his long forelegs, and then lost his temper and fought. The two males were equally matched, and the fight raged through the blackberry bushes, down a bank, and among the trees until the combatants reached an open space where they both decided to have it out. The other fox was an old fighter, and the scars on his head showed white as the tension of his jaw muscles pulled the skin taut around his muzzle. He came in with open jaws. Tod, remembering his first fight, folded his forelegs under him and made a plunge for the stranger, sliding in on his belly. He fastened to a foreleg and began to shake. The stranger rolled with him; Tod lost his grip and the foxes broke apart.

Tod reared up and mounted the other fox from in front, grabbing him by the left stifle. The stranger fought savagely, planting his hind feet against the ground and straining to break the hold. There was no more hissing or screaming, only a subdued grumble as the foxes struggled together. The punishment was more than the stranger could take, and he turned his head away. That meant he was weakening. Tod himself could barely stand and his legs shook under him, but seeing his opponent turn gave him fresh confidence.

Both foxes now fought for the head and nose. Tod grabbed for the stranger's throat but missed, his jaws making an audible snap. Then he got his stifle hold again. He lay down to keep the stranger from getting to his throat and began to work his jaws in to reach the bone. The stranger was almost done by now, and covered with blood, yet he kept fighting. Tod shifted his hold to the other's belly. That did it. The stranger collapsed, lying as though dead, his jaws fixed in a snarl. For a few seconds Tod stood over him, fangs bared before contemptuously turning away. The defeated stranger continued to play dead until Tod was gone.

The vixen showed no more interest in Tod than she had in the other dog fox. She lay on the ground with hardly energy enough to snarl, and Tod, in spite of his frantic sexual urge, did not know what to do. She was so puppy-like and helpless that eventually Tod's memory of his own pups asserted itself and he went off, dug up a squirrel cache he remembered, and brought it back. When he returned he found another dog fox with the vixen, but this male fled at once at the sight of the torn, bloody, and furious Tod. Tod dropped the squirrel beside the vixen and then, retreating a few paces, sat down to watch. After a long, long time she ate it, snarling at him as she did so.

Mating did not take place until the next night, although Tod never left her side and had to drive off two other males during the long wait. The vixen behaved as though she had never been bred before, and whenever he approached her, she spun around to face him with open, grinning jaws. When it was over, she seemed to feel a great sense of relief. He brought her more food and after that she followed him docilely enough, treading in his exact tracks and humbly accepting anything he offered her. He showed her his regular routes and the boundaries of his range, and by spring they were an old, established married couple.

Trapset after trapset was laid for him, but Tod avoided them all. He always came up to anything that could possibly be bait, even a frozen sparrow, with extreme caution; and no matter how ingeniously hidden the traps were, the Man had to leave some traces of scent, for he could not fly. He took to wearing rubber boots when he set his traps to avoid leaving any human scent in his tracks, but Tod came to associate the smell of rubber with the human, and avoided it. Often the boots themselves left almost no odor, but because the Man would walk through grass or weeds, enough of the plants adhered to the boots to alert Tod, for, just as he had learned to connect the odor of rubber with the Man, he learned to associate the odor of crushed herbage with the boots. No matter what precautions the Man took, Tod could detect his presence.

Trotting along the bank of a stream one evening, Tod caught the odor of cat. Of all foods, Tod especially liked cat. He had once found a dead cat thrown out on a garbage dump, and sampled it. It was delicious, and Tod had never forgotten the taste. He followed the smell as easily as a man would have followed a bright light, and found part of a nicely "high" cat on a tiny island in the stream a couple of feet from the bank.

Tod disliked getting his feet wet, and in spite of the cold this stream was free-flowing, for it came from a spring trickling out of the hillside. Zigzagging back and forth to make sure he covered every inch of ground and got every flicker of scent, Tod worked his way in. He found that there were two of the tiny islands; the farthest one had the piece of cat lying on it, and the one nearest the bank was bare. By stepping on the nearest island, he could easily reach the cat.

Tod meticulously went up and down the bank, checking for man scent or signs. There were none. Then he crossed the stream by means of a fallen hemlock log and checked the farther bank. Still no signs. He crossed again and went back to look the situation over.

For all his cleverness it never occurred to Tod to wonder how a piece of cat could get on an island in a stream. He knew only that it was there and that there was positively no man scent. It had to be all right. Gingerly he advanced one forefoot onto the nearest island. It was so small there was only one place he could step.

As he bore down on his foot preparatory to reaching for the cat, he felt something crinkle under his pad. What it was Tod had no idea, but his lightning-quick reflexes made him spring back just as the trap went off. The jaws grazed his pad as he jumped. There lay the trap exposed, and with it was a piece of waxed paper that had been used to cover the trigger mechanism and keep it clear of dirt. Waxed paper had been used so the water would not dissolve it. It was the crinkling of the waxed paper that had warned him.

Tod left the bait alone. He did not know what other traps might be set there. Later, going far downstream, he came on the familiar scent of rubber boots where the Man, after wading along the brook to leave no scent on either bank, had at last come out.

Though Tod came on several of these water sets, he now knew about them, and was never tempted again. Finally, they disappeared.

Tod did discover there was plenty of good hunting along the banks of the stream, especially as spring progressed and animals coming out of hibernation went there to drink. He used the fallen hemlock log as a bridge, and after examining one bank would cross over and try the other. As he approached the log, he would make a quick run, leap on it from the side, and trot across, always putting his feet in the same places, then jump off.

Early one morning, as he started across, he noticed two sticks were lying across the log about a foot apart. Tod instantly stopped and examined them. They were strange, though not startling. He sniffed carefully, but there was no man scent whatsoever. Also, there was no sign of a trap, and this log was solid wood where no trap could be buried. It must be safe, And yet—and yet! Tod recalled those sticks on either side of the scent post in the trail. Though he had seen the other fox jump over one of them and get caught, Tod had learned to connect traps with earth, and there was no earth here. He sat down and thought about it for a long time. While he sat, a rabbit came loping slowly along the near bank of the stream.

Tod slumped down on the log and remained motionless, watching the rabbit. The rabbit was looking for new green stalks; not finding any, he went up the bank toward a stand of young willows that still had bark on them. As soon as he was gone, Tod slipped off the log. Running lightly and silently, he cut around behind his quarry, taking care to keep downwind, and then sneaked up on it. He saw the rabbit standing on its hind legs, trying to reach the still ungirdled bark. When the rabbit was looking away, Tod would lift himself and run forward a few steps, but so low his belly was touching the ground. Then he would drop flat again. Each time he made one of these swift rushes, he always stopped in some shallow depression or behind same well-nigh invisible bit of cover. After a few mouthfuls, the rabbit would turn his head to look around again, while Tod remained stretched at full length, not a whisker twitching. When the rabbit resumed feeding, Tod would slip forward another few yards. As he came closer, his advance was so imperceptible he scarcely seemed to move at all, yet the distance between him and his quarry gradually lessened.

Finally the rabbit suspected something. He could see Tod quite well; though as long as the fox did not move, the rabbit did not recognize him as a fox. Yet there was definitely something there, and it seemed to be constantly coming nearer. Not alarmed but vaguely doubtful, the rabbit began to hop away. Then Tod charged.

Fast as Tod was, the rabbit had seen the start of his rush out of the corner of its eye, and took off as only a frightened rabbit can. The stream was ahead, so the rabbit made for the log bridge, having often used it before. He hit the bark, and with one great bound cleared the first stick. He gave a fearful piercing scream as the trap seized him, and tumbled off the log.

Frantic with the excitement of the chase, Tod ran to the spot. The trap had fallen into the stream, the rabbit in it, and both had gone to the bottom, although the trap was still fastened to the log by its chain. Now Tod saw that a notch about a foot long had been cut out of the log, the trap inserted, and then cleverly concealed by moss and strips of thin bark. The whole business had been done by a man standing in the water and using gloves rubbed with hemlock so as to leave no scent. Though Tod would have loved to reach the rabbit, he had no means of doing so, and was reluctantly forced to continue his hunting.

When spring came and his new vixen showed the typical female interest in holes, Tod decided this time to select the location of the den himself. He was bent on raising this litter, even though he knew the Man and Copper were equally determined to track him and the vixen down when they were tied to the helpless pups. Tod no longer felt confident of being able easily to outwit the Man or even the hound. Still, he was grimly resolved to do his best.

7

Fifth Hunt—Formal Hunting

For several days, Copper had been aware of a growing sense of excitement. Something was going to happen; he did not know what. There were none of the usual signs. The leather-smelling men had not come to the cabin, nor the farmers with their shotguns nor any of the Master's usual hunting companions. Instead, men had been coming who did not smell like people at all, and even their clothes had a curious odor. True, these men often smelled of dogs and horses as did the farmers, but it was all wrong somehow. Their clothes were not saturated with sweat, and their boots did not smell of manure. Even the animal scents clinging to them were unnatural. Whenever the Master brought them up to meet him, Copper sniffed the strangers' trouser legs with interest. He had never smelled dog or horse odors like these. The animals must be on a different diet and kept differently from those he knew.

The strangers not only smelled differently; they spoke in shrill, fast voices very unlike the drawling tones Copper knew. They moved the way they spoke, jerkily and quickly, instead of an easy, swinging lounge. When the Master spoke to them his voice changed. He sounded nervous and respectful. Copper knew he was not at ease with these outsiders. Neither was Copper, although they seemed friendly enough.

As soon as the strangers had left, Copper would jump frantically on the Master, try to lick his face, roll on the ground, and gambol clumsily around him, giving wailing cries. He knew these strangers wanted something done—something that would involve his services, for they always showed great interest in him and when they talked to the Master his name was frequently used. Whatever it was, he would do his best and he wanted the Master to know it. The Master would pat him, scratch him behind the ears, and speak comfortingly. As long as the Master loved and had confidence in him, Copper did not care about anything else.

One morning while he and the Master were returning from the trapline, he heard the sound of a horn. Copper pricked up his ears, for he had never heard a horn like that. It was not the deep note of the cows' horns the jug hunters used or the even deeper call produced by blowing over the barrels of an open shotgun. Then the wind shifted and brought him the information he wanted. There were hounds near—many hounds. He also smelt the tangy odor of sweating horses, tobacco, and the scent of men. Then he heard men's voices, cut through by the clear call of the horn. The Master stopped and Copper stopped with him. There was a crackling in the half-frozen sumac bushes, and hounds began to leak out of the cover, followed by men on horseback, talking and laughing.

Copper had little interest in the men. His attention was riveted on the hounds. Several ran over to him, wagging their tails, sniffing, ears laid back and the skin on their foreheads pulled taut by their open, grinning jaws. Copper stood stiff-legged with upraised, rigid tail, scowling with his massive forehead ridged with wrinkles. These strange hounds were too friendly by half. Copper was no brawler, but even so there were certain formalities to be observed when dogs met; the stiff-legged gait, the upraised tail, the lips half curled in the beginnings of a snarl just to let the other fellow know who you were. He was also baffled by the number of the creatures. Copper had never seen more than half a dozen dogs together in his life.

He sniffed suspiciously, instantly recognizing the curious dog odor that had been on the strange men's clothes. Several of the hounds urinated on trees or bushes, and as the smell reached him Copper realized that they all must eat exactly the same food. It was meal with some meat mixed with it, not table scraps or the remains of wild game shot or trapped. They were all much alike, with long necks, legs straight below the knee, and small, rounded catlike feet. From the way they moved among each other, exchanging signals by motion of heads, tails, and bodies, Copper knew they were used to working as a pack—they even had much the same smell, as though they all slept together. They seemed to have no individuality. Even though Copper was used to hunting with the Triggs, Julys, and Plotts, each hound tended to work independently and was slightly jealous of the others, keeping his distance and avoiding touching another hound. There was no such mutual suspicion here.

The riders came up on their great horses, talking and laughing with the Master while the hounds moved fearlessly among the horses' hooves, to Copper's surprise. Horses were dangerous things; as a pup Copper had been badly kicked by one in a field when he tried to smell the animal's hind legs. Copper had never seen men riding on horses before, but this did not interest him— men did all sorts of queer things of no concern to dogs—but the free and easy relationship that obviously existed between these strange hounds and the horses puzzled him greatly.

The Master seemed eager to have him make friends with these strangers, and Copper politely smelled a few anuses and had his smelled in return, but he had little interest in these foreigners and they had no more in him. He was relieved when the horsemen moved off and the pack followed a quick blast of the horn.

Several mornings after this chance meeting Copper heard the stranger pack hunting. He and the other hounds burst from their barrels at the first faint, distant cry of the pack and, lifting their heads, wailed at the injustice of being tied when other hounds were running. From the sound of the hound music, Copper knew well these strangers were having their troubles, for often the cry sounded more puzzled than eager, it often faded away as the pack checked, and when the cry stopped it was seldom indeed that he heard the excited yelp that meant a hound had picked up the line again. Copper was confident that if the Master would only turn him loose, he could show these noseless foreigners how to work out a line, and he filled the air with his lamentations. Yet days passed and his services were never required.

Then one heavenly morning, just at daybreak, the Master came for him. Copper went mad with joy, while the rest of the pack screamed in jealousy and disappointment. He and the Master got in the car and started off.

They drove into a gray light, for the sun had not risen above the hills. Copper lay in his seat, ardently inhaling the fresh morning smells that he knew would turn stale and weak as the sun grew hotter. Rags of mist hung across the road, whirling apart as the car hit them. Copper sniffed the moisture-laden air anxiously. Too much humidity deadened the scent and made it lie heavily, but he could not tell how conditions really were because the rush of air through the car created an artificial wind that was confusing.

They came to a crossroads, and the Master stopped the car. Instantly Copper smelled the odor of horses, people, hounds, and the exhausts of cars. When the Master opened the door, he jumped out hopefully, yet somewhat doubtful.

There were only three buildings at the crossroads: an old country store, a shipping shed, and a farmer's house under a stand of great elms. The farmer and his family were sitting on the steps, and the children knew Copper and shouted to him. Copper indulgently waved his tail to them, but his eyes and nose were concentrated on the pack, assembled behind a rider and guarded on the sides by two more riders with long whips in their hands. There seemed to be cars and horses everywhere. Copper did not especially object to the horses as long as they did not come too close to him, but he hated the cars because of the stink of their exhausts.

The Master went over to talk to the rider in front of the pack, and Copper followed gingerly at his heels. He knew at once that these hounds were going hunting; they were intent, always keeping one eye on the mounted huntsman, yawning with nervousness and with tilted noses checking the slight breeze. Copper could tell from their actions that they could scent the presence of rabbit, a cat, several house dogs, and even the faint, distant suggestion of deer as well as he, yet they made no attempt to follow these smells, which was more than could be said of some of the Master's younger hounds, who were only too prone to run trash whenever the opportunity offered.

There were crowds of people, some of them mounted and walking their horses around and around in constant circles while other horses were being unloaded from vans or held by men who chewed tobacco and smelled strongly of stables. Many of the people were on foot, and several went up to pat the hounds, who accepted the caresses good-naturedly, grinning at the people with smooth foreheads and drawn-back corners to their mouths. Some people came up to Copper; but he hated to be touched by anyone but the Master; and although he was too well bred to growl, he drew back, and the people, taking the hint, left him alone.

A little drizzle started and coat collars were turned up. Scent dropped sharply as the rain absorbed it and pulled the particles into the ground. At long last the huntsman sounded his horn and rode away, the pack following him in a compact mass, picking their way among the water-filled ruts. The men with whips came next, and then the field trailed along behind. Copper was overawed by the myriad smells, the click of the horses' hooves on the stones, the loud talking, the penetrating tobacco odor from countless cigarettes, and above all by the irritating, all-prevailing cloud of gasoline fumes from the cars, many of which started their engines and followed too.

The Master spoke to him and cut away across country, with Copper thankfully following. He was glad to get away from the variegated blanket of smells that stung his nostrils, as well as from the noise and strange sights. He thought that now he and the Master would go hunting alone, and he trotted along with relief.

The Master headed for a ridge, his boots crunching through curving tongues of frozen snow that streaked the hillside. Copper followed, stepping in the man's footmarks to save breaking through the crust. On top of the hill was a dogwood grove, barely showing behind the curtain of wind-blown rain. As they climbed higher, a wind sprang up and the rain gradually stopped. The sun broke through the clouds, casting a strange light on the fields and the rain wisps now being swept over the ridge. With the wind, scent began to rise from the ground, which was now warmer than the air. Copper could smell where a pheasant had walked through the field earlier that morning, dropped his nose to sniff briefly at a rabbit track, and then hit the line of a fox. He almost broke into a bay, the scent seemed so fresh; but an instant's check told him the scent was really a couple of hours old, only just now released by the change in temperature and the wind swirls. Even so, the fox was somewhere around. She was a vixen, and new to the country—at least Copper had never scented her before.

They reached the grove and halted. The field had been plowed here, and scenting was so bad Copper did not even trouble to cast around him. He sat down and waited beside the Master.

He could smell the horses coming, then the hounds, and then the people. Next, he could hear them. They were mounting the hill upwind of the cover. The huntsman shouted to the pack and waved his arm, whereupon they broke their tightly packed formation and bounded into the cover, spreading out as they did so. Copper could hear them charging about, and trembled with excitement. He longed to go in too, but the Master had said nothing.

Several of the hounds—puppies by their shrill voices—set up an excited clamor. Copper could hardly contain himself and even started forward, only to be ordered back. Those pups had found something, and he could hear the crashing of the older hounds as they tore through the brush to answer the call. Then came a perfect babel of sound, suddenly broken by the huntsman's tooting and the angry crack of whips. Copper could dimly see some large animals burst from the thicket and go bounding off as though they had springs in their legs. As they crossed downwind, he caught their scent. Deer. From the cover came the yelps of the pups, mingled with the gunshot-like reports of the whips. So these men were not after deer.

Suddenly there was another burst of sound, this time the deep cries of experienced old hounds. The pack were on something,

something that was unwilling to leave the cover and was doubling back and forth. The hounds were running into each other in their efforts to follow the crisscrossing trails. Whatever it was, it could not stay in there long. The Master had to grab Copper by the loose skin of his neck to control him.

A few yards away, and downwind, a shadow slipped out and fled across the plowed land. It was the same vixen he had scented on the way up. Copper saw and smelled her, gave tongue at the top of his voice, and would have given chase if the Master had not grabbed him with both hands. The hounds began to burst out of the cover, shouting with excitement. Then the horn spoke, the mounted men dashed between the flying fox and the hounds to turn them. Copper watched with anger and surprise. These men were after neither deer nor fox. What did they want?

The hounds were still questing about, but now there was no sign. Copper could hear the huntsman's voice encouraging them, and recognized the tone if not the words. Clearly the man thought that something else was still in there even though the hounds were growing discouraged. Several ran out, went over to the Master to sniff and wag their tails, and then trotted around aimlessly, hoping someone would tell them what to do. A number were gray-muzzled veterans, and if they could not own a line, the situation was bad indeed.

The huntsman was shouting now, and the Master answered him. The horn sounded, and the hounds ran to the sound. There was crashing in the cover as the huntsman rode out, calling the pack to him. When they were all clear, the Master ordered Copper into the grove.

The old bloodhound joyfully obeyed. He plunged into the tangle, yelping as the prickly twigs tore his great ears, and then began to cast around. The thicket was an almost hopeless mess of hound scents, mingled with horse and crushed herbage, yet

Copper persisted. He found the traces of the vixen's scent but ignored them, as for some reason she was not to be hunted. She had urinated in her terror, and Copper sniffed the damp earth. She was heavy in whelp and could have been run down easily, but the ways of man were inexplicable. He continued searching with head raised, hoping that in the comparatively warm thicket the scent might have risen a few inches from the fouled ground, giving him a better chance. The Master had followed him into the cover and was standing a few yards away so his scent would not add to the already polluted atmosphere. He spoke softly to the hound, urging him on.

There was a movement ahead of him, and a flood of warm scent rushed over Copper like a wave. This must be it, and in his excitement Copper gave tongue. A pheasant rocketed up under his nose, jerking out its alarm cackles as it rose. Copper cringed for the beating he knew was coming, but the Master ignored the lapse and kept repeating softly: "Go get 'em, boy. Go get 'em." Copper did his best. There were ghosts of scent everywhere, yet none distinctive enough for him clearly to identify. Still, Copper's tail began to beat hopefully as he went from one nubbin of scent to the next. The Master knew the signs, and his voice grew louder and more intense.

Little by little the conviction grew in Copper's mind that he recognized this scent. He did not dare to speak on it as yet, and sought desperately for one good spot of odor. He checked the twigs; he thrust his nose under damp logs where the scent might be lying; he scratched the earth and plunged his nose into the scratch, his great ears falling forward to make a pocket around his jowls that held every trace of odor rising from the ground. All he could get was the smell of damp earth from the recent rain, and the earth smell obliterated all other odors. He decided to trust to twigging.

Here it was! Here it was! That scent! It was, it was the odor of the fox he and the Master had sought for so long! That fox was here, or had been here a few minutes before. Now he understood why the pack had been turned away from the vixen. The mounted men, like the Master, wanted only that one particular fox. Copper almost gave tongue, but the scent was still not quite strong enough, and the mistake over the pheasant still caused him to hesitate.

Step by step, he followed the line from the twigs to the edge of the cover. Here he was stopped by the plowed land. The huntsman and his pack were on the other side of the cover, and Copper could see no signs of life as he stood with his head up, hoping to catch some air-borne scent. The Master shouted, and from some distance away came a man's voice answering. Apparently the answer was not reassuring, for the Master wanted him to return to the cover and try again. Copper refused. Faint though the scent had been, it had definitely led out of the cover to this field. Following it over the furrows was impossible, and Copper knew it, yet he decided to make the attempt. He started out into the plowed field.

Away from the shelter of the trees, he felt the full force of the wind on his right jowl. The wind was cold, but the air was still so damp it kept any scent from spreading. He would have to be right on top of a fox before he could scent the animal; and a crouching fox, lying facing the wind so the breeze did not ruffle his fur, was difficult enough to scent at any time.

Crows had begun screaming somewhere over the field. At the sound, the Master suddenly gripped him by the neck and ordered him to stand still. Copper obeyed, although he could see no reason for the command. The Master was calling urgently, yet without daring to shout, to someone. Suddenly the mechanical cawing of the crows changed to shrill screams, and increased in volume. The Master cursed and relaxed his grip.

A gust of wind swept up the hill and hit Copper full in the face. There it was! The fox! And he was running. The burst of energy had thrown his scent into the wind, and he was scudding across the field, doubtless with the crows wheeling and diving around him. The strong scent was too much for Copper. Throwing his full voice, he tore away, regardless of the Master's shouts and curses.

Within a few strides Copper ran out of the scent. He knew the fox had turned and the wind was no longer carrying the body odor to him, so he ran zigzagging, hoping to pick it up again. He could get nothing and finally halted, ashamed, while the panting Master caught up and cuffed him. In the distance he could hear men shouting, and now came the sound of the horn, dulled by the trees. The Master dragged him across the field and, pointing to a spot in a furrow, said, "Here, boy, here!" Copper applied his nose and instantly smelled where the fox had been ying. He must have stolen out of the cover, run a few yards into the field, and then, seeing mounted riders ahead of him, hidden in the furrow.

Copper promptly gave tongue; but once he left the spot where the fox had crouched, the scent vanished. The fox must have run along one of the ridges left by the plow, and the turned earth held no scent. Copper checked, and found the wind had blown the scent into the furrow beside the ridge. Here he could just barely follow it.

Copper hurried on as fast as he could. Behind him, he could hear the huntsman laying on the pack. None of them spoke, and Copper was not surprised. Not only was the scent very faint but its quality had changed considerably from the same scent lying in the dank, protected cover. Here in the open it was much more volatile, and the pack hounds probably could not immediately recognize it as the scent they had found among the dogwoods. The line was not strong enough to justify giving tongue, and besides, Copper needed all his energies simply to detect it. Even so, he gave an occasional yelp to tell the other hounds that he was indeed on the fox's trail.

The hounds recognized the cry, and several ran up and tried to find the line for themselves. When they could smell nothing, they turned away, naturally distrustful of this strange hound who was not a member of the pack and of whose scenting abilities they knew nothing. As Copper progressed, he came on small pockets of scent drawn into hollows in the furrow by heavy, warm air. Here the scent was distinct and he spoke to it clearly. The older hounds, acknowledging the authority in his voice, loped over to investigate, half a dozen loudly sniffing noses in each pocket. Ordinarily having so many hounds to help him would have been an advantage to Copper, as the more hounds spread out up and down the furrows, the more chance there would be of one of them finding a scent trace; but these animals did not have bloodhound noses and they only got in the way, to Copper's intense irritation. Several times he had to stop and snarl at them. Even the gray-muzzled old veterans were unable to match the bloodhound's marvelous nose, although they pressed to his dewlaps in trying to discover what he was trailing. The fox had jumped from ridge to ridge; so Copper had to cut back and forth to get the scent blown into the different furrows; and as the hounds had no idea what he was doing, he had to shove them aside.

Copper came to the end of the field, and hit grass. Now at long last the pack could take over, for here the scent rose strong. At the cry of the old hounds, the younger members of the pack dashed forward. At first it was only the old hounds who gave tongue, pressing forward close together to follow the narrow scent line, but as they advanced, the scent spread out from the pad marks so a dozen hounds running abreast could all carry the line. The wind was blowing so strongly that they ran not where the fox had run but nearly a hundred feet downwind of the line where the scent was being carried.

Copper was outdistanced almost at once and dropped behind, his feelings somewhat hurt, although the hound knew well that he could never keep up with these long-legged, barreled-chested animals. Actually, he was glad for a rest, as the constant strain of sniffing up the phantom traces of scent had drawn so much dust and dampness into his nostrils that saliva had begun to drip from his nose and mouth. Soon he had the satisfaction of seeing the older foxhounds drop back in their turn, letting the younger hounds rush forward, carrying a good head of scent, their puppy voices breaking into the deep, true bay of full cry.

The clouds had shredded away and the sun had broken through, so if it had not been for the wind the day would have been almost warm. Soon the sun would kill the scent, but now it served only to dry the damp air and allow the scent to rise. It was floating breast-high above the ground; and not being hampered by having to drop their heads, the pack went all out at top speed. The riders had had to go around the plowed and planted field; but now they tried to make up for lost time, and pounded past on either side, sometimes so close they made Copper flinch. Copper disliked horses anyhow, but galloping horses really frightened him.

They crossed a stream that was all one brown torrent from the melting snows. Here were several riderless horses which were especially alarming, for they tore along hysterically, quite prepared to ride down man or hound. Men were remounting, the backs of their coats plastered with mud. The Master started running, and Copper loped along behind him, appalled by the whole proceeding. Clearly none of these people knew anything about fox hunting, which Copper regarded as a highly skilled science, not a mad rush.

The fox was running dead straight, clearly making for some definite goal that might be a hole, a thick cover, or a swamp where he could escape. Even the pups knew he must be pressed hard on this soft turf where scenting was excellent . . . with a little luck they might roll him over before he reached his sanctuary. As they gained on him, the scent grew increasingly fresh and strong until even Copper put forth his best efforts, baying with the others. But the fox still had a spurt left in him. He suddenly drew ahead and made it to a stand of hardwoods. Running along fallen trunks and doubling around stumps, he brought the pack to a stop.

Now a hound was calling excitedly that he had found a trace of scent. Only a puppy though, judging by the shrill tones. Still, he sounded sure of himself. Now came the positive voice of an old hound who had run over to confirm the find. The huntsman was shouting, and hounds were running through the trees from all directions to the two finders. A tense wait. Then another hound called from a spot farther along the line. More crashings as the pack hurried to the new spot. Two more spoke, then a dozen, then came the full cry of the pack as they streamed away. The huntsman's horn gave a series of shrill toots and the riders leaned forward on their horses and galloped toward the logging paths through the woods. As there were few paths and plenty of riders, Copper was glad to be out of the jam.

The pack had broken out on the other side of the cover and were flooding down a hillside in full cry. Even though he could not see them, Copper knew they were in the open, for there were no reverberations from their cries as there had been in the woods. Apparently they were carrying a good head of scent and would run for a mile without a check, yet surprisingly the victorious voices gradually died away into total silence. Even though Copper could tell a mile away (downwind) what nearly every member of the pack was doing as long as they threw their voices, he was baffled now. They must have run completely out of scent.

An incessant tooting of the horn sounded. The Master spoke to him and together they entered the woods, following one of the paths now congested with riders smoking and talking. Once clear of the woods, Copper could see the huntsman sitting on his horse with the two whippers-in while the pack swirled around in check, tails feathering madly. The Master took Copper toward them.

Copper refused to work where the other hounds had fouled the ground, and made a quick cast on his own between the pack and the woods. The field had been planted in alfalfa, which made for good scenting, but there was no trace of fox. The fox must still be among the trees, and what those crazy hounds were doing casting about in the middle of a field Copper could not imagine. He cut back and worked the edge of the woods. Ah, there it was, faint but held by wet leaves—the fox scent. It stopped by the border of the grove and then went back. Copper followed it among the trees inch by inch, for the whole pack had so run over it, as well as the huntsman and his two whips, that the line was almost hopelessly fouled. At last he ran out of scent entirely yet still kept on, for the fox had been going in a straight line, and Copper hoped to pick up the trail eventually.

An abrupt exclamation from the Master and a quick rustle ahead of him. Knowing the Master must have seen something, Copper rushed blindly forward. Here it was! The reeking-hot track of fox! It started by the stump of an oak and led away through the trees, but Copper was not sure whether the fox had been lying on top of the stump and jumped off or whether he had run to the stump and was now on top of it. Standing on his hind legs, he smelled the top of the stump. No doubt about it now, the fox had been lying there for some time, but he was not there now. Whirling around, Copper set off on the line in full cry. He knew what had happened. The fox had run to the edge of the grove, stopped, backtracked, and jumped on the stump, where he had curled himself into a ball. The hounds, following the steaming-hot track, had rushed past him, going within a few feet of the motionless animal, yet not winding him, so concentrated were they on the line ahead. The huntsman and the whippers-in had followed the pack; and although, being mounted, they looked down on the stump and passed so close to it they could have touched the fox with their whips, the men had used their eyes no more than the hounds had used their noses, and had torn on, looking ahead. When the hounds had come to the edge of the woods, they had rushed blindly on into the open, carried by their own momentum and each hound's conviction that even though he himself could smell nothing, the rest were making such a hubbub that surely they must be hot on the trail. When they at last discovered their mistake, they were in the middle of the field, several hundred yards from the woods, and hopelessly lost. It was all very well to be fast, Copper reflected bitterly, as long as you did not overrun the line.

Copper started off on the new line as hard as he could go, hoping to keep pressing the fox and prevent the scent going stale. For once, he ran mute, although the line was strong, for he had no wish to bring up the hounds and horses until he was well away from the area fouled by their various odors. Scent was better in the woods than outside, for in the open a warm sun was making it rise higher than a hound's nose. Even so, when he came to a dead spot in the trail, Copper jumped on a log to check if even under the sheltering trees the scent might be rising. He found nothing, and therefore stayed on the ground from then on.

He reached a broad cut through the trees where a high-tension line had been run. Under the steel towers, tall grass and weeds had sprung up that should have been helpful, for the fox left not only the scent of his pads but also body scent rubbed off against the weeds as he went through them. However, the sun was shining full on the cut and although the trees broke the wind, the warm air caused turbulence that made the scent quiver as it rose, and formed tiny whirlwinds that were most confusing. Worse yet, a number of cars had been driven into the cut and one had its engine still running. The line led directly under this car, showing the cars had arrived after the fox had passed. The exhaust fumes clung to the damp grass and obliterated the fox scent. The Master, who had followed, shouted, and the driver shut off his engine. Copper crawled under the car and went on, but the scent had been killed.

Unable to follow by scent, Copper followed the fox's drift—he kept on in the same direction the fox had been going when last scented. He hit the line again under the trees on the far side of the high-tension cut, and this time felt confident enough to throw his tongue. The huntsman's horn called, whips cracked, and soon he saw the pack coming, the lead hounds leaping high to see over the tall weeds. Copper gave another cry to guide them and then voluntarily dropped back, as he was growing tired and was quite willing to let them do the hard running. The old hounds hit the line at once and crackled through the greenbrier with the youngsters hard on their tails. Copper followed at a distance, contenting himself with an occasional sniff just to make sure they were on the right line.

The fox had crossed to a cutting and run down it, and here Copper was nearly trampled by the following riders who belted down the cutting at full gallop and paid no attention to him or to the Master either. As far as Copper was concerned, this was the last time he was going hunting where horsemen were involved. At the bottom of the hill the trees stopped and open farming country spread out to the next ridge, which was also wooded. There were a farmhouse here, a barn, and a springhouse with a stream that widened into a broad, shallow pond full of arrowhead and sweet flag. A farm family was standing by the springhouse, shouting and pointing. The fox, caught between the people and the pack, must have swum the pond, for the hounds took to the water instantly, splashing through the shallows and churning the clay bottom until the water turned a dirty white. Even when swimming, the pack continued to give tongue, for the scent was floating on top of the water and they could follow it easily. Knowing where the fox must have come out, Copper cut around the pond, picked up the line, and started off on it, baying triumphantly. For a few glorious moments he was ahead of the pack, but they soon overhauled and passed him. Content with his victory, Copper dropped back and joined the Master again. Unlike the pack hounds who drove on to kill, the bloodhound was more interested in the scent than in the fox.

It was a good run over open grass fields, and the pack streamed away with the riders after them, allowing Copper and the Master to proceed with the slow dignity befitting true fox hunters. They must have gone half a mile or so when they came to a long mound of earth, made by a construction crew digging a pipe line ditch. The ditch was on the far side of the bank and beyond that was another flat field. The pack had already crossed the mound and the ditch when Copper and the Master reached it, but their baying had ceased.

Knowing something was wrong, Copper sprang to the top of the mound. Ahead of him in the field was the pack, again at check. Copper wasted no time in trying to find the line. He knew exactly what the fox had done. After crossing the mound, the fox had dropped into the ditch and run along it, knowing the hounds would jump both the mound and the ditch and keep going. Being hard pressed and wet, he was probably lying up in the ditch right now to rest, but which way had he run?

Copper jumped into the ditch and took a quick sniff. The ditch ran across the valley from ridge to ridge and the wind was blowing from the far ridge. If the fox had turned in that direction, the wind would be bringing his scent. Copper could smell nothing, so it appeared the fox had run downwind along the trench. Without a moment's hesitation, Copper turned and ran downwind. He had taken only a few strides when he hit the line. The ditch was so narrow the fox had rubbed against the sides, so there was plenty of scent. Three more bounds and he found the place, damp and reeking, from which the fox had just sprung seconds before. At once he shouted "Here it is! Hurry!" and had the satisfaction of hearing the pack racing toward him even before the huntsman's horn sounded. As the lead hounds plunged into the ditch they fell on top of him, but Copper did not care, for they hit off the scent at once and went tearing away, some in the ditch, some running along the sides. Copper's nose had told him something else—that the fox was tiring rapidly. He wondered if the pack knew it, and was relieved to hear a new note of confidence in the voices of the veterans. This was the time to press the fox as hard as possible, giving him no time to rest or play other tricks. As the fox's energy faded, his scent faded with it, and soon tracking would be almost impossible, especially in the heat of the day. The kill would have to be made quickly, and these hard-driving, fast hounds were perfectly equipped to do it.

The fox had left the trench and cut across country, for Copper saw the pack make a sudden turn and spread over the meadow, still in full cry. When the leaders began to suffer from both trailing and running at top speed, they stopped giving tongue, and the other hounds, running in the rear, recognized the signal and pushed forward to take their turn at the dual task. On the side of a hill they came to a brief check, wheeling over the slope like low-flying swallows, for the wind blowing down the grade spread and twisted the scent. Although they were silent, Copper thought they were still giving tongue, for the sound of the hound music was still ringing in his head. Then they were off again, pouring over the hilltop until even the last stragglers disappeared.

The field was considerably reduced by now, but a goodly number of riders still followed the pack. These were obviously more experienced than the original lot, for they did not crowd the hounds or make so much noise, and kept well away when the pack was finding. Copper felt he would not so much mind hunting with people like this. He and the Master followed slowly to the top of the hill, and paused. The pack was out of sight, and Copper could not hear them, listen as he would. The only sounds that came to him were the angry scolding of a jay and the distant barking of a house dog at some farm.

They plodded on and came up with a little knot of horsemen standing near the edge of a cornfield. The corn had not turned out well, and the farmer had left it standing, to the huge delight of the local wildlife. Copper could smell the pack in the corn, as well as the odor of pheasants, rabbits, and a small covey of quail. Occasionally some of the hounds would come out of the field and trot over to the horsemen with cheerfully wagging tails, only to be sternly ordered back by the whips. Copper hoped he would not have to find the line in that cornfield. With all those trash scent of birds and animals, it would be a confusing place to work.

He heard the high-pitched, staccato cry of a puppy, the same one who had found the line among the hardwoods. Clearly a pup with promise. It was immediately followed by crackling as the rest of the pack sprang through the dead stalks to the spot. Soon some of the older hounds were also speaking, but plainly it was a difficult trail to work out. When the pack finally emerged, only the lead hound was carrying the scent, working from pad mark to pad mark, while the rest followed. In the open, the other veterans were able to help, and the pack moved off at a slow yet steady lope.

In a hollow, the scent strengthened and the pack began to run, giving tongue again. Copper and the Master ran too, trailing far behind the horsemen. The pack vanished around some woods, but even as they did so the glorious cry slackened, and then changed to a short chop bark. Copper recognized the sound. They were barking "treed." The fox had either climbed a sloping tree or gone down a hole.

When he and the Master arrived, the hounds were crowded around a drain running under a gravel road. As many as could, collected in the limited space at the mouth of the drain and had their noses pointed up it while they shouted that the fox was brought to bay. At the Master's shout and with some help from the whips, they made room for Copper. He smelled at the drain's opening. Yes, the fox had gone in there, but was he still there? Copper turned and tried to work out the trail to see if the fox had backtracked, but water was running from the drain and the whole area was so fouled by hound smell he could do nothing.

The Master rattled a stick in the drain and threw in a stone. Copper quickly jostled him aside and, sticking his nose inside, inhaled deeply. There was no scent of fox, and no fox could have helped giving out a strong odor at the noise of the stick and the reverberations of the stone. Copper backed out and, lifting one leg, urinated on the drain's side to show the quarry was gone.

The Master spoke to the huntsman, who sounded his horn and took the pack in a long swing downwind. He had to make several circles, each wider than the other before any of the hounds spoke. Copper heard one of the veterans whimper, then yelp, then burst into a deep bay. Even before the huntsman spoke, Copper started running. He was rested now, and when the pack took off he was able to keep up with them for the first few hundred yards.

Half a dozen riders shouted, and the pack raised their heads at the yells, as did Copper. Then he saw the fox. He must have lain down to rest, sure that his trick at the drain would succeed. He was running awkwardly—he must have lain too long and allowed his muscles to stiffen—but still moving with small, neat strides unlike the leaping drive of the hounds, who now broke into the viewing cry. The fox's tongue was lolling, but at the fierce, bloodthirsty new cry he was able to put on a fresh burst of speed, and flashed away so that he was out of sight in seconds, bringing the pack to their noses again. Mad with excitement, Copper extended himself to his utmost, for now was the time to force the exhausted animal to the limit. With luck, they should kill within the next few minutes. Even so, he could hardly keep up with the slowest of the pack; the main body were so far ahead he could no longer see them. Then to his agony the cry died away; the pack had checked again.

Gasping and forcing his tired legs forward, Copper hurried on. The pack had to be put on the line again instantly; every moment they were at check the fox was lengthening his lead. He saw them spread over a gravel road. Judging from their wildly waving tails, they were able pick up bits of scent on the gravel, so they were not entirely at fault. That was to be expected. On the solid turf, the fox's pads left definite imprints saturated with scent; on the rough gravel only the tops of the pebbles had been touched, making tracking more difficult. Copper had no intention of trying to track the fox on the gravel. He had probably crossed directly over the road, and the line could be easily picked up on the far side.

Clearly some of the veterans had the same idea, for long before Copper could come up he heard the authoritative bay that meant "Here it is," and saw the hounds flowing off the road toward the sound. They were off again in full cry and gone before Copper reached the road. He could still hear them, but the cry was not so steady as before. The scent was fading fast now, and there were dead spots in the trail. Copper well knew the fox would pace himself by the cry of the pack, slowing to save his energies when the cry weakened. The thought infuriated him. He would have no trouble with the trail, he felt sure. If only he could keep up with these powerful racers!

Another check. This time Copper caught up with the pack. The fox had made a loop—two rings slightly overlapping each other—and the stupid hounds were running around in circles following the line. Copper wasted no time in such foolishness. He made a wide swing and picked up the line where the fox had gone on. He was about to speak on it when another scent hit him. A cool, damp wind was blowing, and in it Copper suddenly smelled the fox. The fox had made a swing and doubled back. He was really tired and making short, quick turns now. Ignoring the line entirely, Copper cut across country, following the airborne scent instead of the ground odor. The scent vanished within a few seconds, for the fox was running across wind and the breeze no longer carried his odor to Copper, but the hound kept on. As he knew he would, he hit the fresh line and bellowed for all he was worth on it. Luckily the huntsman had enough brains to put the pack to him and they took off instantly. They were only seconds behind the fox now and nothing could save him.

The cry of the hounds took on a shrill, angry note and Copper lifted his head. There was the fox. His brush hung low; his back was arched; his head was down; his jaws dripped white slime. No tricks could save him now, for the pack was hunting by sight and this time there would be no more spurts. Copper made a last effort to be in at the kill.

Forced out of his usual range, the fox was running blindly through a new housing development. There were innumerable cars, children playing on the lawns, and many houses, but Copper hardly noticed them, so intent was he on the slight form that drifted just ahead. In full cry, the pack hurled themselves forward, their voices bounding off the close-packed houses. People were running out of the doors, children were screaming with fright, and dozens of cur dogs had suddenly appeared and were barking hysterically at the oncoming hounds. No one seemed to notice the shadowy form of the silent fox as he glided through hedges, around trees, and ducked past swings and sandboxes. As the hunt tore through the development, screaming women clutched their children, and men dashed out shouting at the riders and kicking at the hounds who were trying to get past them. Utterly bewildered, Copper swerved aside, made a detour, and tried to come up with the fox again, but now there were people everywhere; and judging from the sound, the pack had gotten into a fight with the cur dogs. A car with a siren and flashing light on top came roaring down the street, and Copper decided to get out of there fast.

It took him two hours to lick himself clean, and when the Master finally returned, Copper wisely avoided him. Even before he saw him, he heard the Master's voice; and at the tone of it Copper hurried to his barrel kennel and hid there trembling. As the Master did not call him, Copper knew his fury was directed elsewhere, but even so the wise old hound decided to keep out of his way until he had had a chance to calm down.

8

Sixth Hunt—The Still Hunt

It was spring and there was a sickening stench of violets in the air, so Tod went out to look for some well-rotted manure to roll in. He found some nice seasoned cow flops in a pasture and wallowed in them happily. The rich, soft odor, so much like the partly decomposed meat he liked to feed on, flooded over him as he crushed the manure with his shoulders, and he wriggled in ecstasy for several minutes.

Tod was feeling completely content with himself and the world that spring morning. The foxhounds had never returned. They might someday, but Tod did not worry about the future. Although he never forgot a lesson learned from a danger, he did not brood. In a world full of men, dogs, guns, and traps Tod lived a happy day-to-day existence, while at the same time never relaxing his wariness. He could identify several score of odors, but until a wisp of wind brought him one of those odors, he gave it no heed.

He was feeling particularly happy that morning because after a long and diligent search he had found a large patch of saw-toothed grass and grazed it down like a sheep. He had been increasingly troubled by worms as the winter progressed, and the grass had cleaned him out, so he now experienced a feeling of well-being he had not known for weeks. Tod had good reason to feel relaxed. At this time of year there were no traps set, no one was hunting him, there was plenty of food, and the vixen had recently given birth to a fine litter of pups in a den Tod had selected himself. Tod had picked out a den among a heap of boulders that could not be dug out, and even better, to Tod's way of thinking, it had no less than eight escape tunnels, all well hidden even though the main entrance itself was clearly visible. Tod and his vixen had not constructed this elaborate underground maze themselves; it had been used by generations of foxes, now all gone. He had simply fallen heir to it, and the vixen had meekly accepted his choice. In addition, they knew the location of half a dozen other suitable dens so that at the first hint of danger she could move the pups elsewhere while Tod acted as decoy for the men and dogs. Tod's only real problem was his spring shedding. Because the hair was coming out in great patches, he was almost bare on the flanks. The matted winter undercoat itched him abominably, and he tore out the tangled tufts with angry jerks of his lean jaws.

Finishing with the manure, he trotted to the top of a hogback ridge where there was always a crosscurrent of air, to get the early-morning scent picture. The low-lying mists were still clinging to the tops of the black oaks, and Tod's long brush was damp with dew before he reached the ridge. He sat down with his brush curled around his feet to look out over the valley. Starlings were popping in and out of the grass around the feeding cattle, roosters were crowing in a distant farmyard, and a red squirrel raved at him from a nearby oak with a locust-like buzz, his tail and hind legs jerking convulsively. The sound annoyed Tod and, lying down, he pretended to go to sleep. The action confused the squirrel. After even angrier protests, he came down and darted past the motionless fox. When Tod still refused to move, the squirrel came closer and closer, until at last in his determination to get some reaction from the seemingly dead fox, he approached to within a few feet. In an instant Tod was on his feet and charging. The squirrel tried to run and then to dodge, but Tod's scissor-like jaws caught him by the neck. Tod shook his little victim savagely until the body went limp. He ate the head and then loped off with the body in his mouth to find a good place to bury it.

He selected a spot along a hedge netted by silver cobwebs, dug a hole, and interred his prey, sweeping the dirt in and tamping it down with his nose. He heard a distant horn and stopped frozen into alertness, but it was not the fox hunter's horn; it was blown by the master of a beagle pack exercising his hounds. After the second toot Tod recognized the sound, for he had often heard it before. Having nothing to fear from the little hounds, he relaxed and continued on his way.

He checked a few scent posts, heard the thump of a rabbit, and swung out of his path to investigate, even though he knew the thump meant the rabbit had seen him. Just for sport, he chased the flickering white tail until the rabbit went down a hole. Tod was checking off when he heard a commotion underground that interested him. He bounded back to the hole and found that a woodchuck was in occupancy and was blocking the rabbit's progress. Tod instantly started to dig, his forefeet flying. He forced himself down the hole and, by making a long stretch, was just able to grab the rabbit by the rump. He backed out, dragging the rabbit with him in spite of the wretched bunny's ear-piercing screams, and killed him. Afterward he played with the body for a long time until, reminded of his marital duties, he picked up the rabbit and headed for his den.

Swinging around carefully to be downwind of the boulder heap, he galloped up the hillside stained with flowers. After listening at the mouth of the burrow, he dropped the rabbit inside. This was the vixen's first litter, and she was so fascinated and worried over her offsprings that she never came out. She had done such a good job of licking the fetal fluid off them after birth she had nearly ended by eating the pups themselves, and Tod was rather concerned about her. She had begun to steady down now, but Tod was relieved when he heard her come up the pipe and drag the rabbit down into the main den. He listened with his head cocked on one side until he heard the mewlings of the pups, and then trotted off contentedly to lie up some fifty yards from the den where he could keep an eye and nose on things. The sun was high in the heavens now, making the fresh morning scents stale and hot, so there was nothing to do until evening.

At dusk he rose and stretched, shooting out his claws, and then went over to sniff at the den. He heard nothing, but because the smells were all right he went out on his night's hunting in a cheerful frame of mind. In a field, he came on the tracks of a woodchuck who had traveled back and forth between two holes several hundred yards apart, apparently unable to make up his mind which to use for a den. Tod walked meticulously in the chuck's tracks—as the chuck had a shorter stride Tod was obliged to shorten his own stride to make his pads fit in the imprints—and enjoyed this game so much that after coming to where the chuck had gone down one of the holes, he turned and made a round trip, still stepping exactly in the tracks.

Tiring of the sport, he continued on. By a pond, he came upon a Canada goose who had left her precious nest and eggs to do a little grazing on the tender new grass. She regarded Tod suspiciously, while he, knowing she would immediately take off and land in the pond if he rushed at her, pretended the most elaborate unconcern. He seemed intrigued by every stone and patch of grass, snuffing at each carefully while all the time approaching the goose by a circuitous course. She gradually became convinced that he had no interest in her, and continued her feeding. Tod edged closer and closer, until finally he was able to make his rush. He sprang for her neck, but the goose threw herself backward, honking loudly, and managed to beat him off with her wings. Her cries were instantly answered from the pond, and the gander rushed up the bank and went for Tod, hissing in fury. An infuriated gander was more than Tod was prepared to handle and he turned to run, but there was a fence line here that made a sharp bend, and the gander rushed him into the angle. For a few seconds Tod got a real fright, for the gander was beating him with the knobby elbows of his wings and stabbing him with his piledriver beak, and the combination was murderous. At last Tod managed to break away, and fled across the meadow with the gander in pursuit. Once in the open, Tod could easily outdistance the bird; his fright over, he even turned to play with the gander, making little darts at him and swinging away at the last instant while the gander charged him with cup-bent wings and lunging neck. When the bird saw he could not catch the fox, he retreated with dignity to the pond where his wife was already afloat. Tod ran along the bank watching them, and then loped off as though finished with the game.

Tod had been bored lately, and now that he was recovered from the shock of the gander's savage attack, he rather enjoyed the excitement of the engagement. Swinging around, he stole back toward the pond, taking care to keep downwind, for he did not know that the birds could not smell him. He crept to the top of a little rise and lay there in the fast-gathering darkness, watching them. He lay fully stretched out, his long nose between his extended forepaws, his ears up, and an eager expression on his face, his lips pulled back in a half grin. If ever a fox looked "foxy," Tod was that fox.

Motionless as a stone, he saw the goose swim to a high bank on one side of the pond and climb it to her nest. She carefully removed the gray down with which she had covered the eggs and, after elaborate wrigglings and twistings, sat down to brood. Still not moving a hair, Tod studied the lay of the land. Then he glided off the hill and crept toward the unconscious goose. Rainwater runoff on the slope had made a shallow trench, and at first Tod was able to crawl along that, but then the trench ended and he was forced to cover the last few yards on the almost bare slope. It was almost completely dark now and he inched along by means of gentle pushes with his elbows, nose touching the ground. By imperceptible degrees he reached the nest and softly inserted one exquisite paw under the goose as gently as he had brushed dirt off the trap pans. He found an egg and worked it out until he could slide his thin, pointed nose in and grab it. The goose shifted her weight and gargled to herself, but did not realize what was going on. As soon as he had the egg in his mouth, Tod hastily backed away and then turned and ran.

He went to one of his favorite eating places, for although Tod would eat anywhere, he had certain spots he preferred. Chewing open one end of the egg, he licked out the contents and then gamboled around the empty shell in triumph. The whole adventure had contained just enough danger to give it spice. Hugely content with himself, and glowing with a feeling of well-being, he continued on his rounds.

Tod was so delighted with his smartness that he played with rather than hunted the game, and it was only when the stars began to wash out and the dawn breeze stirred the aspens that he realized he had a family to feed. Sobered, he headed for one of the several housing developments that had mushroomed in the neighborhood over the past year or so. Tod at first had been highly suspicious of these places; but his inveterate curiosity had caused him to investigate them and he had found that they were an excellent source of food.

He went to the nearest and made a cursory check of several yards that a few weeks before had had pens containing rabbits, chicks, and ducklings. Tod had cleared them all out long ago and they had never been restocked. Still, there was always the chance. He then jumped up on a porch railing and ran along it. A parakeet had been left out in its cage here one night, and Tod had attended to it. Nothing like that had happened again, but Tod always investigated. Being thirsty and liking milk, he went to several doorsteps where milk bottles had been left. With quick, hard blows of his long nose, Tod drove in the cardboard lids and lapped up the milk as far as his thin muzzle could reach, going from one bottle to another until he was satisfied.

He then made a tour of the garbage cans. By standing on his hind legs and bracing his forefeet against the side of a can, he could pry off the lid with his all-purpose nose. In one can, Tod found a real prize. A chicken carcass had been thrown away, still with plenty of meat on it. Tod collected the carcass and also picked out several tidbits, which he inserted inside the carcass as though stuffing it. Then with the carcass in his mouth he started off.

He had only gone a few yards when a house dog that had been sleeping in its kennel came tearing out, screaming its stupid head off. Tod could easily have outdistanced the dog, but he had begun to think of the development as part of his range—he had left his scent marks on several bushes and fence posts—and the sudden outburst gave him a bad scare and made him furious. Dropping the chicken, he swiveled around and went at the dog with a fury far greater than its own. Astonished, the dog turned and fled, his angry cries turning into frightened yips. Tod gave him a good slash on the flank with one of his long, protruding canines and then went back, picked up the chicken, and beat a hasty retreat. He hated noise and disturbance, and there might be bigger dogs around.

He dropped the chicken at the mouth of the den and waited until he saw the black nose of the vixen appear, sniff at it, and then caught the quick flash of her white teeth as she seized the carcass and pulled it in. Satisfied that she had accepted his offering, he headed for his lying-up spot.

Peaceful day followed peaceful day until the time came when the pups were able to walk and make short excursions from the den. As they grew stronger and more confident, the pups might come out at any time of day, but they were always nervous and jumpy until twilight. When the long shadows stretched out, and there was no glare and the cool of the evening tempered the breathless heat of the day, they would tumble out and frolic on the yellow fan of hard-packed earth, oblivious to danger. At such times the vixen would lie out above the den and watch them with a devoted, happy expression that was as clearly defined as Tod's mischievous grin when he was watching the geese. Tod kept clear at such times, standing sentinel in case of trouble, but he also enjoyed the pups; and if one of them got involved with a pinching bug or was frightened by a yellow jacket feeding on one of the half-eaten carcasses that strewed the den area, Tod was on to his feet and ready go to the pup's help even more quickly than the vixen.

The only bad days for the pups were rainy days. The older foxes accepted the rain philosophically, but the active pups, cooped up in the den, were miserable. One pup would crawl up the entrance burrow and sit with the raindrops pelting off the end of his nose, dolefully regarding the weather and wishing it would clear. Before long, one of his litter mates would drag him away by his brush and take his place, hoping to detect some change in the weather. When the sun did finally break through, what rejoicing! No matter what time of day it was, the whole litter would come bobbing out to cavort in the open, glad to be at liberty after the imprisonment of the den. Even the damp earth that clung to their pads and brushes was a small price to pay for the chance to stretch their long legs.

Tod was an excellent provider—too good. He brought in far more food than the family could eat, and the den area became littered with putrefying carcasses surrounded by haloes of buzzing bluebottles. Although the foxes enjoyed the smell of carrion, ultimately the den became too odoriferous even for them, and they moved to another burrow. By now the pups were half grown, and old enough to travel on their own. They followed their parents to the new quarters in single file, each pup stepping conscientiously in the paw marks ahead of him so that to a casual observer only one fox would seem to have passed.

Now came the training period. At first, training was indistinguishable from play. When playing, the pups bounced around like woolly balls as they attacked beetles and chased crickets, yet even so they were coordinating their muscles and learning skills that would later stand them in good stead when handling a rabbit or woodchuck. Their play was really a form of exploration and experimentation, for after mastering one technique they would then try another, dropping any that were unsuccessful and retaining any that worked. Generally one lesson was enough of either success or failure, and the pups never forgot either. Even when completely relaxed, the pups were still learning, for their restless eyes and noses were always at work, picking up new sights and smells. They learned to distinguish between taste and smell—no easy task, for these two senses are coordinated. At first, they "handled" everything with their teeth and tongue to get the taste of it. Later, one quick sniff told them all they needed to know. They also learned from each other, realizing when one had made a mistake in tackling one of the crippled animals the parents brought in, and trying a different system when their turn came.

They watched their parents and duplicated their actions. Although very few vocal commands were ever given, the foxes were able to communicate an astonishing amount of information by their brushes, facial expressions, body movements, angle of ears, and even by their fur—when raised it meant danger. They could register fear, anger, joy, submissiveness, and jealousy. The pups learned to know that the screaming of crows or the buzz of a red squirrel meant something was coming. They learned always to get downwind of anything they were curious about. They learned that the den always meant safety and that going to ground was the best of all protections—a lesson they never forgot and one that Tod had never learned because he had been raised by man.

When the time came for their first formal lessons in hunting, either Tod or the vixen took them out one at a time, as foxes never hunt in packs, only in pairs. The first quarry was mice. Watching, the cubs learned that as soon as a mouse was smelled or heard, you stopped with lifted brush (the correct angle of the brush was important, as you needed it to balance you when you sprang). When the exact spot was located to a pinpoint, then came the long, stiff-legged jump with the brush thrown to one side as a counterweight. If you missed, you made a quick series of hard, short jumps to make the mouse move, as it was probably lying motionless, hoping to escape unnoticed.

Although the male pups were more aggressive and venturesome, it was a little vixen who first caught big game. On the same pond where the geese lived there were a number of mallards, some permanent residents and some visitors who dropped in mornings and evenings. Early one morning while Tod's mate and the young vixen were returning from a night's hunting, the little vixen ran down to the pond and began to rush back and forth along the bank, staring curiously at the ducks. The ducks were not frightened—they knew perfectly well that as long as they stayed in the water they were quite safe—but they automatically set up the alarm cry, following the fox around the pond much as the hen pheasant had followed Tod's first mate through the pines.

The young fox began to play with them, making graceful, curving bounds, running in circles, and even lying on her back to pat at her brush with both paws. These were the same motions she made when playing with her litter mates, and she wanted the ducks to play with her. She was naturally playful and had gone through this routine when she first saw sheep and had tried to do it when she first encountered a dog, until the old vixen's actions showed her that dogs were dangerous. The ducks were charmed. They raised their wings and sat back on their rumps to see better. Then they swam in closer and closer, flirting their tails with excitement as they came. The little vixen ran a few yards along the shore to encourage them to chase her, and the whole flock hurried after, pushing each other out of the way. By now they had forgotten she was a fox; she seemed only a strange creature behaving in a curious but intriguing fashion.

The ducks were so close in that now the vixen pup, who was rubbing first one shoulder and then the other in the soft sand, could have reached them with a single bound. At such close range their smell was strong, and the luscious scent made her mouth water. She now thought of the ducks as food rather than as playmates. She crouched, the tip of her brush twitching like a cat's tail.

Most of the flock at once sensed the change, and hastily swam away. One drake, only a yard from the crouching fox, was scratching his head with one foot. His eyes were closed. The vixen sprang. There was a series of terrified quacks, and the vixen hauled her catch ashore, straining with all four feet to keep the drake from dragging her into the pond. She had him by the base of the neck and could not shift her grip without letting him go, yet with that hold she could not kill him. The drake would have eventually torn himself loose and escaped, but the mother vixen came to her daughter's help and broke the struggling drake's neck with a sharp twist. Even then the pup did not know what to do next, and the mother had to break open the drake for her. From then on, the young vixen would deliberately go into her dance to lure ducks ashore, and never made the mistake of crouching before she sprang. She especially liked the wings, and chewed off the feathers near the nubs, leaving the sheared ends scattered in a circle around her.

It had been a warm, dry spring, and many of the housing developments had planted little truck gardens, so there were plenty of rabbits about. Even though Tod and the vixen often killed a dozen rabbits a night, burying those the pups could not eat, they still made no impression on the population. As a result, hawks and owls began to move into the area in great numbers. Often during their hunting, the foxes would hear the prolonged, agonized screaming of a rabbit in the grip of great talons. Assured of an easy meal, the parents would instantly dash toward the sound, drive off the winged predator, and appropriate the catch. The pups soon learned to do the same, and always had one ear cocked for a rabbit's scream. The parents had trouble teaching them to hunt live rabbits, as robbing the raptors seemed to the pups a much easier way of making a living.

The pups were now hunting mainly on their own, although the family still used the den area as a rallying ground, for the litter were not entirely independent. First one and then another of the pups failed to turn up at the family get-togethers. This vaguely worried the vixen, although Tod paid no attention to the truants. When winter came he would have to drive the male pups, at least, off the range, so the sooner they left of their own volition, the better.

Tod was trotting along a timbering slash with a rabbit in his mouth, looking for a good cache spot, when he heard the distant squeal of a rabbit. The sound was far away—although Tod could spot the position of a mouse's squeak with great accuracy, he had difficulty establishing the location of distant noises—and he ignored it. But the cry was repeated over and over again. At last Tod could resist the appeal no longer. He made a quick job of burying the rabbit, leaving both ears protruding from the hastily shoveled-in earth, and loped off to investigate.

Even so, he was still ultracautious. He slipped from one cover to another, stealing along behind tangles of blackberry bushes and taking advantage of every depression that offered a chance of concealment. Somehow the squealing of this rabbit did not sound exactly right, and Tod had a keen ear for such matters. He circled the spot carefully, and as he came downwind of the noise he tasted the taint of man in the air.

Even so, Tod did not run. His curiosity was even stronger than his fear. He sneaked through the cover toward the sound, taking elaborate precautions. Finally he reached a spot near whence the sound was proceeding. A slight motion caught his eye, and he instantly dropped and lay immobile, but his eyes were busy. There was something there and it was alive and it was not a rabbit.

Tod had to watch for some time before he recognized the Man. The Man was sitting behind a small bush, and kept almost as motionless as did Tod, but at intervals he raised something to his lips. When he did, there came the scream of a rabbit. After a few calls, the Man lowered the object, and waited. Then he repeated the performance. It was only when the Man moved that Tod was able to identify him, except by smell. Otherwise, he blended in with the bush.

If the Man was patient, Tod was equally so. He would have lain and watched indefinitely, trying to decide what the Man was doing, but he did not have long to wait. There came a rustling in the undergrowth, and one of his half-grown pups burst out into the open, looking around eagerly for the rabbit. With one swift, easy motion the Man raised a gun beside him, and fired. Tod never twitched a whisker at the explosion as he saw the pup leap stiff-legged into the air, whirl around, drag himself a few feet, and then collapse. The Man walked over to the dying pup and pressed the life out of him with one booted shoe.

Tod had seen enough. He wiggled backward away from his lookout position, then turned and glided away through the cover. Not until winter set in with full force, and made hunting difficult, did he pay any attention to rabbit screams.

A few weeks later there was only one pup left. Tod knew well what was happening to them, but there was no way he could convey his knowledge to the vixen or to the remaining pup. The vixen was frantic, and spent long hours following the trails of the missing pups through the woods, trying to locate them. Tod knew it was useless, yet only by ignoring the calls himself and refusing to join her in the tracking could he attempt to transmit his knowledge.

One evening while Tod was investigating one of his scent posts he heard the agonized scream of a fox pup. It might be his or some other pup, but Tod never hesitated. He raced toward the sound madly, his mane standing up with rage and his teeth bared, knowing only that the pup was in desperate straits, perhaps in the clutches of a dog or an owl. He struck a game trail through the forest and flashed along it, for the first time reckless of possible danger. The sound was growing louder every second and he had almost reached the spot when he saw the vixen cut in front of him. She, too, had heard the tortured cry and was racing to the rescue.

Ahead were a clearing and the remains of a lumberman's cabin. It was from this clearing the cry was coming. The vixen exploded out of the cover and paused for a moment to look around, standing with one forepaw upraised and her ears cocked. Instantly there came the stinging crack of a rifle. The vixen dropped where she stood, dead before she hit the ground.

Tod turned just in time. The plaintive cry of the pup still continued, and in spite of his terror, Tod circled the clearing. Now, together with the scent of the gunpowder, he could smell the Man. Tod saw him walking now. He went over and picked up the vixen. Then he went to a square box that had a spinning turntable on top of it and lifted some stick-like object. At once the noise of the pup's crying ceased. The Man then took a flat disk from the turntable, blew carefully over it, and replaced it. He pressed a button on the side of the box, and the pup's crying continued.

Tod now could tell that the sound of the crying was coming from a large horn-shaped thing lying some distance from the box. He lay watching and listening until the record was over. At last the Man put the record carefully in an envelope, disconnected the amplifier, and carried it and the phonograph to a car. Taking the vixen's body with him, he drove away.

Tod had no idea what was going on, but by listening intently he was able to realize that the crying was not precisely the sound made by a fox pup in pain. It had an artificial quality coming from the horn, and he could also pick up slight surface noises from the record. In the following weeks he heard the pup's crying repeated several times in different parts of his range, but after listening a few seconds he was able to identify the recording. He was never fooled again.

When winter came, the traps reappeared; but Tod was trapwise now, and regarded the trapline as a source of food rather than as a menace. Several times he was chased by small packs of dogs from the housing developments, and Tod actually enjoyed fooling these idiots. He would perform some simple trick to give himself a brief lead and then lay down a perfect cat's cradle of tracks, only to jump clear at the end and canter off to the top of a little hill where he could watch the fun. As the baffled dogs ran in futile circles trying to unravel the maze, Tod would sit in plain sight, watching them and grinning broadly. As the curs' bafflement increased, he could no longer contain himself; but would stand up on his hind legs to see better, and prance with delight at their frustrated rage. When they showed signs of giving up in discouragement, he would run a few paces down the hill and give his short, sharp bark to attract their attention. Then as the pack took after him in full cry, he would whisk away to repeat the trick elsewhere. The dogs usually grew tired of the game before Tod did.

The first snowfall came early that year. Tod was lying up on the hogback ridge under the black oaks and did not even take the trouble to move as the flakes came drifting down, except to bury his nose deeper in his brush-blanket. When dawn came, he found two inches of soft snow covering the ground that scarcely impeded his movements at all. He went hunting and caught a rabbit sleeping too tight in a raspberry thicket where the bunny had been shielded from the storm. Full and content, Tod returned to his old lying-up place under the dead pine, and dozed off.

He lay fast asleep, unmindful of the noises around him. A squirrel ran along the dead pine, his claws scratching loudly on the bark, but Tod slept on. A buck and two does trotted past, and Tod never moved a muscle. From the woods came a loud snap as a dead limb cracked in the frost. Tod was too fast asleep to hear it. The noises of humans came: men shouting to each other on a farm, the sound of an ax in the woods, the swish and roar of cars on a highway. Tod was dead to the world.

Then came a faint—oh, so very faint—grinding sound: the sound of snow packing under the gentle tread of a man's boots. Tod was gone in a wink. He did not stop to look back; he did not worry about heading into the wind. He went all-out, for he knew that sound meant danger. In seconds he was over the nearest ridge.

Once he was protected by the ridge, Tod slowed down and swung around to watch his back track. It was possible that the human meant no harm and would not follow him. The man had come from downwind or Tod would have scented him long before he heard him, so Tod had been running upwind. He had to circle to get downwind of the intruder so his nose could help his eyes.

A fleck of snow leaped up beside him, and with it came the report of a gun. Tod shied sideways. The shot came from his side of the ridge, so it could not have been fired by the man he had heard; but beyond that, Tod did not know from where it had been fired. At random, he swerved to the left. As he did so, he caught the unmistakable scent of man right ahead. Tod turned again and ran back. There was something standing on a rise of ground ahead, but whether it was a man or not Tod could not tell, and the wind was against him. As he ran toward it, he saw the figure move to bring up a gun, and Tod instantly recognized it as a human. There were three men, one on either side of him and one following. Again Tod turned and ran in his original direction, going all-out.

Another shot, and a hole appeared in the snow almost under his nose. At the same instant, Tod could smell the hot metal and stench of powder. He ran as he had never run before. Another shot sounded far behind him, and where this bullet went he had no idea.

Tod ran for nearly a mile before slowing down. This time he jumped on a stump to watch his back track. He watched for half an hour, and when nothing moved he decided the men had given up the pursuit. He started off to look for another lying-up place, zigzagging back and forth as he quartered the area to find a good spot. At last he picked a location at the base of a choke-cherry where the wind had left a spot fairly free of snow. He curled up but still continued to watch the back trail.

An hour passed and Tod dozed off again. Then he heard the angry scolding of a jay, and was instantly alert. He saw the figure of man moving on his left and almost at the same time another coming up on his right. Tod watched them without moving. The men came on and on. Then he saw, farther away, the third man. This man was following his track in the snow.

Tod had a wide range of vision, so he could watch all three men at the same time without moving his head. The tracker came to where Tod had begun his zigzag, and stopped. He waved his hand to the others and pointed down. They waved back and started forward while the tracker stood still, waiting until they were well advanced.

Tod saw the man on his left suddenly stop, stare at him, and then start to raise his gun. Tod waited for no more. He ducked around the tree and started running again. This time there was no shot.

Tod went nearly three miles before lying up. He deliberately chose a hazel thicket heavily overgrown with wild rose, and hid in the heart of it. For a long, long time he remained awake and listening, but finally, deciding the chase was surely over, he fell asleep.

Here there was no jay to scream a warning. Instead, he heard the crackle of the bushes on either side of him. Tod waited only long enough to make certain of the men's positions and that the tracker was with them, before slipping away. This time he did not rely on half measures. He kept right on going; and when he did finally lie up, he broke his invariable rule of always going into the wind to make a great U and lie up where he could not only see but also smell his back trail. Even so, he lay awake until it was almost dark, but the men had given up.

Tod now added the technique of still hunting to his list of dangers. He realized it was not the tracker who was the menace but the men on the flanks. Running from the tracker, it was easy to ignore the presence of the two men ahead and on either side. So from now on when he was disturbed, Tod ran with an eye out to both the right and left.

In late November there was a heavy snow that seriously inconvenienced Tod until a crust formed and he could run across it. Even so, it was so deep that he was unable to dig down to his caches except with the greatest difficulty, and if it had not been for the garbage cans in the developments he would have been hard put to it to make a living.

He was returning one morning from a night of can pilfering when he heard a curious noise. *Ding! Dong!* it went. Then again, *ding, dong, ding!* Tod paused to listen, head cocked to one side, a dainty black foot raised, his ears straight up. The sound was repeated over and over. The constant repetition drove Tod mad with curiosity. He started toward it.

The sound was getting closer. It did not sound dangerous, and Tod might have kept on had he not noticed a ridge that offered him a better view. He turned off and made for the ridge. Even from this elevation he could not see what was making the remarkable noise. *Ding, dong, ding, dong.* It was coming through an alder swamp, not frozen solid. Tod decided to run down and meet it.

As he began to move, he saw the Man come out from among the alders and move forward across an open field. He was swinging something in his hand that gave off the ringing note. Tod watched him go by, and then, still fascinated, trotted down over the snow crust and followed in his footprints. The Man had a gun over his shoulder, but surely he could not be up to harm, behaving in this fantastic way. Consumed by curiosity, Tod pressed close behind the figure until they were scarcely twenty feet apart. So they traveled across the open field, the Man stopped at intervals to ring the bell and stare out across the flats; and each time he stopped, Tod also stopped and stared too, wondering what the Man could be looking for. When the Man resumed walking, Tod walked too, stepping exactly in his tracks.

The Man came to a road where a car was parked. With a groan, he opened the door, threw the bell inside, and then broke open his shotgun and unloaded it. He dropped the shells into his pocket, took a case out of the car, and carefully put the gun away. All the while, Tod stood not fifteen feet behind him, watching intently, turning his head from one side to the other the better to follow the Man's actions. What could he be about?

The Man replaced the gun case in the car and shut the rear door. Then he turned to open the front door by the wheel. As he did so, he saw Tod standing behind him, watching him with a friendly, interested expression on his lean face. The Man stood staring at the fox, and then lifted his head to survey the broad expanse of snow-covered meadow, unbroken except for his own footprints with Tod's dainty tracks in each one where the fox had been following him only a few feet away.

Then the Man began to talk. Tod, listening intently, thought he detected a note of irritation in the voice. The magical spell was broken. In an instant, Tod became a wild animal again. He turned and fled across the snow crust, going like a drifting cloud shadow. Even when he was safe over the nearest ridge, Tod was still unsatisfied. His curiosity was unassuaged. Whatever had that Man been ringing that bell for? It was an entrancing problem.

9

Seventh Hunt—Coursing with Greyhounds

As the years passed, the countryside began to change, and Tod hated changes, especially changes like this. His was basically a world of sound and scent; and when the sounds and scents altered, he felt lost and bewildered. Also, although he could see considerable distances when on some elevation, in running his route he went from one fixed object to another because he was small and his view was cut off by bushes, hedges, and even tall grass. Now he found his familiar trails cut by highways, new buildings, and other strange objects, and he had no idea how to get around them to resume his old course.

Every year, scenting grew more difficult. Huge, stinking bull-dozers had moved in, tearing the guts out of the land, and when they were finished they left great, glaring rivers of concrete over which poured a constant flow of traffic, filling the air with fumes that polluted all other odors. Most of the trees had been cut down, and the air was drier, hotter, and lifeless. Hunting grew increasingly difficult, for the animals not run over on the highways had migrated to more open country. The farmers had followed them, and nearly all the farms were gone now, their places taken by the housing developments or by gigantic factories that added their quotas of filth to the atmosphere.

The people who were moving in were unlike any of the people Tod had ever known. They came in great hordes, as though fleeing some terrible natural catastrophe, like animals running before a forest fire. As with all fugitives, there was an air of panic about them. Instead of going about standard tasks like the farmers, they rushed around in pointless activities, always in automobiles. They raised no food, they kept no livestock—except countless dogs—and as the houses increased, the groundwater level sank until the earth was hard under Tod's feet. There was an unpleasant taste to the streams; the fish were dead; and the wild plants that had once been a stable part of Tod's diet grew increasingly difficult to find.

Yet Tod lingered on. This was his beloved home, his range for which he had fought, the place where he had known so much happiness and so many triumphs. Changed though it was, there were still a few trees, a few bushes and a few rocks he could remember ever since he was a pup, and he clung to them. He could not be happy anywhere else. All the foxes of his generation were dead or gone, but he could not bear the thought of seeking a new range. He was too old to start life over.

Although most of the other animals had gone, there were foxes in plenty. They were not like the foxes of the old days; they were more like alley cats, for they had become complete scavengers. They looted garbage pails, hung around the dumps looking for scraps, and knew exactly when the newly built grocery stores put out their refuse. Not one of them could have caught a rabbit to save his life, or stalked a field mouse. Yet they proliferated at an amazing rate, often building their dens under garages or among the junkyards that now littered the landscape. At one time, it was highly unusual for a litter of fox pups to live through a winter; finding food was too hard, and trappers, gunners, and hounds took their toll. Now there was no trapping, the new people had no guns, and the packs had long since disappeared. On the other hand, food was plentiful, and even the most witless pup could find garbage in the dumps. So the foxes increased at an alarming rate even though they were mangy, rickety, and stupid.

Tod avoided this new generation. He hated the odor of slops that clung to them, and their skulking, catlike ways. Although in the rutting season he would breed the vixens—and often more than one—he took little interest in them or their progeny. The old thrilling courtship through the deep woods and the brave battles with worthy opponents were gone; these creatures were openly promiscuous, and none of the scrawny, flea-ridden males dared to stand up to him, although sometimes a number of them would attack in a gang if they could catch him in one of the maze of passages through the junkyards that they knew so well. As there was now no need for a pair of foxes to hunt together as a team or for the males to catch game for the vixens and their pups—food being provided free by a benevolent society—there was no bond between the couples except momentary sexual gratification. Once the longer a pair lived together, the better they learned to know each other's almost invisible signals, the partner's hunting methods, and the range. Now there was no need for communication; there was no hunting, no range. Therefore there was no need for monogamy.

Of the human beings Tod had once known by sight or smell, there was left only the old trapper who had tried for so many years to catch him, ever since the death of the Trigg hound so long ago. The trapper had only one hound left, old Copper, who lived in the shack with him, for the hillside where the barrel kennels had once been was covered with new houses. The trapper had nothing but a tiny patch of land left around his cabin, and on every side the new developments were pressing in on him. The trapper, Copper, and Tod were the last three living creatures in the district who could still remember the old days and loved them. Everything else was new, alien, and bent on destruction.

When winter came, the old man and his old hound would still set out after Tod through what little open land was still left. They usually started out after a night snowfall, and Tod had gotten to expect them. When he awoke in the morning to find a sprinkling of fine, powdered snow on the ground, Tod would run to the nearest hogback to look for the two. If they did not come, Tod would feel upset and go looking for them. He recognized them as dangers, but even so they were part of his life, and he missed them. Besides, they were the only danger left, and Tod enjoyed dangers as long as they did not become too dangerous.

When spring came that year, the rains did not come with it. Tod went to all the usual places where the first spring buds and long grasses had always grown, but this year he was hard put to find any. Even the tough, cleansing saw grass he depended upon to rid him of worms after the long winter diet of meat was rare. At least, he had the satisfaction of not having to share his finds with any of the other foxes. They knew nothing of these woods foods, and ate garbage winter and summer.

June continued hot and dry, and by July Tod had trouble finding water for the first time in his life. The streams were now run through culverts and used as sewers, and the ponds had been drained to make room for the houses. Tod knew of a few pools in the woods, but these were dry now and he had to dig to find moist earth he could chew. He took to licking stones damp with earth-morning dew and ate the bulblike roots of May apple and snakeroot for moisture. There were still mice and a few rabbits and squirrels around; and now when Tod made a kill, he first eagerly lapped the blood of his quarry and then, breaking it open, drank the water in the bladder. So, in spite of the drought, he was able to maintain himself while waiting for the precious rain.

One night while making his rounds, Tod heard the barking of a fox. For a fox to bark at this time of year was strange enough, and never had Tod heard a bark like this. The voice was hoarse and choked, sending out no message, and ended in a series of long howls. Puzzled, Tod stopped and listened with his head turned slightly toward the sound. Then, driven by his still potent curiosity, he loped toward the cry.

He found the fox in the center of a little clearing. It was a wretched-looking animal, one of the scavengers, and standing with arched back and head down, barking. Then came the awful howls. Tod started at it unbelievingly.

Suddenly the fox began to snap at the air as though catching invisible flies. Bemused, Tod drew closer. The moon struck the surface of an exposed bit of quartz, making it glimmer, and the strange fox rushed to the stone, biting it. Lured on by this remarkable performance, Tod took a few steps closer.

The fox saw him now, and ran forward, crouching and whimpering. This was female procedure, but Tod was quite sure by the stranger's smell that he was a male. Tod tried to circle the creature to smell his anal glands, but the fox kept turning toward him, still going through a submissive procedure. Slowly Tod realized the stranger was begging for help. He was not in a trap and he did not seem to be pursued by an enemy. Tod could not imagine what was wrong.

The stranger fell on his side and clawed at his throat with his forepaws. Tod could hear him gasping for breath. Tod reared up on his hind legs and struck at the stranger with his stiff forelegs, partly because he thought the stranger wanted to play and partly out of sheer confusion. The stranger continued to roll on the ground, choking. Then, suddenly and unaccountably, he leaped to his feet and started to run. He passed so close to Tod that his brush touched, but the stranger paid no attention to him and vanished among the trees. Tod stood nonplused, listening to the stranger crash through the underbrush as recklessly as one of the stupid dogs. When the sounds ceased, Tod went over and gingerly smelt the stranger's trail. It told him nothing, and after checking to make sure the creature had left no urine or feces that might be more informative, Tod went on his way.

A few mornings later, Tod was cutting across the lawn of one of the new houses after a night of mediocre hunting when a rabbit, mad with terror, dashed past him. Tod swiveled around and was after him in a fraction of a second, but the rabbit knew of a special hole in the picket fence, and dived through it, leaving Tod running up and down on the far side. Baffled, Tod turned away just as a fox exploded out of an ornamental yew hedge and rushed across the lawn.

Tod hesitated a moment, watching the newcomer. The fox's lower jaw hung down, his eyes were glassy, and he seemed to run blindly. Glutinous saliva coated his mouth, and he swayed as though unsure of his balance. His appearance was so curious that Tod snarled and turned sideways, guarding with his brush. As Tod was much the bigger animal, he took for granted the other fox would avoid him.

To Tod's astonishment, at his motion the other fox turned and charged him. Tod flirted his brush across his face and gave him a blow with his rump that set his adversary reeling. Instead of being dismayed or putting himself on guard, the other fox attacked again, blindly and with a silent fury that was terrifying.

As he could not close his jaws, he could not bite, but he muzzled Tod's brush and side savagely, covering the bigger animal's soft fur with the sticky white saliva coating his jaws.

Tod was now raging. He reared up, striking stiff-legged at his opponent and looking for a good hold. Before he could close, the door of the house was thrown open and a man came out shouting. Instantly Tod was a fleeting shadow headed for the yew hedge. He slipped through, turned to the side, and ran along it. He could look through the bare stems, and to his astonishment he saw the strange fox turn and charge the man. The man kicked him away and then dodged back in the house, slamming the door behind him. The last Tod saw of the raving animal, he was charging again and again into the door in frenzy of pointless rage.

A week later, he saw another of these uncanny animals. A flock of pigeons came down in the early morning to feed in a small field that had not yet known the bulldozer's blade; and by hiding in a sassafras patch, Tod could occasionally catch a cock intent on courting a demure hen. Below the field a new concrete sidewalk ran to a corrugated shack where children collected each morning until they were picked up by a gigantic bus.

Lying in his sassafras ambush, Tod was watching flock of pigeons feeding, and especially a cock with his throat swelled out to show its iridescent colors for the benefit of a slender little hen who was trying to pick up bits of seed without being mounted by her admirer. A group of children walked along the sidewalk, shouting and talking, but neither Tod nor the pigeons paid any attention to them. Tod was still concentrating on the cock when he heard the children scream.

At the shrill sound, the flock took to the air with a hard rustle of wings and Tod looked in annoyance at the children. Most of them were running frantically, giving ear-piercing shrieks that

Tod instantly recognized as cries of mortal terror. A few were dancing backward, the girls with their skirts wrapped around their knees and the boys kicking wildly. A strong wind was blowing from the children to Tod, and immediately he smelled such an odor of abject fear that he sprang to his feet.

The slim form of a fox was darting among the children, biting right and left as he turned. At each flicker of his head, a horrible screech went up from the bitten child. Not daring to look away from their insane foe, the children tried to run backward, often falling down or colliding with one another. The fox seemed to be everywhere at once. Tod could tell from his actions that he was slashing with his canines rather than biting, and doing terrible execution.

A little girl tripped and fell. At once the fox turned from the other children and sprang at her. There was no slashing here—the fox tore at the child's arms and legs in a delirium of fury. Paralyzed by terror, the girl lay helpless, squealing like a rabbit. The other children, free at last of their tormentor, turned and ran.

Adults were coming, mostly women who as soon as they saw what was happening screamed louder than the child. Several of them rushed at the fox, who promptly turned on them. Now indeed the women screamed, leaping to avoid the attacks and trying to run in their turn, but they were almost as helpless as the children. One found a stick and lashed at the fox wildly. The insane creature easily avoided the blows and, slipping in, locked his teeth in her ankle. She plunged forward on her face, her fearful cries sounding even above the squalling of the others.

The wailing moan of a siren sounded, and a car tore up with a flashing, rotating light on top. Two men sprang out and went toward the women. The fox attacked them, but these men had some sort of guards on their feet that made it difficult for him to take hold. Tod saw the men kick and jump backward. Then he heard a succession of revolver shots and saw the fox knocked kicking onto the ground. The men fired again and again into the now lifeless body. When they finally stopped, the place was a shambles. Children were limping about, sobbing and moaning. Women sat on the ground, clutching their bitten legs. Several people had gone to the little girl who had taken the full brunt of the attack. She lay on her back, drumming on the ground with her open hands. When the breeze carried the acrid stench of gunpowder to Tod, he slid away. He was both curious and frightened. He could not conceive what had happened.

Almost nightly Tod in his wanderings smelled the odor of other foxes. Formerly he would have ignored them or even driven them away, but now he fled from them. Something awful was going on, although he did not know what. Once he saw a fox appear out of nowhere and attack some clothes hanging on a line to dry. A wind was making the clothes wave, and the frenzied animal tore at the cloth, covering it with the gluey saliva that clung to his jaws. A woman rushed out of the house yelling, and the fox spun around and went for her. Tod heard the woman's hysterical screams as he galloped away. When he went back to the sassafras thicket in the hope of finding a pigeon in the field, he saw that the children on their way to the bus were surrounded by men armed with guns and clubs.

In spite of all his precautions, Tod was once attacked by one of these lunatic foxes. Confident of his great speed, Tod ran from the animal at an easy lope, but to his astonishment the raving animal sped after him at such a terrific pace that Tod had to exert his best powers to escape. For a quarter of a mile his lunatic pursuer was close on his brush. Then the maddened animal's speed slacked. When Tod finally stopped to look around, he saw the fox spinning in circles, slashing at himself until he dropped. The creature lay there, his muzzle strained upward, his head twisted to one side, his legs kicking wildly.

Other animals were also affected. Tod was attacked by squirrels, rats, and once even by a rabbit. This was too much, and he killed these mad creatures with a swift, expert nip before they could bite him. He also met several dogs in the grip of the frenzy, but he could easily avoid these clumsy brutes.

There were several buildings with towers, and bells rang in these towers at certain times, always in light peals that Tod had grown to recognize. Now these same bells rang nearly every day, and sometimes several times a day, but with deep, slow, muted voices. Long trains of cars moved slowly away from the buildings at such times, keeping their lights on even though it was day. An atmosphere of terror hung over the district that Tod could vaguely sense. He stayed as deep as he could in the few remaining woods, living largely on mice and on an occasional bird.

Traps began to reappear, and soon they were everywhere. Traps no longer bothered Tod, for he knew them too well; but often he passed foxes caught in them, exhausted creatures sinking with panic, their jaws bloody from chewing on the iron. Then he began to come across dead foxes and other animals lying in open fields or along the hedges. They were rigid, their lips curled into a snarl, and when he sniffed at them there was an acid odor clinging to their mouths that he soon came to associate with their deaths.

Game was scarce, and Tod was delighted to run across some small balls of lard lying along one of his routes. Tod was not especially hungry at the moment, so he picked up one and, instead of swallowing it at once, carried it in his mouth, looking for a good place to bury it. He chased a rabbit, dropping the pill in his excitement, and when the rabbit escaped down a hole, went back for the ball. The ball had broken open, and Tod smelled the same acid odor he had detected on the dead foxes. Tod rolled it over with one foot thoughtfully. He was of two minds what to do, and might have swallowed the ball after all if he had not heard the angry squeaking of two fighting mice some ten yards away. In three bounds Tod had reached the spot and by a quick bite managed to get both of the contestants. Delighted with himself, he trotted on, forgetting the ball.

The next night his hunting was unsuccessful, and he went back to look for it. The ball was gone; and after sniffing about, Tod picked up the line of a cat. The cat must have eaten his ball; and Tod, feeling that he had been robbed, followed the trail. He did not have far to go. Halfway through a wire fence was the cat, cold dead. The desperate animal had managed to worm himself that far before collapsing.

The cat had been almost entirely eaten by crows during the day, and the stomach had been torn open. It reeked heavily of the same acid odor, so Tod left it alone. As he walked through the darkness, his nose near the ground to pick up any useful scents, a shadow flickered over him. Tod crouched automatically, but the shadow was a barn owl, a harmless bird as far as Tod was concerned. He heard a terrified squeak and sprinted forward, hoping to rob the bird of his mouse-kill or, better yet, get both owl and mouse, but the owl was already in the air when he arrived. There was a dead crow there, partly eaten by mice. It must have been one of these feeding mice the owl had caught. Tod did not care for crow; and besides, the bird also had the acid odor, although now quite faint. He kept on.

Just at dawn he managed to catch one of the few remaining rabbits, and started for his lying-up place. On the way, he shied abruptly from a dark mass at the foot of a cottonwood. The barn owl lay there dead, and a skunk was eating it. Tod tried unsuccessfully to drive the skunk away, but the wood pussy refused to move, stamping with his forefeet and keeping his tail with its white tip extended rigidly in the air. Tod was far too wise to risk being blinded by the skunk's musk, so he finally left it alone.

The next night he returned to the spot and found the remains of the dead skunk beside the owl. Both animals had been almost completely devoured by scavengers, and a few feet away was a dead blue jay, quite untouched, so Tod made a meal of that. He had gone only a few hundred yards before wrenching paroxysms of pain gripped him. Tod instantly vomited the entire contents of his stomach, and as the food came up he could taste a faint suggestion of the acid. The spasms came repeatedly, while Tod strained so violently to vomit again he brought up smears of blood. The convulsions returned at regular intervals, and each time that Tod thought he had at last freed himself of the poison they came again, while he writhed on the ground, biting at his own stomach in his agony. By dawn he was so weak he could hardly move, but he was still alive. He managed to crawl under some bushes, and lay there, semiconscious, until nightfall. It was two days before he had recovered enough to hunt again.

By now the woods and fields were full of dead or dying animals, but Tod left them severely alone. He lived on a vegetable diet. He finally picked up enough courage to kill a muskrat he found badly wounded from a fight, and after carefully smelling the animal all over, dared to eat it. He suffered no ill effects, so he caught a rabbit. That was all right too, so he resumed his hunting; but never again would he eat any dead animal, no matter how hungry he might be.

Wild animals were not the only victims of the poison pellets. Several times Tod found dogs whose horribly distorted bodies showed how they had died in torture. Near a road, he came on some hog cracklings thrown about, and was examining them when he heard the voices of children and stole into a hedge. From his hiding place he saw the children stop and a little boy pick up one of the cracklings and chew it. The children continued on, and Tod was about to go about his own affairs when he heard the boy begin screaming. Tod stopped to listen. He heard the anxious cries and questions of the other children, and then the screams stopped. Tod knew what had happened; he had been hearing similar screams followed by sudden silences from wild animals for the past weeks.

The wholesale destruction was incredible, and for a while it seemed to Tod that all life had been swept away. But the rabbits, gray squirrels, muskrats, and most songbirds remained, and Tod was still able to exist. There were even some foxes left, animals who, like Tod, had been smart enough or lucky enough to discover the danger and avoid it. They took refuge in the few patches of cover still left, and lived as best they could. Meanwhile the lard balls and hog cracklings disappeared; after the death of the boy, Tod saw men driving around in cars and collecting the poisoned bait. He had seen no rabid animals of any kind for a long time now, and perhaps the time of terror was over.

Shortly after sunup, while Tod was lying on his oak ridge, he saw a long procession of cars driving slowly down a back road that had been newly hard-surfaced. Tod had never seen so many cars before, and he lay watching them with both ears cocked. He was ordinarily not afraid of cars, but this seemed to be something new. The cars stopped, and many of the people got out, lining up along the road. They all carried sticks, and several had guns.

One man moved forward in front of the group, opening a large piece of paper. He talked to the crowd, pointing to the paper and then to different parts of the ridge, woods, and fields.

When he finished, the people spread out in a long line and started to move across the field.

Tod waited to see no more. He slipped over the ridge and cantered away at a long, swinging lope. He was not unduly disturbed, but he decided to get away.

He ran to the next ridge, stopped, and looked back. There was no sign of the people, so Tod, his mind now at ease, continued at a walk. He reached the top of the ridge and froze to a stop. Coming toward him was another long line of people, also carrying sticks and guns.

This was alarming. Tod had learned long ago not to give way to panic, and now instead of running he stood poised and watching. The people were coming slowly, stopping to examine every ditch and furrow, bending over patches of soft earth, and sometimes shouting excitedly and pointing with their sticks at the ground. Tod could not imagine what they were doing, but he did not like the look of things at all.

Above him came a loud drone, but Tod did not bother to look up. He knew it was one of the huge, noisy things that passed by in the sky occasionally but never did any harm. This time the flying thing did not pass on as they usually did, but circled and came back over the ridge, its shadow sweeping over Tod and making him wince.

A man in the crowd stopped and lifted a device, holding it to his ear and to his mouth. He seemed to be listening, then talking, then listening again, while all the time the flying crea-ture circled the ridge above Tod. The man lowered the device and looked directly at the ridge. Then he raised something that flashed in the sun, and pointed it directly at Tod. He looked through the object and raised a shout.

Tod needed no more. He ducked over the hill, and ran. There was no use going back toward the other line of men, so he turned left, the flying thing following him until he reached the shelter of a patch of woods. Here he stopped to get his breath before going on.

A fox dashed past him, going all-out. Tod hesitated a moment and then kept on. Two more foxes ran by, obviously highly agitated. Tod headed for a wild-rose and grapevine tangle that was one of his favorite hideaway spots, but before he could reach it he heard shots and yells ahead of him. Now he knew why the foxes had been running—men were coming from that direction too.

Tod whirled around and ran. There were men on both sides of him and behind him, but straight ahead might still be clear. As he broke out of the cover he saw long lines of men coming down both ridges, and they raised a shout as he appeared. Overhead the plane still droned around in great circles, but Tod paid no attention to that now. He sped for the far end of the valley before he was trapped.

As he ran he heard shots. A fox, wild with fear, cut in front of him and flung himself toward one of the lines of people. Terror-smitten, he ran up and down the line until a shot paralyzed his hindquarters and a boy rushed forward and beat him to death with a stick. Tod had no interest in the other fugitives. He put forth his best speed and reached the ends of the encircling lines before they could close. Here was a vast, broad field without cover enough to hide a rabbit. For a fraction of a second Tod hesitated, but he had no choice. He dashed out across the field, entirely exposed, tensing himself for the shots he knew would come.

There were no shots, only yells, and Tod felt himself to be in the clear. There were no humans ahead of him, only a single car stopped on a rise of ground. Tod naturally avoided the car and made for a distant hedgerow beyond which showed a patch of woodland.

Out of the tail of his eye he saw the car start to move and swing in a wide arc to head him off. Tod altered his course slightly to avoid it. The car put on speed, leaping and bucking over the uneven ground. Then it reached a plowed stretch and came to an abrupt halt.

The door flew open and two tall, thin dogs leaped out and raced toward him, slipping in the soft earth. One was brown and one was white. The brown was in the lead, the white one following as though tied to the first by an invisible leash. Tod was so supremely sure of his ability to outrun any dog that he even slowed down to watch the curious sight. He had never seen any animals like these before and was not even sure they were dogs. They ran at an undulating pace, almost like weasels, at first making a few spy-jumps to see over the rough terrain, and then flattening out with ears laid back as they got their positions. Tod was loafing along, watching them with half-turned head, when he suddenly realized that these animals were covering the ground at an alarming speed. Then, indeed, Tod ran, putting every last essence of energy into his speed, bitterly regretting the few vital seconds of delay.

To his unbelieving horror, he saw that the long, skinny creatures were fast overhauling him. He could never reach the hedge now, yet he continued to do his best. The white dog had pulled up even with the brown and they were racing in competition, each trying to reach him first. At least they had not spread out to take him from both sides. Coming in from an angle, the brown dog put on a final burst of speed and was on him with wide-stretched jaws.

But the greyhound was going too fast to stop, and ran right over Tod, rolling him on the grass, the snapping jaws missing their hold. Before Tod could regain his feet, the white hound was on top of him, but she also was going too fast in her effort to keep up with her partner, and missed. Tod came up on his feet and was off again, now forced to run parallel to the hedgerow instead of straight toward it. Both hounds had recovered themselves and were after him. Tod had taken advantage of his little lead to duck into a shallow dip deep enough to have hidden him from an ordinary dog, but these long-legged creatures stood so high they saw him easily.

The tan hound was up to him now, clearly the faster of the two. Tod managed to duck around a thistle, and the hound went by, going almost over on his side as he tried to turn. Then the white hound was there. She had been running cunning, following behind her partner, prepared to grab if the tan hound bowled him over again. She swung in from the side, expecting him to dodge again. Tod knew it and instead dropped flat. She went over him, turning within her own length as the tan hound came back. Side by side they charged him. Tod dived between them, and they bumped into each other trying to grab him. This gave him a few instants' start and he made another try for the hedge.

The hounds easily cut him off, and again the tan hound was in the lead. Tod doubled under the gleaming white teeth. With his great brush serving as a counterweight, he could turn quicker than the hounds, although not much quicker than the white bitch. She was on him now, but another thistle was there and he spun around it, the hound going wide. Tod now had a clear field for the hedge, and made the most of it. By the time the greyhounds were up with him again, he had almost reached his haven.

Frantically snapping, the hounds plunged at him; but now Tod knew that although the tan was the faster, he was slow at turns. He ducked under the tan hound's stroke and gained a few more feet toward the hedge before the white hound turned him.

Again and again, he seemed to be in the hounds' jaws, but each time he managed to twist out of the way, sometimes flirting his brush across their eyes as they struck, sometimes ducking under their long legs, sometimes twisting to the left or right, but always after each of the turns working his way closer to the hedge. At last he was almost there, and Tod decided to make a dash for it.

He broke away from the white bitch and made his last bid for freedom. Their backs bent like snakes, the hounds were after him. He saw them, smelled them, felt their gasping breath on his ears but was too tired to dodge again. His whiskers were touching the poison ivy covering the locust posts when the bitch grabbed him.

She was going too fast to pin him down, so she tossed him. Tod felt himself go up in the air, and writhed desperately so he would land on his feet. As he hit the ground, he saw the tan dog, who should have been underneath waiting for him, lying on one side. The greyhound had made too close a turn, and fallen. The white bitch was doubling to grab him, but Tod had a moment's respite. As he flung himself under the ivy, it closed around him.

Even now he was not safe. The hounds easily jumped the hedge and rushed up and down looking for him. They had poor noses but were not utterly devoid of smell, for the bitch found him and with an eager yelp tried to pull him out. Tod bit her hard in the nose, and the yelp turned to a scream of pain. The tan hound was there now; he was too big for Tod to fight. Tod wormed his way through the ivy with the hounds raging outside, forcing their long, thin muzzles in after him and vaulting from one side of the hedge to the other, trying to find an opening among the ropy stems.

Tod heard the car come roaring up, and the men jumped

out, shouting excitedly. Tired as he was, he had to make another effort. Waiting until both his oppressors were on the same side of the hedge as the car, Tod made a break across the next field.

He got a good distance before he heard a shout that meant he was seen. This was another vast, open field, and Tod knew he could never make it to the distant woods. He was too tired to dodge any more and he heard the greyhounds coming. He nerved himself for the death fight as they closed in.

Ahead was a barbed-wire fence. Tod slipped under the lower strand, ran a few feet, and turned at bay with bent back and jaws open for the finish.

The tan greyhound was going all-out, intent on the fox ahead of him. Astonished, Tod saw him hit the almost invisible wires, rebound from them doubled up like a ball, and fall helpless with a broken back. The white bitch saw the danger at the last instant and tried to turn, her whiplike tail thrashing as she twisted. Tod saw her slide on the wet grass and hit the barbs sideways. He heard the barbs tear through her hide and saw gashes flash up along her white coat as she screeched in pain. She limped off past her partner, who lay hopelessly crippled and scarcely alive.

The men were climbing over the hedge. Tod did not wait for them. Turning, he started off again, now going at little more than a trot. He was thoroughly drained of all energy, and had the men put forth their best efforts they might even have been able to run him down, but they stayed with the hounds. Tod made it to the woods, crawled into the deepest cover he could find, and then collapsed, utterly and completely beaten.

No matter how hard a run had been, Tod had always been able to snap back the next day; but this time he could not, nor the day after that, or after that. Even when he could hunt again, he had to rest going up a steep hill; and, after a fast, hard spurt when chasing a rabbit, a burning pain often shot through his chest and he was forced to stop, gasping for breath. He began to live more and more on mice and whatever plants he could find in the receding woodlots.

10

The Last Hunt

Copper no longer dreamed of deer hunting or fox hunting. His dreams now were disordered nightmares that made the hound twist and moan until the Master shook him awake. Copper had once loved to sleep, taking a dozen little catnaps a day, but now he feared sleep because of the torment of his dreams. When he slept, it was only because of exhaustion, and he spent most of his time dozing in a corner of the cabin on a heap of sacks.

One by one Copper had seen the other hounds go, at first indifferently and then with increasing concern. Even though he had never been especially friendly with the other dogs, he missed them now they were gone. Even the constant quarrels they had had—the fights over food, the barking, the jealousies—gave a purpose to life. Each dog had had his own special barrel kennel and own domain marked by the length of his chain that he knew belonged to him. Now the kennel hill was gone, covered with new houses; the old familiar dogwoods, buttonwoods, and elms that shaded the dogs during the summer had been cut down, and Copper had been brought into the cabin to live alone with the Master.

Copper knew why these strange, unnatural dreams came to torture him. Even when asleep he had to breathe, and the air was now polluted. It brought him no delightful, intriguing messages, for it was poisoned with the stench of exhaust fumes, factories, and dozens of dead, lifeless odors. Perhaps even worse was the constant noise—the continual droning whine of traffic on the highways, the drumming beat of the turbines of a giant pumping station that had been recently erected and ran night and day. Often this station filled the air with a sickening stench of gas, while the factories gave off a fine soot that covered the ground like a poisonous black hoarfrost. He missed the pleasant smell of the trees, the pure quality of the air under their leaves, and the damp, clean earth that lay under their shelter. With his delicate nose and acute sense of hearing, Copper was extremely conscious of these changes. He could not see the traffic or the factories, and wondered why the Master when he stood in the doorway looking over the once lovely valley so often sighed.

It was many months since he and the Master had gone hunting, and hunting was Copper's life. When the Master took him walking now, it was always on a lead and over hard concrete pavements that hurt his feet and gave out no interesting smells. The Master never shouted and laughed or played with him anymore; he was always silent and sad, and increasingly there was a smell of alcohol in the little cabin. It frightened Copper to see the Master stagger and sometimes fall, for he could not understand what was wrong with him. The old hound cowered in his corner, and was always relieved when the Master finally collapsed across the bed and after a few minutes began to snore loudly.

But no matter how bad things might be, as long as he had the Master, Copper could not be really miserable. Then something had happened which, although he could not understand its import, Copper sensed meant ultimate disaster.

The new people who had moved in did not like the Master. They seldom spoke to him, and when they did there was a contemptuous note in their voices that Copper felt. The Master was always cast down after these encounters, but they bothered Copper not a whit, for to him no humans except the Master really existed.

Then one day a group of these new people had come to the cabin. With them were two of the leather-smelling men, and Copper had cheerfully wagged his tail when he smelled their leggings, for always before this had meant his powers would be called upon for tracking. But these were not the interested, admiring leather-smelling men of old; they did not like him or the Master. With the crowd was a lean, nasty-voiced man who smelled of antiseptics. He had intoned what had seemed to Copper like an endless speech while looking at a piece of paper. The Master had protested, and Nasty had appealed to the leather-smelling men, who seemed to support him. At last Copper and the Master had gotten into a car and been driven many, many miles to a place Copper disliked at first smell. It was composed of big, barren buildings inhabited by men and women reeking with the sour odor of old age. Nasty had pointed at Copper and ordered him back in the car, and Copper realized dogs were not allowed here. Then the Master had yelled and shouted until even the leather-smelling men gave off a faint whiff of fear. The upshot of the affair was that they had been driven back to the cabin and allowed to stay there, to Copper's great relief. In the most terrible of his nightmares, Copper dreamed of that dark, gloomy place where no dogs were allowed and he would be separated from the Master.

Everyone had avoided them after that, to Copper's intense relief. Then an inexplicable change had occurred. The Master suddenly came into great demand. The leather-smelling men had brought in a dead fox, still smelling of powder where it had been shot and of some new, frightening scent that Copper could not identify. They and the Master had talked a long time. Then dozens of people had arrived, pleading with the Master and all talking at once.

That evening, the Master had taken down his old traps and boiled them in hemlock chips over the fire, whistling to himself. Copper was sorry to see the traps, for it meant he could be of use only as a trap-dog, but he was happy to see the Master happy. Once again they had run a trapline, and in the morning Copper had tracked the captured animals to where the drags had brought them to a halt. Strangely, the Master did not let him go near the captives even after they were dead; still, Copper felt needed and he and the Master were working together.

Later, the Master had taken to melting balls of fat by the fire and carefully putting little kernels of an acid-smelling substance into each one. Copper had been sternly ordered to keep back when he had come over to sniff inquisitively. He was not allowed to go out anymore with the Master on his rounds; but at least the Master was always cheerful now, shouting and talking to the new people, who all were eager to talk to him and often arrived bringing baskets of foods, snacks for Copper, and some-times bottles that smelled of alcohol, though the Master seldom bothered to open the bottles now, and when he did, never stag-gered or became unwell. It was nice to be liked; and although Copper did not know what had happened, he knew they were surrounded by friends, and he dreamed no more of the dark cluster of buildings where dogs were not allowed.

Copper had been allowed to go on the great drive where hundreds of people had beaten the countryside so that no fox would be left alive. Copper's work had been to check drains, holes, and thick clumps of greenbrier to make sure there were no fugitives lurking inside. As always he had done a conscientious job, and when the day was over he was sure he had not missed a fox.

During the next few days everyone was happy, and there was a glow around the Master that Copper could almost smell. Then people came in at all hours of the day and night to talk seriously. The Master listened to them. One evening he—oh, glories of glories!—got down his old shotgun. Copper went mad with joy and the Master fondled him just as he had in the good old days. They slept together that night on the bed of the Master, his arm around the old hound and Copper's head resting on his shoulder. Even so, when the Master rose as the first scent of morning came into the air, took the gun, and whistled to Copper to follow him, the hound could hardly believe the wonderful truth. Once again they were going fox hunting.

They walked until they were out of the poisonous miasma that overhung the district and into the good clean air of open country. Copper drank in the breeze in eager gulps. He had almost forgotten there was air like this, for the world came alive when the wind blew. It was a perfect scenting day, moist but not wet with a light breeze. The ground felt warm under Copper's pads, but the air in his nostrils was deliciously cool. Joyfully he plunged into the white mist that rolled toward them as they entered the hollows, zigzagging to pick up the grand odors that told of rabbit, pheasant, mouse, and woodchuck. He was no longer old and tired and unneeded. Copper was young again, going hunting with the Master, and all he needed was the trace of a fox to make him completely happy.

But he could not find a single fox trail. They checked the old runs, once well padded but now without a trace of scent. Copper squirmed hopefully under the overhung tendrils of the multiflora rose hedgerow. The bushes closed over his head as he worked his way down the long tunnel over roots covered with moss and splashed with blobs and patches of sunlight. No foxes had been here for many a week. They went from crossing to crossing, and still Copper never so much as feathered his whip-like tail. All the foxes were gone.

Then the Master called him and together they went along the railroad tracks, turned off by the juniper tangle and, passing over the culvert under the road, started up the hill where they had first tracked that fox who killed Chief many years ago. Up they went toward the top of the knoll, when suddenly the Master shouted, his voice shrill with excitement. Copper dashed forward and, under the rotten remains of an old fallen pine, hit the well-known scent. It was The Fox he had hunted so often before—the last fox left in the whole area.

Copper's great voice boomed out, and they were off. The scent leaped from the ground and rushed at him. There was no need for him to lower his head as he ran shouting for the Master to follow. Ahead he could just make out the white tip of the brush drifting over the fields while he plunged after it, more slowly than the fugitive but with a powerful drive. He pressed hard, for the sun was rising fast and it would burn out the scent.

Away they went, and soon Copper stopped baying to save his breath; furthermore, the scent was so strong there was no need to tell that he was carrying it. Once he was sure of the fox's drift, he even avoided using his nose, taking only an occasional sniff, as the scent was so strong it would fill his nasal passages and tire them. The fox followed a line of bluffs to a river, turned and ran along the bank. Then he made a sharp turn into a cornfield. Copper was forced to drop his head, and as he worked out the line he heard the raging cries of crows as they dived into the corn ahead. Copper knew they were screaming at the fox, and he raced ahead, picking an occasional wisp of scent from the cornstalks as he passed.

Outside the field, the fox had doubled and run back on his own trail. As Copper followed, he heard the blast of the Master's shotgun. Wild with hope, Copper dashed on. He found the Master staring into some woods, and as soon as the hound appeared the man pointed and cheered him on. Copper swerved and hit the scent almost immediately; it was stained with the odor of panic, but there was no blood. While backtracking, the fox had run into the Man following the hound, but the Master had missed. Ah, well, it was still early.

Ahead was a little field entirely surrounded by a stone wall. Copper knew the place well. Inside were a number of thin, flat polished stones standing erect, each with a small mound before it on which were often vases with flowers. The upright stones made excellent scent posts, and Copper had often used them for this purpose. His nose told him the fox had jumped on the wall and run along it. A common trick. Copper sprang heavily to the top of the wall and followed him, watching for the spot where the fox had jumped off. He went completely around the field and back to his original starting point; being hot on the line, he continued to run around another time before he realized what he was doing.

Annoyed, Copper jumped off and tried the ground both inside and outside the graveyard. The Master came up and spoke to him in low, encouraging tones, but Copper was baffled. The fox had clearly sprung on the wall and run around it several times, jumping over the small entrance opening as he passed it, but how had he gotten off the wall again? The most scrupulous checking gave him no trace of scent on either side of the wall, and finally Copper was forced to give up.

There was a halloo from the road. A farmer came up and talked to the Master, making motions with his hands, and pointing. The Master listened, then called Copper and took him to where the fox had first run into the wall and ordered him to backtrack the animal. Copper looked up reproachfully—all his training was against running heel, but he reluctantly obeyed. He had gone only a few feet along the old trail when the suspicion grew in him that there was a fresh trail laid over the old—and the fresh trail was not going to the wall but away from it. Yes, that was it. The fox had run to the wall, jumped on top of it, run around it a few times, and then jumped off on his old line and backtracked it. Furious, Copper gave tongue in indignation. Another few feet and he found where the fox had turned off from his old line. They were off again.

The fox had swum a pond, but Copper was able to pick up the scent along the edge where it had been blown in from the surface of the water by the fresh breeze, and followed it around the pond to the place where the dripping fox had emerged. The shock of the cold water kept the scent glands in the fox's pads from functioning for a while, so Copper followed the wet trail across the grass, guided by the dampness rather than by an odor until the glands began giving off scent again. Being cold and faint, it was quite different from the fox's former scent, and the hound was forced to stop and sniff loudly to adjust his sense of smell to the altered odor before going on.

The sun was high now, cooking out the scent in the open, but vestiges still clung to the sides of mounds or in the shade of hollows. The scent was no longer rising, but among the dead leaves and damp grass it was holding well. Copper's long, bagging lips sucked it up from the earth; he could not have told if he were scenting or tasting it.

Only twice during that long afternoon was Copper seriously at fault. Once was when the fox crossed a burned field where no scent would lie and the ashes got into Copper's nose, making him sneeze and gag. Even so the hound was able to follow by catching traces of scent from tufts of dried grass that the fox had touched in crossing. The second was in a firelane where the trees had been felled, and there Copper had a hard time, for the fox had jumped from one to the other of the trunks as lightly as a cat, while the heavy hound had to blunder through them. He might have lost the fox for good that time had not the Master come up and, by staring at the soft ground along the borders of the flashing, been able to put him on the line again. Shortly before sunset a thunderstorm had come up, and at the first peal the scent had dropped so sharply that Copper thought it was gone for good. But the storm had passed away to the west, and the scent had come back.

When night came, Copper was still on the trail. It mattered little to him whether it was dark or light, for he put small reliance on his shortsighted eyes. It was the scent that mattered to the half-bloodhound: how it grew faint or clear, rose above the ground or clung to it, the quality of its texture—if it showed fright, weakening, or strength—if it were consistent or spotty. During the day, Copper knew from the scent that the fox was suffering more than he from the heat of the sun. Now that it was cool, the quarry's odor did not have the hot, thick quality of an overheated, exhausted animal. On the other hand, in the cool of the night the scent was stronger, and Copper could follow it more easily.

Several times the fox had tried to double back toward his old range, but each time something had frustrated him. Copper came to one place where he had tried four times to cross a highway, each time to be turned back by the traffic. Another time he had found himself in a new development and been chased by dogs. The shock had killed his scent, and it was more by sheer good luck than skill that Copper had been able to pick up the trail again. The quarry had tried to cross a bridge over the river, only to find people parked there in cars. At last the fox had given up trying to return to his home range, and cut straight across country.

Copper could soon tell that the fox was now in unfamiliar territory, and running aimlessly. Before, the fox had always had some definite goal—a certain crossing, a fence or wall he could run, or as a last resource a hole where he could hide. Now the fox was plunging blindly ahead through brambles, across streams, over walls, and forcing his way through fields of tall grass that delayed him far more than the long-legged hound. When dawn came, Copper was still doggedly following, while the fox was noticeably weakening every hour.

The old hound was near the point of exhaustion himself. His pads were worn off his feet, and he left dabs of blood. His hind-quarters wavered as he ran. But now he was getting scent from the fox's breath as well as from his pads and body odor. As the fox gasped for air the hound could smell the spots where his breath had caught among the vines and bushes. The fox could not be far ahead now. The hound raised his tired head to look, but there was still no sign of the white-tipped brush.

Far away, he heard the sound of the Master blowing across the opened barrels of the shotgun. Copper bayed in reply, tired as he was. The call was repeated, closer this time. Again Copper summoned up enough breath for a feeble call that was more howl than bay, for not only his feet but his lungs were torturing him.

The trail led through a mass of briars, and Copper could hear the fox ahead of him. He struggled on. Still again came the call on the shotgun barrels, and Copper managed to give a weak and faltering reply. Then he broke out of the briars and saw the fox ahead of him.

The fox's head was down, his back arched; he was panting

and his tongue hung out, greatly swollen and almost black. His brush was covered with mud, and dragged. Ahead of him was a fallen tree trunk. The dying animal made an effort to climb over it, and fell back. At the sight, Copper gave a clear, long-drawn out cry of triumph, and staggered toward him. The fox made a last effort to mount the log, and then fell to the ground, limp and motionless. Copper reeled forward, fell, got up, and managed to reach the fox. He gave the body a feeble shake and then collapsed on top of the corpse.

Copper was scarcely conscious of hearing the Master's call or of being lifted and carried to the car. Back in the cabin, he felt a sting of alcohol in his lips that made him choke, strangle, and struggle feebly. Only vaguely he knew that people were crowding into the tiny room, shouting and laughing. He felt the Master massaging his legs and chest. Then came the sting of the alcohol again, and more massaging. At long last, he was able to lift his head, although his vision was still blurred.

He was shown the dead fox, but Copper was too tired even to sniff at it. While the Master held the fox, men pointed boxes at him and lights flashed again and again. When they finally left him in peace, Copper sank back and slept as though he were dead.

Slowly the Master nursed him back to health. Many times a day people came to pat and talk to him, and there were more of the flashing boxes. The fox was skinned and the pelt hung with a skinning board in it, just as in the old days. Gradually Copper regained his strength until he could walk again with the Master.

He was blissfully happy now. Everyone liked him and liked the Master. The Master's voice was always cheerful, and when he was cheerful, Copper was cheerful. He even learned to tolerate the strangers with their never-ending pawings and strange talk.

Gradually Copper was conscious of a change. Fewer and fewer people came. The Master grew increasingly silent and began to drink again, more heavily than ever. He seldom took Copper for walks now, and the old hound lay on his pile of sacks, puzzled and disappointed. He tried his poor best to make the Master happy again, clumsily trying to play, licking his hand, running to the door to show he was all ready to go hunting again—if there was anything left to hunt. Nothing he did won even a smile or a caress from the Master.

Then one day the nasty sour-smelling men from the great, somber place where dogs were not allowed came back. With him were the leather-smelling men, but now they were not friendly. There were some other people too, people who had exclaimed over Copper and patted him when he and the Master came back with the last fox, but now their voices were angry and they pushed him aside. They talked and talked to the Master, while Copper listened in dumb misery.

He heard a sound he had never heard before. The Master was crying. He sat on the edge of the bed, sobbing, and tears came through his fingers. Copper forced his way through the people and anxiously licked the Master's hands, asking to help. The Master stroked his head just as he had in the old days, and Copper wriggled joyfully.

The Master went to the wall, took down the gun, and loaded it. Copper barked and cavorted happily. They were going hunting again, and surely the Master would take him? Yes, the Master called to him and, leaving the people, they went outside.

The Master led him a little way from the cabin and, sitting down beside him, stroked his head. Copper licked his face, and whined. They had killed the great fox, the fox that had eluded them for so many years. Now they were together again, and happy, for nothing could separate them.

The Master made him lie down, and then held one hand over his eyes. Copper lay trustingly and contentedly. The Master knew best. Did he recall the many good times they had had together and this last great run—a day and a night and part of another day? Of course he did. Copper gave the Master's hand one last lick. He did not care what happened as long as he would never be separated from the Master, for he had killed the great fox, and in this miserable, fouled land there was no longer any place for fox, hound, or human being.

Author's Note

Any author who writes a book with an animal hero automatically lays himself open to the charge of anthropomorphism— often with justification. We can guess at what goes on in an animal's mind only by comparing his mental processes with ours. This is a poor system, as an animal's way of thinking is so different from ours that he may perform an act which seems to us the result of reason from some quite different motive. I believe that animals can reason but on a very rudimentary level compared to a human.

In the problem of scent, the situation is exactly reversed. Many animals have powers of scent so greatly superior to those of a human that we can only vaguely understand what scent means to them. Yet here again we must interpret the behavior of a hound following a trail in terms of human scenting ability, for we have no other technique to guide us.

A fox's cunning is proverbial. Hundreds of stories are told about him. Two questions must always be asked of these stories: (1) Did a fox actually perform this feat and (2) If he did, why did he do it?

For over a year now I have kept a pair of foxes who are so tame I can turn them loose and watch them hunt, fight, make love and live almost a normal life. I have also watched many wild foxes and I have talked to dozens of Masters of Foxhounds, trappers, hunters and game wardens. Unfortunately, I have never met two men who can agree on what a fox will and will not do.

I have frequently been told that no fox will run among sheep or cattle to throw hounds off his scent. Twice I have personally seen a wild fox followed by hounds do exactly this. From the window of my bedroom I have watched foxes run across our pasture until they located our flock of sheep, crawl into the center of the flock and lie there motionless, watching the baffled hounds who could not own the line because of the heavy sheep foil. A well-known writer has denounced Ernest Thompson Seton as a "nature faker" because Seton on the basis of his own personal observation says that a fox will run along rails just before a train is due in order to kill hounds. This writer adds sarcastically, "Just where the fox procured a copy of the time-table is not made clear." Mr. William Batchelor, Master of the Whitelands Hunt, tells me that his pack is no longer able to hunt the Whitford Sales area because a fox consistently takes the pack in front of trains on the Trenton Cutoff. Whitelands' huntsman tells me that when the fox hears the whistle of a train, he will immediately leave his run and head for the Cutoff. There is no question at all that he knows precisely what he's doing.

There are two famous stories about foxes which I have not included in this book. One tells of foxes leaping on the back of sheep and riding them across a field to break the line. I can find no record of anyone who claims he saw this happen with his own eyes. The other tells of a fox slowly backing into a pond while holding a bunch of grass in his mouth. When he is completely submerged, all except his nose, he drops the grass and runs off.

It is said that foxes rid themselves of fleas by this method as the fleas leave the fox to get on the grass. In my experience, it takes carbolic soap to move a flea off a domestic dog, so I cannot understand how simple immersion would do the trick with a fox. On the other hand, the story that foxes will carry a dead bird and several mice by tucking the mice under the wings of the bird is quite true. I have seen my foxes do it.

I was especially interested in whether foxes are monogamous, promiscuous, or whether they mate for one season and then separate. With almost mathematical precision, exactly half of the men who had observed foxes all their lives believed them to be monogamous and the other half were equally sure they were as promiscuous as the domestic dog. I believe that Mr. Paul L. Failor, supervisor of the Predator Control Section of the Pennsylvania Game Commission, has the answer. Mr. Failor points out that at any time of year when you see a fox you will almost surely see its mate nearby, a strong indication for monogamy. The male helps in feeding and raising the pups, which would be impossible if he had no interest in one, individual female. Lastly, in fox farms only mated pairs will breed except under rare circumstances; it is very seldom a male will serve more than one female. However, as Mr. Failor points out, it is seldom that a pair of foxes can live together more than a few years without one or the other being killed. In this case, the survivor mates again during the next rutting season.

I believe that the American and European red foxes are quite different animals, although it has often been stated that only the gray fox is a native American, and that all our red foxes were imported from Europe by fox hunters. The remains of red foxes dating from pre-Columbian times have been found in Indian burial mounds near Ralls, Missouri (*Journal of Mammalogy*

40:401–405 Aug. 20, 1959). From all accounts the European red fox is definitely promiscuous, but the American red fox clearly seems to have different habits.

Fox hunters must pardon me for speaking of "pups" rather than "cubs." As an indignant zoologist told me, "Foxes are dogs, not bears." Foxes are actually little wild dogs and so would have pups.

Those familiar with the history of American fox hunting will instantly recognize in my chapter "The Last Hunt" the famous story of Baldy, a Virginia red fox, and Boston, a part bloodhound, part foxhound cross. Hunting alone, Boston followed Baldy for a day and a half, covering a distance of 150 miles. Both animals dropped dead at the end of the hunt and were buried together. The story appears in *Recreation* magazine, July, 1898, pp. 3–7, and Seton quotes it in *Lives of Game Animals*, Vol. 1, pp. 549–552.

It is certainly conceivable that an experienced zoologist might question some of my views on foxes, yet I hope that even he can pick up an idea or two from my accounts. If so, perhaps he will treat me as a good fox hunter treats his horse:

"Be to his virtues ever kind,
    Be to his faults a little blind."

D.P.M.

About the Author

Daniel P. Mannix was an award-winning American author and journalist, as well as a magician and filmmaker. Mannix's magazine articles about his experiences in the carnival, where he performed under the stage name "The Great Zadma," became popular in the mid-1940s and were compiled with the assistance of his wife in the book *Step Right Up!* His dozens of books and extensive essays range in subject from children's animal stories, environmental issues, and hunting accounts to historical examinations of the Hellfire Club, the Atlantic slave trade, and the Roman gladiatorial games. Mannix was particularly interested in the Wizard of Oz canon and composed a biography of L. Frank Baum for *American Heritage* magazine in the 1960s.

DANIEL P. MANNIX

FROM OPEN ROAD MEDIA

Find a full list of our authors and
titles at www.openroadmedia.com

FOLLOW US
@OpenRoadMedia